QUEST OF THE WOLF

MAGNETIC MAGIC
BOOK 4

LINDSAY BUROKER

1

Morning frost blanketed the grass of Sylvan Serenity Housing when I walked out of my apartment carrying a sword and a backpack full of rope, tools, snacks, and other items that might be useful in staging a rescue. I felt like Frodo heading off to Mordor with the One Ring on a quest to save the world. Except I was off to a lavender field to save a werewolf.

"Almost the same."

I strode toward my truck, glad the tenants who'd started staking out the parking lot in search of ghosts weren't there with their paranormal-monitoring equipment. On the way, I passed Duncan's Roadtrek van.

The night we'd confronted my cousins, he'd driven it to Lake Sammamish. It hadn't been until a few days later, when I'd gone to seek sign of him, that I'd found it parked on a side street near a dock, with his jeans, phone, and keys inside. When he'd slipped into the water carrying his demolitions, he must have assumed he would end up changing forms. I'd driven the van back and parked it here, hoping he would return for it of his own accord. He hadn't yet. That was why I had to rescue him.

When I reached my truck, an SUV rolled into the lot with my son Austin in the passenger seat. I was relieved to see him, even though I had determinedly *not* worried about him when he hadn't come home the night before, and I hadn't called to check on him. Okay, I hadn't called more than *once*. He was eighteen, in the Air Force, and visiting for the holidays. Tracking his every movement wasn't my duty anymore.

Fortunately, Austin didn't appear drunk or stoned when he hopped out of his friend's SUV, waving a thanks for the ride. Given that he hadn't likely slept, he looked quite alert, but he eyed me warily when our gazes met.

A year ago, I would have read him the riot act for staying out all night, but a year ago, he'd lived with me and had a curfew. Now... I didn't want to be an overbearing mother lest he not visit anymore. Like his older brother, Cameron.

"There are eggs and bacon on a plate on the counter." I pointed toward the apartment.

"Oh, good. I'm starving." Austin started in that direction but paused. "Uhm, I need to ask you something."

"Go ahead."

He didn't usually hesitate, but he did now. Was something wrong? Did he need money? A confidante? A kidney?

No, they wouldn't have allowed him into the military if he had an organ deficiency. I was less certain about the rest.

"Did you like the chocolate-covered crickets?" Austin asked. "Do you want me to get more?"

I squinted at him, certain this wasn't the *real* question he wanted answered. "The chocolate is waxy and is desperately in need of sea salt."

"I saw the canister in your truck." Austin arched his eyebrows. "If you're taking them on the road, that means you're eating them. They can't be that bad."

"I wouldn't say they're *good*."

"I looked in the container yesterday. They're half gone."

"Because they came in a handy travel tin."

"So their appeal is that they're..."

"Convenient," I said firmly, refusing to classify them as palatable. "Like bags of chips by the checkout counter."

"Convenience crickets."

"Exactly. What's your *real* question, my son?"

Austin smiled ruefully. "I was wondering if I can spend a few days at Mount Baker."

"What? Now?" I waved at the outdoor Christmas tree I'd put up near the leasing office. The holiday was quickly approaching.

"Yeah. For skiing. Snowboarding, actually. We wouldn't technically be staying *at* Baker, but Oakley won a week at an Airbnb on a lake in Maple Falls, so it's really close. You can drive right up to the mountain in the mornings. He has the cabin over Christmas."

Over... Christmas?

I wanted to blurt *no*, that Austin was only in town for a couple of weeks before returning to finish his Air Force training and being assigned to his first duty station who knew where. On the other side of the world, probably. More, he'd spent so much time with his friends since he'd come home that I'd barely gotten to talk to him.

"He's never won anything," Austin continued. "I haven't either. A couple of my friends are home from school and going too. It'll be really epic."

Trying not to let my disappointment show, I groped for something to say. Something that was in line with my attempts to be a mature, and certainly not overbearing, mother who acknowledged that her sons had grown up and could now live their own lives.

"I think the law dictates that I can't forbid you from doing anything anymore, but know you'll be abandoning your lonely, divorced mom on the biggest holiday of the year." That hadn't come out as maturely not-overbearing as I'd intended.

"You could come up to visit on Christmas morning. It's not that far of a drive."

"Oh, sure. I'd love to spend Christmas morning with a bunch of hungover frat boys."

"Nobody's going to be hungover, Mom. We're not twenty-one."

Like that would matter.

"Besides, we're going to snowboard, not get smashed."

"You don't know *how* to snowboard." I knew that for a fact. We'd never had enough money to engage in expensive winter sports.

"I've been once, remember? Jae-jin's mom took us up to Steven's Pass a couple winters ago."

"From what I heard, you spent the day on the Daisy run."

"*All* beginners start on Daisy. I'm going to take lessons at Baker. They've got a beginner package that includes equipment rental and doesn't cost much."

I attempted to rein in my disappointment. If anything, this was a blessing. Rescuing Duncan would be simpler if Austin wasn't home. I had spent the boys' entire lives taking an alchemical potion to sublimate my werewolf magic, but these past few weeks, I'd stopped, and the magic had come roaring back. Now, when my emotions got the best of me, I turned furry and fanged—whether I wanted to or not.

Further, members of my pack, in addition to numerous other troubles, had started showing up regularly at the apartment complex. If I wanted to keep my secret identity from my normal *human* children... this trip would be for the best.

"Mount Baker is supposed to be a great place to learn," Austin added in a cajoling tone. Maybe he hadn't realized that he could do whatever he wanted, no matter what I said. "It's known for its great powder, steeps, trees, chutes, and cliffs."

I didn't know what steeps or chutes were but waved away the brochure description. "It's fine. You can go. I appreciate you asking my permission, like my opinion still matters."

Austin smiled in relief. "Your opinion *does* matter."

"But you were still going to go if I said *no*, right?"

"Of course. Snowboarding is a life skill that I need to learn."

"Uh-huh. For the record, *trees* and *cliffs* are things you want to avoid while careening down a mountain."

"I'll keep that in mind." Austin saluted me before jogging up the walkway toward my apartment in the back of the sprawling complex.

Surrounded by acres of grassy lawns, paths, and manicured trees and shrubs, Sylvan Serenity hadn't been a bad place to raise the kids. Other than the increased crime in Shoreline lately and the nearby freeway traffic audible through the greenbelt, it was a pleasant place to live. As the property manager, I *ensured* it was.

Before getting into my truck, I looked wistfully at it all, hoping that after I found Duncan, I could figure out a way to keep the owners from selling the complex.

"A problem for another day." I put the truck into gear.

While backing out of my spot, I had to brake abruptly as a kid on a bicycle wheeled past. My beat-up truck lacked modern amenities like rear cameras. Something clunked around under the passenger seat. Curious, I paused to pull out an unexpected item. It was wrapped in the colorful comics section of a Sunday paper, a red ribbon holding it closed.

A gift?

It had some heft, which gave me an immediate inkling about what it was.

Untying the ribbon and unwrapping the paper revealed a substantial cylinder-shaped magnet with a coil of twine attached to an eyelet. A slip of paper read:

.   .   .

To help you with your future endeavors.
    ~ Duncan

My first thought was that Duncan had escaped from imprisonment and left it for me during the night. But wouldn't he have knocked on my door if he were free to do so?

I rubbed the comic pages he'd used to wrap the gift. They lacked the crinkle of a fresh edition. Instead, they were limp and damp, like they'd been out in the truck in Seattle's damp winter air for a few days.

"He must have left this before we stormed Augustus's mansion," I reasoned.

Maybe he'd had an inkling that he would lose the battle to Lord Abrams's control device and end up abandoning me.

How a magnet would help me deal with my problems, I didn't know, but moisture welled in my eyes as I set it on the seat and pulled out. Duncan was a good guy. I needed to rescue him.

"Easier said than done."

My nerves fluttered in my belly as I merged onto the freeway and headed north. Though it had only been a couple of weeks since I'd escaped from the lavender farm and potion-making facility where I believed Duncan was held prisoner, so much had happened since then that it felt like ages had passed. Before long, the full moon would return. I needed Duncan back so I would have someone to hunt with.

"Sure, that's the only reason."

I shook my head at my sarcasm, admitting that Duncan made me smile. He was good company, and we had things in common, more than a love for dark chocolate. I wasn't always sure I could trust him—or that his creator wouldn't magically compel him to attack me—but I liked having him in my life. I wished we'd gotten an opportunity to be together physically too. We'd been heading in that direction... until my seventy-year-old mother had shown up and started talking about how Duncan would be a good mate and that I should have babies with him. As if *that* was an interest of mine at forty-five with two grown sons.

Having a companion, however, was of interest. I'd only recently come to realize that.

Traffic wasn't bad, and it didn't take as long as expected to reach the Arlington exit. The last time I'd come this way, the self-driving car of one of our enemy's minions had been handling the navigation. But I remembered the route. Despite recent development around Arlington, it was still more rural than suburban out here, and there weren't many roads to choose from.

Even so, I doubted myself when I headed down the street toward TBL Luxury Perfumes and Potions. It had been nighttime when we'd come before. By daylight, the lavender fields I'd expected were visible, but a sign staked by the long stone-paver driveway hadn't been there before. Momentarily, I wondered if I'd gotten the wrong lavender fields. But, no. The Southwestern-style mansion that didn't fit in with typical Pacific Northwest architecture was distinctive. This was the right place. But no cars were visible up the long driveway, nor did I see any indications of activity.

I pulled to a stop in front of the sign. FOR SALE, it read and included the name and number of a real estate agent.

Unease crept into me. I drove slowly up the long driveway, halfway expecting the sign to be a ruse, that I would sense werewolves and security guards amped up on strength-enhancing potions. And what about the werewolf boy who had howled at us from the fields? The clone brother Duncan had only recently learned he had. The residents and workers couldn't all be gone, could they?

Not only did I not sense any magical beings inside the compound, but I didn't pick up the slighter magic of the potions that had been brewing in the factory. I climbed out of the truck and peered in a few windows. The gift shop was empty. So was what I could see of the mansion.

I slumped against the front door. Duncan wasn't here. Nobody was.

2

After returning to the front of the property, I called the real estate agent. Angelica Simons. If she'd listed the lavender farm, she would have contact information for the owner. Whether she would give it to me was another matter.

"Hello?" a woman who was presumably Angelica answered.

"Hi, I'm calling about the lavender farm for sale outside of Arlington." Actually, I was calling about the werewolf that I believed had been held prisoner in it until recently...

"Yes, it's zoned agricultural and includes more than one hundred acres of mature lavender as well as a five-thousand-square-foot house, gift shop, and state-of-the-art perfumery."

Perfumery? More like a *potionry*. Or whatever the proper name was for a facility full of burbling vats of alchemical concoctions.

"It looks really nice." In a loaded-with-bad-guys residence-of-an-evil-overlord kind of way. "Do you know why the owner is selling?"

"He didn't say." The agent's tone turned a little suspicious. "Are you a qualified buyer?"

"I'm the property manager for qualified buyers who own

numerous commercial facilities." Technically, that was true, though my employers exclusively held multifamily properties. I could imagine the stern Kashvi Sylvan pursing her lips with disapproval at the idea of picking up a *perfumery*. Afraid I would have to lie to continue on with that charade, I switched to, "I'm also a potion, erm, perfume buyer." I made the slip on purpose to see what kind of reaction I would get. Did the real estate agent know what had *really* been manufactured on the premises?

Angelica didn't answer at all. Hm.

"I've visited the gift shop before and was disappointed to find it closed," I continued. "Do you know if the owner is still in business? Do they have another shop I could visit?"

"I don't know. The property is listed at twelve million, firm. If your employers want the details, have them call me." Angelica hung up.

"Well, that's rude. I called it *nice*." After my experience escaping from the place, that wasn't a descriptor that came easily to mind.

My next call, as I walked around the property, looking for clues that might have been left behind, went to my niece, Jasmine.

"Hey, Luna," she answered. "Do you want to be a *reference* for me?"

"For what? A job application?" I stopped at the wrought-iron gate leading into the walled courtyard. The bar I'd bitten and bent while in wolf form hadn't been fixed.

For twelve million dollars, wouldn't one expect all repairs to be done in advance? And for fang marks to be buffed out of the gate? I peered into the stone-paver courtyard.

"Yeah, my mom's business is *dead*," Jasmine said. "I'm going to have to use my fancy real-estate-finance degree to work for another agency, hopefully one that's getting more leads right now."

"I can tell you an agency *not* to apply to." I stuck my tongue out toward the for-sale sign. For some reason, maturity was difficult to achieve today.

"A reference would be better."

"I haven't worked with you in a professional capacity."

"I recorded a heroic battle for you while risking my own life. I also threw a pan at a seething wolf that I'm related to, all to help you out."

"Is that night something you want me to go into detail about when your prospective employers call to ask about your character?" I tried to step sideways between the bars, but they were too narrow. As a wolf, I'd escaped that way, but my hips were trimmer in that form.

"Maybe you could leave out the werewolves. They might not be a selling point."

"They usually aren't."

We, both werewolves ourselves, shared a sigh.

"But you could mention the pan-throwing," Jasmine added. "That's a point in my favor, right? It shows initiative."

"*I* appreciated it." I tested the lock on the gate. It was, alas, sound.

If it hadn't been midday and more than a week until the full moon, I might have been able to call upon my magic to change into a wolf, but that was always difficult without a threat stirring my blood. Even if I *could* shift, there was no guarantee that wolf-me would remember what human-me wanted. Some prey sauntering through the fields might distract me, and I would end up ten miles away in Lake Stevens with a rabbit dangling from my jowls.

"Good. That's all you have to tell them. Whoever. I haven't sent out any résumés yet, but I have to soon. I *can't* keep living in the ADU at my parents' house, not when they insist on a curfew. If it's not a hunt night, I have to be home by one. Like I'm a *teenager*. Have you ever heard of any people so repressed?"

"I have not." I pressed my forehead to the gate and peered around the courtyard. I wanted a clue, damn it.

"If I had my own condo, I could live by my own rules."

"I wish you the best in fulfilling your career and financial goals, but I called about something else." I would probably cave and let her list me as a reference if she kept asking, but I felt squeamish about vouching for someone's employment skills when I hadn't observed them. Besides, wasn't there a rule against asking relatives to be your reference?

"Oh, right. You called me."

"Yes, I did. Remember when your father looked up the business that's been buying werewolf artifacts? He got a list of places they own, right? I remember you mentioning a few."

"That's right."

"The owner, and his mad-scientist buddy, have moved out of their Arlington location. Do you think you can get me the list so I can check their other facilities? What was the name of the business that owned everything? The Tumwater Tonic Corporation. I think that's it. Oh, and can your mom check the MLS to see if the other addresses have also been listed for sale?"

"Anyone can check that, but sure. I'll get them for you." Jasmine hesitated. "Is this about Duncan?"

Since she had been with me the night he'd disappeared, she'd witnessed him being called away.

"I'm trying to find him, yes."

"Good. He's got that sexy accent."

"And is thus worth rescuing?"

"*Obviously.*"

After hanging up, I finished walking the perimeter of the facility, but I didn't find a way inside. I considered getting my rope out of the truck. I might be able to climb the courtyard wall, but I hadn't sensed any remnants of magic inside the compound. My gut told me that Radomir and Abrams had completely cleared out. If Duncan had been here at all, he was gone now.

Disappointed, I leaned my forehead against one of the cool adobe walls of the main building.

"I shouldn't have waited so long to come looking," I said, though it was possible that those guys had moved their operations and listed this place for sale before they'd summoned Duncan. They'd probably decided to leave the night I'd gotten away with the artifacts, maybe figuring I would gather the rest of my werewolf pack and come after him. "I *wish* I had."

Unfortunately, I didn't have much sway with my fur-sprouting kin. I was lucky the pack hadn't ostracized me for killing my cousin, Augustus.

My phone rang. I pounced on it, hoping Jasmine already had leads for me, but Bolin—spelling-bee champion, fledgling druid, and my intern at the apartment complex—was calling.

"Hi, Luna," he said. "Are you here?"

"At Sylvan Serenity? No, I'm... running an errand." Even though Duncan was a priority, I couldn't help but wince since my *errand* was taking place during work hours. I vowed to stay late this evening to tackle whatever deluge of tenant requests had come in that day.

"You might want to come back."

"Trouble?"

"Yeah."

3

HEADING BACK SOUTH, THE TRAFFIC WAS WORSE, AND I GRIPPED THE steering wheel, knuckles flexing. Bolin hadn't given me any more details before hanging up, and I worried that the motorcycle gang was harassing the apartment complex again. Or, what if my cousins who had been kicked out of the pack had shown up to exact revenge?

My skin buzzed with heat, magic pricking at my veins. I almost laughed. The wolf magic that hadn't wanted to let me draw upon it when I'd been thinking of breaking into the lavender compound was stirring now, my strong emotions calling to it.

But turning into a wolf while driving down the freeway was a bad idea. A very bad idea. I took a few long, slow breaths, willing my body to calm. Fortunately, I reached my exit without fur sprouting from my arms.

When I turned into the parking lot for Sylvan Serenity, there weren't any motorcycles, police cars, shattered windows, or other signs of fresh chaos. Instead, it appeared peaceful, the wan winter sun gleaming on cars and throwing long shadows from the evergreen trees edging the lawn. Bolin's blue Mercedes G-Wagon was parked under some of those trees, his translucent portable garage blown up to protect it from bird droppings.

"Such a strange druid." After pulling in beside the SUV, I peered around for the promised trouble.

An unfamiliar BMW in a guest parking spot was the only thing potentially amiss. Neither it nor Bolin's ride were the types of vehicles that my tenants owned.

The door to the leasing office was open, and Bolin leaned out as I walked up. Behind him stood an older man with lighter skin than Bolin but who had his same mussy red hair. My step faltered. That was his father, Rory Sylvan.

Were both of his parents here again? Hopefully, they hadn't come to discuss selling the property. When they'd shown up the week before, that had been the first time I'd seen them in years. I preferred that frequency of visitation from the owners—my employers.

Since my *errand* had taken me away from the property in the middle of the workday, I quickened my pace. Until werewolves— and thieves of werewolf artifacts—had inserted themselves into my life, I'd never randomly taken off during the day unless it was to pick up parts to repair one of the units. But now... I grimaced with guilt, hating that I had become a less-than-ideal employee, especially during a time when the owners were paying extra atten- tion. At least the place still looked good. It hadn't always been during office hours, but I'd kept up with all the maintenance requests and regular seasonal issues.

Bolin stepped outside to meet me, and I heard Kashvi Sylvan's voice. Yes, both of his parents were in the leasing office. She seemed to be talking to someone besides her husband.

"Is this the trouble you mentioned?" I nodded toward the office but also rested a hand on my chest, half-wondering if *I* was the trouble. Or the one *in* trouble, rather.

"I thought you might find it concerning," Bolin said.

"People in the leasing office? Nah, I dusted and took out the trash this morning. It's not that concerning."

His grave look told me that *wasn't* what had prompted his call. "They're showing a potential corporate buyer around the property."

I groaned, my gaze drifting back to the BMW.

Before, I'd dreaded the idea of motorcycle thugs, but now I wished vandals would roar through the parking lot. Or what about my ghost-hunting tenants? Couldn't they wander past with their glowing and beeping equipment? I needed something to happen to convince a buyer that this place was too weird to be interested in. Especially a *corporate* buyer. Yuck.

Sure, the Sylvans had gotten super rich over the years and were a long way from qualifying as a mom-and-pop business, but they also weren't a heartless, publicly-traded company cutting costs at all expense to make their wealthy shareholders happy.

Alas, the sun was doing an excellent job of highlighting the well-tended grounds, the recently pressure-washed roof, and birds flitting about as they chirped appealingly in the trees. There wasn't even any freshly chewed gum stuck to the side of the cluster mailboxes. If I were a real-estate photographer, I would choose this day to take pictures.

As if the thought had summoned such a person, a young man with a drone tucked under one arm wandered in from the parking lot.

"I'm here to take the photos," he called when Rory Sylvan looked out the door and waved at him.

I groaned again, managing to muffle it when Rory noticed us and acknowledged me with his wave. I attempted a smile as I returned the gesture, not wanting to share the bleakness I felt, that I was about to lose my home and job of twenty-plus years.

Would a new *corporate* owner want to keep on someone

without a college degree? Someone who kept drawing trouble, especially werewolf trouble, to the complex?

"Any chance the prospective buyer has read the news and has concerns about the rising crime in the area? And the incident that happened here?" I pointed casually toward the parking lot, though I felt guilty about downplaying the night Duncan and I had changed into wolves to battle the thugs Radomir had sent to kidnap me. It had been self-defense, but there had been *deaths*. Multiple deaths. Thanks to my crazed wild werewolf instincts taking over, I had been responsible for them.

"It did come up," Bolin said. "The guy is negotiating and trying to imply that this place should go for a steal, due to those incidents, but my parents had me get out the financials and show them off. The complex is extremely profitable, great cap rate."

I bared my teeth. That *was* something I'd always striven for, but, in this situation, it wasn't a boon.

"It's amazing how much work you do that they would normally have to pay contractors and other service providers for." Bolin looked at me with bemusement, as if I were odd. "Was that part of your original deal when you first got the job?"

"No, but I've never seen the point in paying for things I can do myself."

"I don't know where you find the time, especially considering how busy your life is." Bolin glanced at Duncan's Roadtrek in the lot and also toward the greenbelt.

"It wasn't that busy until recently."

"Well, you're a hard worker. That's good."

I squinted at him. "You don't usually throw compliments around. Are you about to let me know I'm being fired? Or do you want something?"

"It's in the job description of an intern to suck up to one's superiors."

"Two days ago, you didn't know the meaning of the term *suck up*."

Bolin's eyebrows flew up. "I know the meanings of *all* terms. Suck comes from the Middle English *souken* and Old English *sucan*, to use the lips and tongue to draw liquid into the mouth. As for slang variations, those are more twentieth century and imply, er, sexual acts. Though the terms are removed enough in the present to rarely suggest vulgarity."

"That's a relief. What is it you said that you want from me? If not to warn me of my impending firing?"

Bolin hesitated, no doubt recognizing me trying to trick him into confessing. Ultimately, he shrugged and answered. "I was wondering how your niece, Jasmine, is doing. You know she asked me where I get my coffee, right? Did she go visit Rocket Espresso? And get an orange mocha? That's my favorite drink. It's the one I gave to her. She must have liked it, right?"

His expression reminded me of a golden retriever seeking attention. If he'd had floppy ears, they would have been perked with hope.

"I'm not sure if she's been there." I tried not to bare my teeth at the photographer as he put his drone into the air for aerial shots. Damn it, why had I removed all the moss from the roofs a couple of weeks ago? The place would look *great* in his photos. He would doubtless take them in such a way as not to include the traffic-filled freeway on the other side of the greenbelt.

"Oh." Bolin's shoulders slumped.

Busy scowling at the drone, I almost missed his disappointment.

"She might have gone there." I figured I should bolster my intern, not wallow in my own worry and distress. He'd helped me out numerous times. But, thus far, Bolin hadn't proven himself to be the kind of guy that girls fell head-over-heels for. Or even the kind they noticed was flirting with them. "I can ask her the next time I talk to her."

"That would be great. She's pretty. And vivacious. I had to spell vivacious to win my fifth-grade spelling bee."

"That was a good memory for you, huh?"

"Oh, yes. That was before the words got excruciatingly obscure and difficult and the competition stiff."

"Before I talk to Jasmine, I do feel compelled to ask if you realize she's my relative. And all that that entails." I raised my eyebrows.

Bolin paused before answering. "More than that she inherited the same sense of sarcasm that you have?"

"That *does* run in my family, but yes. More."

"Your son didn't get more, right? He seems normal." Bolin had only met Austin in passing, but, as a fledgling druid, he had the power to sense if people were magical.

"Because his father was a normal human, yeah." I refrained from making that *a normal sleazy human who stole money and cheated on me*. After all, I was working on my maturity today.

"And it takes two... unnormals to make... one of you." He gestured at me.

"Essentially."

"Or a bite."

"Yes. But hardly anyone can pass along our magic that way anymore."

"Is Jasmine hardly anyone?"

"No."

"Okay." Bolin brightened. "Good. Will you see her soon to talk to her?" A hand on his chest implied *about me*.

"I'm not sure. She's researching something for me now."

"The wolf case?"

"No, that's...." I hadn't *forgotten* that our elusive wolf-lidded magical case had finally opened, revealing a metallic mushroom-shaped artifact that had saved Duncan from a fast-acting poison, but I'd been worried about his disappearance. I had mentally and physically put the case aside to mull on later. It, the lid again closed and locked, was back in the heat duct under my bed. At the moment, Jasmine, who'd witnessed the miraculous healing, was the only person besides Duncan who knew about its contents. But since Bolin had been studying it, maybe he deserved an explanation. It might also take his mind off his disappointment in realizing Jasmine probably wasn't at home, writing his name in her journal with hearts around it. "The case has had a new development. I'm not sure what to think."

"Oh?" Bolin's brows rose with interest.

"When I was fighting my cousins, it popped open." Speaking quietly so we wouldn't be overheard, I explained how the artifact inside had healed Duncan's wound.

"That's amazing, but how did the case just *pop* open? We tried everything from pliers to reading the translation aloud in English and the original Ancient Greek to unlock it. We even used lubricating potions on the hinges while chanting *open sesame*. It seemed fused in place."

"It's not fused." I debated how to explain what had prompted it to open without admitting that Duncan had been cloned from an ancient werewolf with the power to turn into a bipedfuris, the towering two-legged version of our kind with the ability to spread lycanthropy through his bite. "We believe that it opens when one of the threats that it—the artifact inside—was designed to protect against is nearby. Like it senses something with venom or poison." I didn't bring up werewolf bites, the third item mentioned in the inscription. "And then it makes itself available to help the person nearby."

"Oh, how handy. It sensed that the sword your cousin used was poisoned? And that's when the lid opened?"

I was fairly certain Duncan's presence in the two-legged form had been the catalyst, but I nodded. It hadn't occurred to me before, but there *was* a possibility the poisoned sword had caused the case to open. Maybe I'd wrongly assumed the bipedfuris had been responsible.

"We didn't get a chance to experiment, but Duncan asked if we had rattlesnakes or scorpions around," I said. "He wanted to see if a venom-producing creature would cause it to open. Strangely, I don't keep any of those in my truck, so we still don't know."

"Did you try waving the poisoned sword over it again?"

"No. The house was on fire by that point."

"On fire," Bolin mouthed.

"When my family fights with each other, we go all out." Technically, Duncan and his underwater demolitions had been responsible for the explosion that had started the fire, but my vile cousins had prompted that need. "You have siblings, don't you? Or cousins? You know how chaotic things can get, I'm sure."

"I guess so. My little brother and I wrestled on the couch once, knocked over a candle, and spilled hot wax on our mother's newly installed carpet."

I scratched my cheek. Such an incident wouldn't count as worth recalling in a werewolf family. Hell, Cameron and Austin had caused more of a mess than that on a weekly basis, and the lupine magic hadn't even passed along to them.

"We were grounded for three weeks," Bolin added.

"If you'd been one of my kids, I wouldn't even have denied you dessert for that crime." As an ardent dark-chocolate fan, I'd always considered withholding sweets a far worse punishment than *grounding*. That was more of a torment for the parents than the kids since it meant the rowdy ones were stuck at home, plotting more trouble.

"Really?" Bolin looked wistfully at me. "Every time my parents grounded me, they took away all my electronics. I had to either read old-school physical books or practice the violin."

"I forgot that was on your résumé." I pantomimed running a bow over strings. "Maybe you should be serenading cute girls while you hand them fancy mochas."

"I've tried that before. It didn't work as well as the chick flicks would lead you to believe."

"Did you play super boring classical music or something good?"

"Classical music isn't *boring*. And some of it takes amazing mastery with the violin. How could you *not* fall for a guy who flawlessly played Niccolò Paganini's 'Caprice No. 24' under your window?"

Only the serious earnestness in his eyes kept me from laughing at the question.

"Jasmine likes rap," was what I said.

I expected my spelling-bee champion to be affronted by the thought of such pedestrian music, but he squinted at me, as if I'd offered him a challenge.

"Which rappers?"

"I'm not sure. I can ask."

"Would you? Like, gather *intelligence* for me?"

I hesitated, not certain it was my duty to help Bolin hook up with my niece, but he kept assisting me with my crazy life, and he was doing a good job keeping things running on the property when I was gone.

"Maybe a little." I texted Jasmine, asking what music she wanted me to load to play in the truck the next time we stormed a castle. A prompt reply came back, and I showed Bolin.

"Kendrick Lamar, Eminem, Doja Cat, 50 Cent," he read slowly.

"Do you know who any of those are?" I only did because of my sons. Probably a testament to how pathetically unhip I was, my tastes ran toward the eighties music I'd grown up with.

"Of course. I'm just... I need to think about how to use a violin to serenade a woman with rap beats. They're not exactly..."

"Romantic?"

"Easy to recognize if you're playing the beats on one instrument."

"You'll have to sing along."

That earned me an aggrieved look.

"*Can* you sing?" I asked.

"Of course. I was in my church choir all through high school."

"You had a lot of extracurricular activities."

"Learning music improves cognitive function in children. My mom insisted."

"You're a good son. I don't know if Jasmine will fall for you, but I bet her parents would like you." I watched the Sylvans walk out of the leasing office with a gray-haired man in a business suit. Instead of heading for the parking lot, they meandered down a walkway toward one of the buildings in the back. For a full tour?

"Don't say things like that," Bolin said. "No girl under thirty wants to date someone her *parents* approve of. They want to go out with guys who are edgy and rebellious."

"You'd better start practicing your violin rap beats then."

The rumble of a motorcycle made me spin toward the parking lot.

It wasn't one of the big Harleys the thugs had ridden but a bright green Kawasaki dirt bike. Swept back in a man bun, the rider's long green-dyed hair almost matched it. Wooden sticks stuck out of a holder on his back, and I imagined him applying them to car windows.

Scowling, I strode toward the parking lot. Even if I'd been fantasizing about trouble scaring off prospective buyers, I could not, in good conscience, want vandalism to take place.

The rider pulled into a spot meant for bicycles, parked, and hopped off the Kawasaki. He didn't look to be more than twenty, but that didn't mean he couldn't be trouble, and I bared my teeth.

My canines were sharper than typical for a human, a testament to my lupine heritage, but not so noticeably that people jumped back in alarm. Only those with magical blood of their own sensed that I had power. This guy merely raised his eyebrows.

"Hi. I'm Yuto. Are you Ms. Luna Valens?"

I stopped a few feet away and gave a wary, "Yeah."

"He said you were pretty, snarky, and kind of feral."

I blinked at the description. "Who said that?"

The kid—Yuto—pulled out a phone and looked at a note on his screen. "Duncan Calderwood."

"You've seen him? When?" I almost pounced on my visitor.

Maybe Yuto sensed that—and my feral vibe—because he took an uncertain step back. "A few days ago. It might have been almost a week. Sorry about that. We run a camp at the dojo over the holidays when kids are out of school, and it's been busy."

"Dojo?" I looked at the sticks on Yuto's back again. Maybe those were practice swords, not cudgels for vandalizing cars.

"Yeah. I work there for my uncle to help pay my way through school. I heard you're looking to learn how to fight with swords."

I *had* vowed to find some lessons, but... "Are you sure you're old enough for that? I figured I'd get a Mister Miyagi and have to learn how to wax-on-wax-off first."

Yuto looked blankly at me. Apparently, making students watch the *Karate Kid* hadn't been part of his uncle's training program.

"I've got a lot going on right now," I said.

"We all do this time of year, but the lessons are already paid for. I came by to get your contact information and have you sign a waiver, but we can have the first practice here, if you like. It's nice out today, and any flat area would work."

"Duncan paid for lessons for me?"

"The first ten, yup."

A lump of emotion formed in my throat. Duncan was

watching out for me even though he wasn't here. Even though he was... Where the hell *was* he?

I owed him, damn it. He was the one who'd given me the sword and suggested I use it to protect myself—and others—when I couldn't take, or *shouldn't* take, my more powerful lupine form.

"Ten?" I asked lightly, not wanting to admit my emotions to a twenty-year-old stranger. "Is that how many it will take for me to master swordsmanship?"

Yuto opened his mouth but didn't seem to know if I was joking or not. I was, but with my limited time, I didn't know how many lessons I could fit in.

"I started training in martial arts when I was four," he said, "and I'm still learning."

"So, it'll take more than ten lessons?"

"For mastery, yes."

"What if I just want to be able to prong werewolves?" I kept my tone light to indicate it was a joke—even if it wasn't. With Augustus gone, I might get lucky and not *need* to prong any more lupine family members, but luck hadn't favored me lately.

"I... guess that would depend on the defensive skills of the werewolf."

"They're pretty badass."

"You might need twenty lessons then."

"Okay. Let's plan on that."

"Are you ready to get started?"

I looked toward where I'd last seen the Sylvans. They'd disappeared from view, but I wasn't about to wave swords around on the lawn while the owners were on the premises. If anything, I needed to check my email and see what maintenance orders tenants had sent in while I'd been away.

"I can after work hours. I'm the property manager here," I added, figuring he might wonder how someone wandering out to meet visitors in the parking lot at an apartment complex could be at *work*.

"I thought you might be security." Yuto grinned. "You looked like you were going to kick my ass when I rode up."

"As someone who's been studying martial arts since you were four, you had to be terrified by the prospect of being attacked by a middle-aged woman."

His grin widened. "All my experience has informed me that middle-aged women can be some of the scariest people you'll encounter." Yuto held out his phone, a form to sign on the screen. "Here's the waiver. You have to promise not to sue the dojo if you're injured while training."

"No problem." As I signed, I casually asked, "How much are these lessons?"

I couldn't imagine private sword-fighting instruction came cheaply. How much had Duncan spent? I appreciated him looking out for me, but I didn't want to take his money—or the equivalent. After I rescued him, I would find a way to pay him back, assuming I could afford a ten-pack of sword-fighting lessons. Maybe there was an installment plan.

"I believe Mr. Calderwood and my uncle bartered and came up with a non-financial arrangement."

"Does that mean Duncan paid with something he dragged up from a lake bottom?" I asked with certainty. That was, after all, how he'd found my magical sword.

"My uncle is a great fan of military history, and he has a cannon collection. I understand it now has one more item in it."

"Is collecting cannons *legal*?" Maybe that was a silly thing to ask since I was now friends with someone who regularly purchased grenades and underwater demolitions.

"Historic muzzleloading black-powder cannons are. They're considered antiques. The rules around other things are fuzzier, I gather." Yuto glanced at the signed form and took his phone back. "I'll be ready to start when you are."

"Okay, thanks." As I headed to the leasing office, I debated how I could repay someone for sword-fighting lessons that had been financed with a *cannon*.

4

AFTER WORK, I ENDURED MY FIRST SWORD-FIGHTING LESSON AT A
dojo a mile from home. Had I not had so much on my mind, I
might have enjoyed learning new skills, but, during rest breaks, I'd
kept glancing at my phone, hoping Jasmine's dad had a lead on
where Duncan might be. The only message that came in was a
note from Austin saying he'd headed up north for his holiday
snowboarding vacation. By the end of the lesson, with blisters
forming on my palms, I'd vowed to do some more research into
Duncan's captors on my own.

Back at the complex, I walked up to the threshold of an apartment recently rented by Rue, the alchemist who'd formerly
resided in downtown Seattle.

I issued the special knock I'd used with my *previous* alchemist,
a retired nurse who'd been scared off by Jasmine in werewolf form.
Rue hadn't mentioned such things as being standard in the field,
but who knew?

The door opened, a grayish-blue cloud of incense smoke
wafting out over the shoulders of the white-haired, wizened-faced
Rue. Before long, the ceiling would be dingy with the stuff. In a

saner moment, I wouldn't have leased an apartment to someone who dangled desiccated chicken feet, dried twists of herbs, and odd tufts of fur from the walls. But my life had gotten strange—and dangerous—suggesting I might repeatedly need the services of an alchemist.

"Yes, good." Rue nodded firmly at me. "Knocking is less obtrusive than the doorbell, which agitates my familiar when she is on the premises. Why do the delivery persons insist on ringing the bell even when you've left instructions for them to place the items on the threshold, and the app alerts you to their arrival?" She lifted her smartphone.

I scratched my jaw, somehow finding the thought of sending out for groceries incongruous with a grandmother alchemist. "It's a busy neighborhood. They want to make sure nobody steals your ingredients."

Rue blinked. "It is not safe?"

"Sometimes, there are werewolves in the woods."

"Oh, they do not concern me." Rue flicked her fingers as if such powerful creatures were of little consequence. Given all the potions—and doubtless *poisons*—she had on shelves and what looked like medicine cabinets mounted all around the living room, she probably believed she could handle them. "Though the rabbit spleens I ordered earlier might have been tempting morsels to roaming werewolves."

"You got those through Instacart?" I eyed her phone.

"There are other services those of us in the paranormal community find handy." Rue stepped back, waving me into the smoky living room. "What do you require? Something I can make for you?"

"Maybe. That's what I came to find out."

"You are aware of my fees."

"And that you don't lower them, despite me giving you two months of free rent and both senior and veteran discounts." The *senior* discount was her legitimate right; I had been looser when entering her status as a veteran. Why I'd negotiated at all, I wasn't sure, except that her concoctions *had* been useful. With luck, they could be again.

"I allow you to enter and request my services without an appointment. Were you not the property manager who was presuming to tread upon my threshold near my bedtime hour, you might have found yourself doused with my skunk-thistle spray."

"Bedtime? It's 7:30 at night."

"I go to sleep early. It's good for the skin and one's overall health." Rue squinted at me. "Have you been applying my wrinkle cream?"

"No, but I will. It's been a trying month. I need help finding something."

Someone.

"You seek your missing werewolf mate. I observed that his vehicle is in the parking lot, but I have not sensed his presence in several days."

"He's not my mate, but yes."

"Is he not itinerant in nature? Perhaps he departed to seek fine treasures elsewhere."

Fine wasn't an apt word to describe most of the rusty junk Duncan pulled out of lakes, ponds, and seawater, but I didn't dispute the description, saying only, "Not without his van. It's full of all his magical equipment for locating things. And also his sardine stash."

"A tasty treat. I can see why one would not leave such behind."

I crinkled my nose at that descriptor for the canned fish. "I think bad guys have Duncan—the same bad guys who employ the thugs who tried to get you to supply that Tiger Blood potion."

"Their willingness to imbibe substances that require illegally acquired ingredients did disturb me."

"Yeah, that's why I hate them too. Do you have anything that could help me find Duncan? He's..."

Rue arched her eyebrows.

"I owe him," I said to stave off further suggestions that we were mates. "I want to make sure he's okay."

"I see." Rue headed for a shelf lined with books and tiny jars of colorful liquids. "I do have numerous recipes for location potions."

I rubbed my eyes, the pungent haze making them water, and thought about stepping outside, but if she could truly help...

"I believe all of them require cells from the body of the being one wishes to locate."

"Cells?"

"Yes, a physical manifestation of the person's essence." Rue pulled down a thick tome with yellowed pages, the binding loose. Very slight magic emanated from it. An enchantment to keep it from falling apart with time, perhaps.

"So, more than their scent, such as would be used for tracking?"

"Correct. I would need something from the body."

"A hound could sniff a T-shirt he'd worn."

"Should the services of a four-legged *animal* be what you required, you would not have come to my door." Rue sniffed and opened the tome, the binding creaking.

"True." Besides, I could have turned into my wolf form to track someone if I'd thought that would work. But days had passed since Duncan's disappearance outside my cousin's burned-down home, and it had rained since then. There wouldn't be much of a trail. Even if there had been, tracking someone twenty miles through the suburbs wasn't easy, and if he'd gotten into a car at any point...

"Here is a tried-and-true formula." Rue rested a finger midway down a page near the front. The text had been handwritten who knew how many years—centuries?—ago. "I have many of these ingredients and could acquire most of the others."

"Is rabbit spleen one of them?"

"It is not, but the same supplier could get most of these." Rue looked at me. "If I were properly compensated."

I sighed and checked my phone to see if Jasmine had called or texted yet. Thus far, her *father* hadn't asked for compensation when researching things. But no new messages had popped up.

"I'm willing to pay a fair price," I said.

"I would also, as I said, need some of his cells. Not very many. If you've had intercourse recently, I might be able to take a sample of his essence from your vagina."

I crossed my arms over my chest. "His *essence* isn't in there. Even if it were, I bathe frequently to clean my body of sweat, grime, and other people's cell samples."

"Unfortunate." Rue lifted the page to show me the recipe, though it wasn't written in English. "This mentions that blood, saliva, semen, or excrement would do."

Excrement? Ew.

"I can let you into Duncan's van," I said. "Maybe something in there would work. If you want, you can swab the inside of his composting toilet."

Her lip curled. "That... could be sufficient. However unglamorous. I do charge extra for travel."

"The van is in the parking lot." I pointed in its direction, the lot only fifty yards away.

"I charge *extra* for travel," Rue said firmly.

Since swabbing a toilet might be involved, I decided not to object. "Okay."

Rue set the book aside, plucked a small leather kit out of a drawer, and gestured for me to lead.

Outside, rain pattered on the concrete-aggregate walkways and the asphalt parking lot. One of the landscaping lights along the way was burned out, and I made a mental note to change the bulb in the morning. I'd finished my maintenance to-do list before my sword-fighting lesson, but new duties came up every day here.

"Here you go." I unlocked the door of the Roadtrek and opened it for her. A magical ceiling lamp turned on, emitting a warm glow. "Sample away."

Rue curled her lip again, but she did climb into the van and open cabinets.

"The toilet is in that one." I pointed, though I suspected she was looking for alternatives to collecting *that* kind of sample. Maybe she could find a used tissue or hairbrush or something else that would work for her recipe.

"How can you tell? All these doors are tiny." Rue did locate the one that opened to the little lavatory, though the closet door beside it was of similar size.

"This van should make you appreciate the square footage of your apartment and give you a desire to pay more."

"I thought you weren't the owner and didn't make any more money if I paid a higher rent."

"That's true, but I like to manage the property to the best of my abilities and ensure my employers make what they need to cover all the expenses of maintaining the complex." A statement that was especially true now, though I doubted a two-hundred-dollar increase from one tenant would keep the Sylvans from selling.

"I guess I cannot fault you for that." Rue took a bracing breath as she looked at the composting toilet and drew out her kit.

I thought about asking if she needed help, but the rumble of loud engines turning onto our street stopped me. As I faced the parking lot entrance, four big men on motorcycles sped into view. They headed straight for the complex's driveway, and I groaned with the certainty that trouble had arrived.

5

HALF-WISHING I HAD THE SWORD, THOUGH A SINGLE LESSON HAD barely taught me how to hold it, I left the van and walked onto the pavement where the motorcycle riders wouldn't miss seeing me. The first time thugs like this had rolled into the lot, it might have been chance—a little vandalism partaken in for fun—but this time... I had little doubt these guys were here for me. Or at least *because* of me.

Engines roaring, all four men rode around the lot, circling the cars, going up and down the lanes.

I didn't sense anything magical about them, nor did I recognize them. These weren't Radomir's thugs, amped up on Tiger Blood potions. That didn't mean they weren't dangerous. Each of the big men wore black leather pants and a studded jacket and carried cudgels or tire irons as they eyed the windows of parked cars. They hadn't come here to tour one of the vacant units.

"On second thought," I murmured, "that one looks a little familiar."

Had he been one of the thugs present when Duncan jumped

into the fray to help? On the day he'd first arrived to metal-detect in the woods next to the apartments?

Back then, the intruders' eyes had been bloodshot and glazed, as if the men were on drugs. Today, they looked more alert as their gazes fixed on me. Two kept riding up and down the lanes, waving their cudgels in the air, though they hadn't yet struck anything. The other pair slowed to a stop a few paces from me.

My phone was in my pocket, and I thought about calling 9-1-1, but I remembered the *last* time the police had shown up. It had been in the aftermath of Duncan and me changing into were-wolves and tearing out throats. The authorities had found mauled bodies and heard reports of wild dogs—or wolves. If another inci-dent like that happened, with me in the middle of it, someone might figure out that the property manager for Sylvan Serenity Housing was a werewolf.

At least none of the tenants were in the parking lot at the moment. That was a small blessing, but it wasn't that late at night, so people might come and go. Bracing myself, I groped for a way to deal with these guys quickly.

"Luna Valens," one of the stopped men said. He had a faint accent, a wispy black mustache, and dark eyes that bored into me.

"Congratulations on your ability to read my name off the mail-box," I said, though I doubted these thugs had read anything. "How can I help you?"

He gave me a long once over, like he was checking me out, though he was probably trying to tell if I had weapons. I bared my teeth, letting him see my canines—my *lupines*, one might call them. Too bad my five-foot-three-inches of height and one-hundred-and-ten pounds didn't lend any extra menace to my sharp teeth.

"You've been making trouble," his partner said, a bald guy with a similar look. Maybe a brother.

"*I'm* the one making trouble?" I touched my chest, then pointed to his cudgel.

It rested across one of his handlebars, but he still gripped it.

"This town doesn't belong to you. Mind your own business, or we'll tear up your place." He looked toward the van where Rue's nose was pressed against one of the windows as she watched. "*And the people who live here.*"

My skin warmed, my blood tingling as indignation at the threat filled me. Indignation and anger.

This was my territory, protecting the people who lived here my responsibility. The rational part of me knew I should avoid changing, but emotions rode higher, and, in case I couldn't control the magic, I tugged off my jacket and pulled my phone out of my pocket, tossing both to the sidewalk. But I didn't want to change in front of witnesses. I had to *talk* these guys into leaving. Somehow.

The other two men revved their engines and continued to ride around. Rue probably wasn't the only one nearby with a nose pressed to a window, watching.

"What are you talking about?" I asked, though I had an inkling. The thugs who'd tried to rob the convenience-store owners had also ridden motorcycles, and they'd had a similar vibe as these guys.

"The police know better than to mess with the Fellowship," he said.

"The Fellowship? Are you on a quest to save Shoreline from the Dark Lord Sauron?"

If he caught the reference, he didn't show it. "Mind your own business, or we'll make sure you don't have a business to mind."

"That's a clever play on words, but you need to be more specific. What is it you want me to do? Or *not* do?"

"You attack our people, and we'll attack yours."

His buddy thumped him on the arm and pointed at the Roadtrek. No, at Rue. "Valens needs a lesson. To see what happens to her renters if she gets in our way."

He turned off his motorcycle and hopped off, heading for the van.

Skin pricking and adrenaline rushing hot through my veins, I strode over to intercept him. Rage rode with the adrenaline. How dare this guy stomp presumptuously into my territory and threaten those under my care?

Rue might have a potion she could throw at the man, but she also might have come out with nothing but the sample kit. She needed protection.

"You girls need to leave men's business alone," the first speaker said.

When I planted myself in the path of the man heading toward Rue, he hefted his cudgel. The threat called to my magic as surely as the presence of a full moon would. When he swung, I ducked. The cudgel whistled over my head, missing by inches. Instead of rising back up, I dropped to all fours as the change took me.

Fur sprouted from my skin as magic morphed my limbs, torso, and head, and my mouth elongated into a fanged snout. The thoughts and emotions of a wolf took over as my body changed, shoes and clothes disappearing into the ether. Abruptly, I smelled everything around me, fir and pine sap from the woods, gasoline from the vehicles, the body odors of the men around me—the *enemies* around me.

"Shit." The man backed away, cudgel raised. "I *told* you she was a werewolf. Pedro saw her change. He said so."

"Hit her before she finishes," the other rider barked. Instead of raising his cudgel, he reached inside his jacket, withdrawing a handgun.

Even as a wolf, I recognized the danger. When the closer man stepped forward, swinging for my skull, I jumped to the side, using his body to block me from the firearm. I also caught the cudgel, my powerful jaws snapping down on the wooden weapon, and tore it from his grip.

Out of the corner of my eye, I glimpsed his pack mate jumping off his wheeled conveyance and aiming the handgun in my direction. I darted toward the closer man, using his body as a shield, and bit him in the thigh.

He screamed and tried to kick me with his free leg. I jerked back, pulling him off balance. He pitched to the pavement and clutched the bite wound, out of the fight for the moment. That left me without cover. Further, the other two riders had turned down this lane, their noisy vehicles roaring. I sprang between two cars.

With a crack that hurt my pointed ears, the firearm went off. A bullet took a chunk out of the pavement where I'd been standing. The two riders came through, their cudgels raised, but such weapons couldn't reach me as long as I stayed between the cars.

A thunk sounded nearby. It came from Duncan's rolling den, and I remembered a human ally was within. Or had she exited the vehicle and put herself in danger?

I backed out from between the cars to circle around several and come at the men from another direction. The roar of the motorcycles made it easy to track the riders, but I couldn't hear the gunman who'd stepped off his. I also couldn't smell him over the pervading odor of gasoline.

Needing a better view, I sprang lightly onto the hood and then the roof of one of the parked vehicles. The gunman crouched on the other side—he'd been trying to sneak closer to me. He shouted in alarm when he spotted me. Before he could point his firearm at me, I jumped down, jaws snapping.

Some vestige of my human brain remained, despite the overpowering wolf magic, and I remembered that I did not want to kill these foes, lest it make trouble for me later. At the last second, I diverted my aim from his throat to his shoulder. My fangs sank deep through clothing and muscle and flesh, and bone crunched.

The man screamed in my ear and dropped his gun as we tumbled to the pavement. I came out on top and bit him again, this time on the hand he'd used to fire that weapon.

A motorcycle roared right behind me. I whirled and sprang as the rider came into view. His cudgel was raised to strike me, but he wasn't fast enough. I arrowed into his side, my momentum taking us both tumbling off the motorcycle. Like a mountain cat, I twisted in the air to land on my paws. Freed of its rider, the motorcycle ran into a car. The wrenching of metal assailed my ears and made me want to run from the area.

But another rider remained. He was angling toward the human woman who'd come out of the rolling den. I sensed power from her but recalled that she brewed magical concoctions; she wasn't a fighter. Or so I thought. She gripped a large cylinder on a rope that she twirled, then flung. It struck the rider in the face, knocking his head back. He released the handlebars and lost control of the motorcycle. As he fell off, it nearly ran over the man I'd bitten in the thigh. Struggling to rise, he barely managed to scramble out of the way.

"Do not underestimate the power of a grandmother," the woman called, reeling the cylinder back in.

Nobody answered her. Our enemies were hobbling away. Only one managed to salvage his motorcycle, get back astride it, and ride out of the parking lot.

Hackles up, I growled, considering taking a few more bites of flesh from those who weren't leaving as quickly. But the human woman—Rue, that was her name—lowered her coiled rope and cylinder and approached me without fear. Though I believed her an ally to me in my human form, I watched her warily. Not all those who allied with humans were willing to ally with werewolves.

She stopped at my side and patted me on the back.

"I believe the incinerated ashes from the toilet droppings will do for the location formula. As long as they don't belong to you, that is." She cocked her head, regarding me curiously. "No, you probably go in the woods. Yes."

Even though I mostly understood the words, they did not make much sense to me. As I waited for the wolf magic to fade, I growled again, irritated that the men had dared intrude upon my territory. Perhaps my instincts had been right and I should have killed them so they could not prove nettlesome again.

Looking in the direction I was growling, Rue asked, "Do you want me to make a formula so you can locate *them* too?" She withdrew a napkin from a pocket and dabbed the corner of a dented fender, hair and blood darkening it, not yet washed away by the drizzle. "This is fresher than the ashes. Yes, indeed." She patted me on the back again but paused, looking up at the sound of a car driving in.

I noticed it but also spotted another human in the area, a woman with an electronic device. She was on the far side of the parking lot, many vehicles in between obscuring my view, so I hadn't noticed her before. She was pointing her device in our direction.

"You may wish to disappear into the woods and hope she didn't get a good photograph or video." Rue stepped away, lowering her hand. "I believe from what I have heard that the tenants do not know of your alter ego."

I was already backing away. My wolf instincts cared nothing about humans and their electronic devices, but I remembered that it would matter to me in my other form. Trouble might yet come of this night.

6

IN THE WOODS NEAR THE APARTMENT COMPLEX, I WAITED BETWEEN two trees for the wolf magic to fade. The battle with the humans had been unsatisfactory, and I longed to go off and hunt, but what if I needed to again defend my territory?

That thought kept me in place, though I would have struggled if I'd caught the scents of more than sleeping squirrels and smog as human vehicles passed on the other side of the woods.

As I sat on my haunches, a sense of loneliness crept over me. The last time I'd taken my wolf form, I hadn't been by myself. Duncan, the male I had almost made my mate, had been there. In the ancient form of the bipedfuris, he'd fought with me, helping me battle my enemies. He'd been a good companion, and I missed him.

Sometime after Rue left the van and returned to her apartment, my magic faded. Soon, I crouched naked among the damp fir needles, the chilly air much more noticeable against my bare skin, especially with droplets of rainwater dripping from the branches above.

With my arms wrapped around my torso, I headed for the back

of the complex, hoping to avoid notice. A few cars had rolled into the lot, tenants returning home late, but the girl who'd been taking photos or recording the fight had disappeared. In my lupine form, I hadn't recognized her, but, as I considered the memory through the fuzzy thoughts of the wolf, I believed it had been one of the ghost hunters. At least I hadn't *killed* any of the intruders this time.

A distant phone call, the ringtone familiar, made me groan and remember that I'd had the wherewithal to cast aside some of my belongings before changing. That was good, but now I needed to retrieve them from the puddle-filled sidewalk next to the cars.

"A task for after you're dressed," I told myself, continuing toward my apartment. But the rings continued, and I paused.

What if it was Jasmine? With urgent news about Duncan?

I peered toward the lot, didn't see anyone around the cars or on the walkways, and darted that way. The grass cold and damp under my bare feet, I hoped I could grab the items and escape before anyone saw me.

It *almost* worked. After I snatched up my jacket and phone, only glancing to see that Jasmine had indeed been the one to call, I ran down one of the covered walkways toward my unit—until a man came around the corner ahead of me.

Even before he issued a high-pitched yelp of alarm, I knew he wasn't one of the motorcycle thugs—or a physical threat of any kind. He carried a laptop bag and a Pop Tart. It was my fifty-something divorced tenant who'd once proudly shown me his Darth Vader toaster. Was that a faint Sith-Lord helmet imprint on the back of his Pop Tart? Probably.

"Ms. Valens." He clutched his laptop bag to his chest, like I might be a mugger.

No, just a damp werewolf in naked human form...

"Yes. Sorry to startle you. I'm..."

He glanced down but jerked his gaze back up again, up and

then some. Instead of locking his eyes onto my face, he studied the ceiling of the covered walkway.

"...practicing for the Polar Bear Plunge," I finished. "It's only a couple of weeks away."

"You... went swimming?" He didn't look down again to consider how damp I might be. "Without, uhm, a towel?"

"You need to harden yourself for the coldness of jumping into Lake Washington in January," I said, glad he hadn't asked *where* I'd found a place to swim this time of year. The pond by the convenience store where Duncan had magnet fished came to mind, and I felt the same twinge of loneliness I'd experienced in my wolf form.

Not the time, I thought firmly.

"I'm progressing well and looking forward to the event." I scooted around my tenant. "I do believe I've earned a shower though. Excuse me."

"Are there any tickets left?"

"I think it's free to anyone who registers."

He looked at my backside as I strode away, but when he noticed me glancing over my shoulder, he jerked his gaze to the ceiling again.

"Thanks!" He walked away with his face tilted up as he waved awkwardly.

When I'd fixed his faucet, he'd given me a big tip and also tried to offer me Pop Tarts. Or had it been Darth Vader toast? I couldn't remember, but as I ducked into my apartment, I worried he would be at Matthews Beach on Polar Bear Plunge Day, looking for me.

"Too bad I'm going to come down with a cold that morning." I shut the door firmly behind me and grabbed my robe before tapping on the phone to call Jasmine back. Since I'd been gone all day, the heat in the apartment wasn't on, so I turned it up. A hot shower sounded appealing. "Later."

"Hi, Luna," Jasmine answered before it went to voicemail. "Did you listen to my message?"

"Not yet. I was... inconvenienced."

"Does that mean you were furry?"

It was hard to hide that kind of thing from another werewolf.

"Yeah. Some idiots on motorcycles came to threaten my apartment complex."

"That happens a lot, doesn't it?"

"Kind of, yeah. I'm taking care of it." I glanced at the sword leaning in the corner of the living room, wondering if events would have turned out differently if I'd had it, along with a few hundred lessons under my belt. With my tenants—and alchemist—being threatened, I probably would have turned wolf regardless.

"Let me know if you need help. I want to earn your recommendation for my résumé."

"Let me know if you've got any leads on Duncan, and I'll be sure to tell them what a good researcher you are. That comes in handy in the real estate industry, doesn't it?"

"Oh, sure. Especially with atypical properties. You always have to dig up stuff. But Dad was the one doing your research. Here, I'm going to text you a list of addresses that the company owns in the Puget Sound area. I looked them up. None of them are on the MLS yet. Not the commercial listing services either."

"Probably because the other facilities haven't been raided by werewolves yet."

"That type of thing *can* prompt a property owner to sell. They hardly ever mention it in the notes though."

"Odd." I eyed the list that came through via text. She'd sent a number of them before, but some were new, with addresses located all over the Puget Sound area, everywhere from Tenino to Port Orchard to Issaquah to Deming. Wasn't that a little town on the way to the Canadian border? "This is going to take some driving."

"Do you want help?" Jasmine offered again. "I *love* driving and cranking my music."

I recalled Bolin's request to acquire information that would help him woo Jasmine, but setting up young people wasn't my priority. "It'll be dangerous. You'd better skip this adventure."

"Are you sure? I don't mind danger, and I've got time on my hands until I start getting job interviews. Oh, and I've got some networking events next week. Mom says I have to go so I can schmooze." Jasmine's tone shifted to mimic her mother's. "You get jobs by being in *proximity* to people, not filling out applications on the internet." In her own voice, she added, "That was her way of saying I need to go kiss some asses."

"That sounds right." I hadn't needed to apply for a job in a long time—the internet had barely existed when I'd started working at Sylvan Serenity—but even back then, merely dropping off résumés hadn't done much. "I may need to join you at those networking events if... things don't work out here."

"Because of the idiots?"

"No. Well, not *only* the idiots." As I explained about my employers getting ready to list the apartment complex, I looked up the addresses, hoping one of the "street views" would show me a facility that jumped out as a likely place to restrain a werewolf. Something with barbed-wire fences, cannons mounted on crenellated walls, and a dungeon, ideally... Unfortunately, most of the addresses were for unassuming warehouses. I didn't even see any barbed wire. What kind of evil-overlord lairs were these?

"Huh. Well, it could be cool if we went to networking events together. It's easier to schmooze with backup. We could talk each other up."

"You almost make it sound fun."

The problem was that I didn't *want* to leave my current job. Even if some of my tenants were weird and wandered around with

Pop Tarts and ghostometers, this place had been home for a long time.

"It *will* be." Jasmine said more, but my instincts twanged as I sensed someone magical approaching my apartment, and I didn't hear the rest.

What now?

"Oh, by the way," Jasmine continued, unaware of my distraction, "Emilio wants to know if you're coming to visit the pack anytime soon. He craves salami and summer sausage."

"Doesn't he have a job and the ability to purchase his own salamis?" I walked to the window and peered between the blinds but didn't see anyone.

Could it be Rue that I sensed? Already coming to deliver my potion?

"Emilio is pursuing a number of entrepreneurial ventures while living with his parents," Jasmine said.

"That's a *no*, right?"

"Correct."

The being I sensed didn't feel like Rue. It felt like a werewolf.

I grabbed the sword from the corner. So soon after a change, I wouldn't likely be able to turn again. I might have to defend myself in the human way. "With a swift poke to the eye."

"What?" Jasmine asked.

"Someone's here. I'll call you back."

I waited for the doorbell to ring. It didn't. As I leaned close to check the peep hole, I decided the werewolf's aura was familiar. Someone from the pack.

When I peeked through the hole, I realized *why* my visitor hadn't rung the doorbell. The big white male was in wolf form.

"Lorenzo?" I set aside the sword, tied the belt on my robe, and opened the door.

Maybe I should have found clothes to put on first, but after the fight and sitting in damp pine needles, I craved a hot shower. Besides, it wasn't as if a wolf cared about human nudity.

"Where were you when I was hoping something would scare away the prospective buyer and real-estate photographer?" I asked.

From the threshold, he gazed at me with soulful blue eyes, and I regretted making a joke. Mud spattered his chest and paws. Had he traveled all the way here in wolf form? Had something happened to my mother?

"Everything okay?" I asked, certain it wasn't.

Lorenzo turned his head to gaze toward the woods. To draw my attention in that direction? It looked more like he sought answers out there than that he wanted me to look at something.

"Is... *Mom* okay?" I clarified.

His bushy white tail drooped. By the moon, had she passed?

I gripped the doorframe. She'd been getting weaker from the cancer, but I'd thought... The last I'd seen her, she'd still been walking around and eating and drinking. It hadn't been that long.

A hint of magic swirled around the wolf, and Lorenzo sat back on his haunches as the change overtook him. Once he returned to his human form, he straightened and met my gaze again.

"We need to speak," he said.

"I was afraid of that."

7

AFTER INVITING LORENZO IN, I WENT TO THE BEDROOM TO GRAB A blanket. If he hadn't driven down here, he wouldn't have a vehicle —or a change of clothes. Wordlessly, he accepted the blanket and wrapped it halfway around himself before sitting on the couch.

Despite his proclamation that we needed to talk, Lorenzo took his time getting started. I sat in the nearest chair and thought about getting him something to drink, but he'd worried me, and I wanted whatever news he had to share.

Finally, he spoke. "Last night, your mother went on a hunt alone. She didn't invite me along or even tell me that she was going, even though... I had asked her to do so. On the hunt, she battled a bear. Having been disturbed from its winter hibernation, it was particularly belligerent."

He paused, a long pause that had me wringing my hands.

"Is Mom okay?" I asked.

A solo werewolf in his or her prime might handle a bear, but Mom was a long way from her prime. Unfortunately. My throat tightened. For so many years, she'd been so powerful, so indomitable. In the past, I never would have worried about her hunting alone. But now...

"She did survive the encounter. She received numerous wounds, however, and is now resting in bed."

I sagged back in the chair, relieved she was alive, but Lorenzo didn't appear to share my relief. He gazed pensively at the kitchen cabinets.

"I believe she only survived because I showed up in time to help. Even though she hadn't told me she was going, when I went by for a visit and found her cabin empty, I had a hunch. If I hadn't gone to see her and hadn't been able to track her into the woods..."

"Why did she pick a fight with a cranky bear?" I asked. "Especially in her condition?"

"She would not answer me when I asked that same question, but I believe it was *because* of her condition."

"What do you mean?"

Lorenzo swung his gaze back to mine. "She doesn't want to die in bed."

"Oh," I said as the realization sank in. I wanted to shake my head in denial but didn't. Right away, in my heart, I knew he was right. After a lifetime of being strong, Mom didn't want to be weak. After surviving so many hunts and so many battles, she didn't want to die of an illness.

"I was not sure who to seek out for help," Lorenzo said. "The pack's wise woman... can only treat her body, not her mind. When I left home tonight, I thought to hunt, but I could not focus on seeking out game. Eventually, my paws brought me here."

Was that hope in his eyes when he looked at me?

"What can I do?" I wanted to help but doubted Mom would listen to me any more than to Lorenzo or anyone else in the pack.

"Talk to her. I've tried, and your half-siblings have tried, but... you're her favorite."

"That can't be true. I left for years. *Decades.*"

"You're special to her. You were of his loins, the one she never stopped loving." Lorenzo's mouth twisted. With bitterness? Regret? It was hard to tell, but he seemed more accepting than angry. "I think when she wakes in the night and feels her mortality close... I don't know. When I confronted her, she said I was silly, that she wants to see things resolved with the artifact thieves and you—she hopes you mate with the lone wolf and promise to have werewolf offspring. Then she can die in peace."

I rubbed my face. Would I have to promise her that Duncan and I would get horizontal and make werewolf pups? At my age, I didn't want that, and Duncan hadn't given any indication that he wanted to stick around and father offspring. If anything, he'd been alarmed by Mom's suggestion. After traveling his whole life, he probably couldn't imagine settling down in one place.

"Talk to her," Lorenzo urged again. "Please. I don't know what you plan for your future, but even if you could only convince her not to do anything suicidal, I would appreciate it. I understand wanting to go out like a warrior, but surely she still has time. She's not ready for..." He swallowed. "*I'm* not ready for her to pass."

"I know. I get it. I'm not either. I wish there was a way to heal her, that she would have listened to the human doctors and considered their treatment options."

"She trusts magic, not human medicine. She is from the old days. The old *ways*."

"I know that too."

A thought came to me, and I returned to the bedroom, fishing in a drawer. As I stood above it, I felt the magic of the wolf case under the floor and paused to consider it.

The artifact inside it was not what I'd come for, but it *had* healed Duncan from what would have been a fatal sword wound. No, from the *poison* that had edged the sword. The artifact had great power, but nothing in the translation said anything about cancer or illness. The words carved into the case spoke of protecting against poison, venom, and werewolf bites. Maybe later, I could take it up to Mom's cabin and wave a vial of poison over it to see if it would open and do anything for her. Just in case.

Leaving it in the heat duct, I withdrew the magical talisman that Duncan and I had found in the river the first time we'd hunted together. I'd since put it on a new chain so one could wear it around one's neck.

Known as a longevity talisman, it lacked the power of the other artifact, but it supposedly helped with pain—arthritis and the like —and promoted long life. I'd rubbed it and called to its magic a couple of times, and it had seemed to make the wounds I'd received in battle less grievous than they should have been. Maybe it would make Mom feel a little better.

I returned to the living room. "I'll come up to see her when I get a chance, but give her this in the meantime."

"A witch's talisman?" Lorenzo must have encountered such items before. "I believe the wise wolf has similar enchanted items that she's tried on your mother."

"Well, this one is a gift from me, so it'll obviously be more effective."

He smiled faintly. "Perhaps it will do something. She did receive a few wounds in the bear battle, wounds that would have once healed quickly but are lingering." He flexed his hand, then waved to his neck. The locations of the injuries she'd received? "Her body and her magic are not as strong as they once were. I wish I could lend her *my* strength."

"So do I. Here. Give her this too." I grabbed one of the sea-salt-and-bacon-bits dark-chocolate bars from my kitchen stash. "This *has* to help."

When he accepted it, his smile widened. "I would think so. And also you visiting."

"I will." I dreaded showing up, only to have Mom ask about

Duncan and offspring, but if my presence could help her in any way, I felt obligated to go.

"Thank you." Lorenzo inclined his head toward me, draped the blanket over the back of the couch, and headed for the door. He paused with his hand on the knob. "I almost forgot."

I raised my eyebrows.

"One of your half-siblings was leading a hunt up north, in the currently unclaimed territory between Skagit and Whatcom counties. He thought he sensed a powerful werewolf, one he'd met briefly once before."

My eyebrows climbed higher. Did he mean...?

"Duncan was his name, yes?" Lorenzo asked. "The one you brought, the one with old-world blood."

"Yeah. Was this recently?"

Like since Duncan had gone missing?

"The night before last," Lorenzo said.

"Was it near a town? Specifically near a perfume factory that could double as a dungeon capable of holding a powerful werewolf?"

Judging by Lorenzo's confused expression, he hadn't heard much of that story. Radomir and Abrams might not be holding Duncan in a perfume factory again, but their lair wouldn't be in the middle of interesting wolf hunting grounds, surely.

"It wasn't near a town. They sensed him in the foothills of the mountains." Lorenzo waved toward the northeast and the Cascade range.

"That's unexpected."

Lorenzo spread a hand, then opened the door. "I'll let your mother know you'll visit soon."

"Okay."

As soon as he left, I dialed Jasmine's number as I again perused the list of addresses she'd sent.

"Everything okay?" she asked as a greeting.

"Lorenzo stopped by. He's worried about my mom."

"Oh, yeah. The bear thing?"

"Word gets around."

"There are no secrets in a werewolf pack."

"Deming," I murmured, plugging the town for one of the addresses in on my map app. "That's in Whatcom County, isn't it?"

"Yeah, near Bellingham."

There wasn't a "street view" option for the address, and Google didn't pop up so much as a Zillow listing for it. Unlike the previous evil-overlord-perfumery lair, this place didn't have a business associated with it, at least not anything publicly listed.

"I need to take a road trip," I said.

"Tomorrow?" Jasmine asked.

Tomorrow was Saturday, so I could more easily slip away from the apartment complex. "Yes."

"Do you want company?"

I hesitated, not wanting to get my little niece in trouble, but she'd been helpful when I'd faced off against Augustus and my other cousins. Besides, she was the line to her father, geek werewolf researcher. I might need him to dig further into this place.

"Sure," I said. "Bring gas money."

"It's not *that* far to Deming."

"I know. I was joking." Sort of. I had money budgeted for gas for the month, but the new uncertainty about my job and future prospects made me want to conserve even more than usual.

"How about I bring provisions?"

"Deal."

8

BEFORE DAWN, MY PHONE RANG. I'D ALREADY BEEN UP, MAKING espresso and quaffing a protein shake, but I hadn't expected any calls that early and jumped.

Figuring it might be Jasmine asking when I would pick her up, I trotted into the living room to answer. Rue was my caller, her name finally programmed into my phone.

"The potion?" I asked without preamble, though I hadn't expected her to finish it so quickly. "For finding Duncan?" I added with hope.

If the address didn't pan out, the potion could be handy. Since my half-brother had apparently sensed Duncan out in the wilds, I wasn't sure this Deming location would lead us to him.

"I've created an Elixir of Locus for him, yes," Rue said, "and also the motorcycle brute who assailed me."

"Didn't you technically assail *him*? That was one of Duncan's magnets, wasn't it?" As a wolf, I hadn't recognized it, but the memory of her hurling a cylinder on a rope had stuck with me after I changed back into human form.

"I believe it was a magnet, yes. I only assailed him because he attempted to assail *me* first."

"That is true. I'm not sure I want to hunt those guys down, but..." I paused. Being able to find them might be useful. I needed to rescue Duncan first, but the convenience-store owners *had* requested that I do something about crime in the neighborhood. Duncan had even suggested I use my werewolf powers, and possibly the sword and a cape, to become a superhero crime fighter. Normally, that wouldn't have appealed, but Shoreline *was* an extension of my territory, one could argue. If the crime was organized and I could figure out a way to drive out the leaders, I would try. Later. "I take it back. I need both potions."

"I thought you might. I'll bring them over with your invoice."

"You're not going to forget to bill anyone, are you?"

"What kind of businesswoman wouldn't *bill* someone? Don't forget the travel fee I'll be adding on."

"Oh, I haven't." Maybe I should have objected further to paying a fee for travel to the *parking lot*, but I remembered that she'd had to delve into the innards of the composting toilet.

After grabbing my pack, the sword, and more substantial food to have for lunch—and dessert after lunch—I headed for my truck. Rue met me there, holding a cloth bag tied closed with a gold ribbon.

"The elixir for Duncan has the gray label," she said. "The color of wolf fur. You need to be within ten miles of him when you imbibe it. If he's out of range, you won't feel anything."

"Imbibe?" Even though logic suggested that was what one typically did with potions, I hadn't imagined drinking anything. Especially not anything that had been made with samples derived from the composting toilet.

"Imbibe." Rue nodded firmly. "The whole thing at once. Chug it like a frosty beer on a hot August night with no air-conditioning present."

I made a face.

She must have guessed which ingredient I objected to imbibing.

"Will it help if I tell you I strained and filtered the liquid before pouring it into the vial?" she asked.

"It would help if you promised intense sanitation and irradiation was involved."

"Oh, yes. I do that with all potions." She smiled.

"Liar."

Her smile widened. "Ten miles. Then chug, chug."

"All right, thanks." After tucking my gear into the truck, I accepted the bag and her invoice.

"I gave you a ten-percent discount since you're a repeat customer."

Words that didn't keep me from choking over the price. I would have to take work on the side if I continued to need the services of the alchemist.

"Generous," I managed to murmur as I delved into my purse for my labeled budgeting envelopes.

"Naturally. Do you want me to start a stamp card? When you order nine potions, the tenth of equal or lesser value is free."

"I'd like to say that's not necessary, but..."

"Your life is most chaotic and dangerous. I suspect you'll continue to order from me."

"I suspect so too. Stamp me up."

"Excellent. I also included a free trial of my delightfully versatile blue-spider acid." Rue pointed at the bag. "It's in the small vial. Be careful not to break it. It can eat through almost anything."

I held the bag at arm's length.

"I thought it might be useful if you need to destroy steel bars in order to rescue someone from a cell."

"I actually *have* needed to get through steel bars and doors of late."

"As I suspected." Rue nodded and turned back toward her apartment, but a police car rolled into the parking lot.

I had the urge to spring into my truck and peel out. Too bad I was the property manager and responsible for the place. At least there weren't any mutilated bodies on the pavement this time. I looked for the car with the dented fender that Rue had taken her blood sample from, but its owner had moved it.

"Did you call the authorities?" Rue looked at a dainty silver watch on her wrist, the four quarters of the hour marked by vials, the hands represented by syringes. "It is quite early for visitors."

"The police have people who work around the clock."

My muscles tensed as the black-and-white car pulled into the empty *staff* spot next to my truck. The male and female officers inside were familiar; it was the duo who'd come to my apartment the night of the incident with Radomir's brute squad, the night of their deaths to werewolf jaws. *My* jaws.

The certainty that this visit had to do with me filled me with anxiety. Stern-faced, the officers stepped out of the car, hands resting on sidearms. Oh, yeah. They'd figured things out. I barely held back a groan. What was I going to say?

My only thought, as the female officer stepped onto the sidewalk, was that I was glad Austin had taken off on his trip so that he wouldn't see me getting arrested—or being accused of being a werewolf. Her name tag was visible on her uniform today. Dubois.

"Luna Valens," she said, though she only glanced at me, instead focusing on Rue.

That was odd. When had she seen my alchemist before? The officers had questioned a lot of tenants the night of the deaths, but Rue hadn't yet lived here then. If anything, I expected Dubois to confront me on where Duncan and I had disappeared to that night. I'd hoped they had been too busy to notice the bad guys' crashed Tesla slipping away, but I hadn't been certain.

"That's right. Can I help you?" I nodded to her and the male officer, trying not to let my gaze linger on their hands—their hands resting on their firearms.

"Is this one of your tenants?" Dubois pointed at Rue.

My alchemist folded her arms across her chest, gave her name, mentioned her grandchildren, that she was a widow, and that her cat was a service animal and thus allowed in her apartment. I'd forgotten about that cat—her familiar—when I'd helped her fill out the application, but I wasn't going to object to its presence now. Judging by the officers' scowls, the *cat* wasn't what had brought them.

"She moved in recently, yes," was all I said.

"Were you aware that she was in your parking lot with a wolf yesterday?" the male officer asked me.

"Uh." I blinked slowly as realization swept over me. The woman who'd been taking photos with her phone. She must not have come out in time to see me change, but she'd seen Rue and me together after the fight. Maybe also *during* the fight. "We've had some trouble with coyotes lately." I waved toward the woods.

"That wasn't a *coyote* in those photos. Ma'am." Dubois finally addressed Rue directly. "We would like to ask you some questions."

Rue lifted her chin. "I have nothing to hide."

"Good."

"Not even your chicken feet or rabbit spleens?" I murmured when the officers leaned into their car, presumably to grab recording equipment.

"Neither is illegal," Rue said.

"It's about a fight that was reported." Dubois stepped back close to Rue, her eyes narrowing. "And also an incident earlier in the month."

"Is that wolf still here?" The male officer eyed the parking lot, the grassy lawn, and the woods.

"I haven't seen any wolves today," I said.

That was true... since I didn't usually look at myself after shifting.

"What, it only comes by on Tuesdays and Thursdays?" Dubois asked.

I spread my hands and attempted to look bewildered, not guilty.

"The photos sent to us by a tenant showed the wolf fighting men on motorcycles," she continued.

"If it did that," I said, "then it's a hero. Those bikers have vandalized this place more than once. I had to replace that cluster mailbox a few weeks ago, thanks to them."

Not paying attention to me, Dubois pointed at Rue. "The photos also showed you standing next to the wolf afterward, *petting* it. Like it's your faithful hound."

"That's silly," Rue said. "As I said, I already have an animal companion. My cat would object vociferously if I came home with the scent of a forest predator clinging to me." A quick glance at me suggested that might have happened. "Besides, wolves aren't allowed to be kept as pets."

"It wasn't a cat that attacked those men," the male officer said. "Not yesterday and not the night of the murders. We think someone might have trained that wolf to carry out those deadly deeds."

I bristled. When Duncan and I had battled those thugs, it had been in self-defense. Yes, I'd lost it when my wolf instincts had taken over, but if the men hadn't been trying to kill him and kidnap me, we wouldn't have shifted forms and attacked in the first place. But I couldn't say that without admitting everything.

"I don't know what you're talking about," Rue said. "Perhaps someone seeks to blame me for some reason. I have lived many years and acquired a few enemies. Rivals who are envious of my skill and success in my field, among others."

Afraid they would ask what *field* she was in, I hurried to add,

"Where did you get the photos? Such things can be computer generated now, you know."

"Of course we know that," Dubois snapped.

"If Tia Aandahl was the one to call you and send them," I said, dredging the tenant's name from my memory, "you should know that she and her roommate spend their evenings out in the parking lot with ghost-hunting equipment. They seem to believe this is a hub of paranormal activity. I'm surprised you didn't get a photo of Rue petting a ghost."

"My cat would also find that distressful," Rue murmured.

Dubois looked at her partner, a touch of uncertainty in her eyes. "That girl *has* made a report to the station before. About... paranormal activity."

"Those photos looked legit." The male officer gazed around the parking lot, his eyes pausing on one of the security cameras mounted on a light post. "You record footage of what happens here, Valens?" He looked at Dubois. "Did we get that last time?"

"Sergeant Mendez was going to check on it. I'm not sure he remembered though." A chagrined expression replaced some of Dubois' earlier sternness. "I should have followed up on it."

"That footage gets deleted after a week," I said.

I'd made sure the footage of Radomir's thugs had been deleted even sooner.

"But you would have yesterday's recording," Dubois said.

"They should be there, yes. But I believe you need a warrant to demand to look at it."

By the time they got that, I could arrange for them to be deleted.

Dubois' eyes closed to slits. "You wouldn't share the footage with us to help show your tenant wasn't involved?"

"I'd have to call my boss and get the passwords and log-in information for the files." I shrugged. "I'm just the property manager. If you want to rent a unit, I can help you."

Her eyes remained slitted, but it was Rue she focused on again. "Will you willingly answer our questions?"

"As I said, I have nothing to hide." That wasn't a *yes,* and Rue shot me a baleful look as Dubois led her away.

At least they didn't handcuff her and stuff her into the back of their car. Still, I felt guilty. If Rue hadn't been out here collecting *samples* for her potions, potions she had made at my request, nobody would have photographed her.

"I'll see about getting that warrant." The male officer gave me a long look before he got in his car and called someone.

I resisted the urge to sprint into the leasing office, get on the computer, and delete the previous night's security-camera footage. The male officer might follow me and catch me. I would do it later, after I picked up Jasmine and went to find Duncan. The officers shouldn't arrest Rue on the basis of a couple of photos. Even knowing that, I continued to feel guilty, and I worried she would be surveilled and eventually arrested because of her association with me.

She might also tell Dubois the truth about everything. About *me.* After all they'd seen, the police might be ready to believe that werewolves existed. Then *I* would be the one surveilled and arrested.

9

"DEMING IS A SURPRISING LOCATION FOR A POTION FACTORY OR whatever those guys have at their facility up here," Jasmine said as we drove north on Highway 9, a mixture of forested land and rural farm properties to the sides.

Since I'd waited until the police departed to leave and pick up my niece, we were getting a later start on the Duncan search than I'd wanted. Cold rain pattered on the windshield, the clouds making it feel more like night than afternoon, and the heat blasted from the vents in my truck. We drove through puddles, spraying the sides of the highway.

"It's a surprising location for *anything* except some farms," I said, though I hadn't passed through Deming in a long time, and I didn't remember it well. It was close enough to Bellingham that civilization might have grown out in that direction by now.

"The population is a little over 500." Jasmine had her phone open with a map to the property, but she'd tapped over to a browser to look up the town.

"People or squirrels?" I noted one alongside the highway that hadn't survived a crossing attempt.

"Oh, I'm sure there are way more than 500 *squirrels*." Jasmine showed me a photo of a gas station with a towering forest behind it.

Seeing the trees made me reassess the town as a possible place that a werewolf could be imprisoned. Who there would think anything of howling in the woods?

"Seven miles to the address." Jasmine lowered the phone. "The road it's on is a little ways out of town, after the turn for Mount Baker Highway."

Mount Baker Highway. I hadn't realized we were heading so close to where my son was staying for his snowboarding trip. It was, I assured myself, a coincidence that he was taking his vacation in the same area where Duncan had possibly been spotted—sensed. And where Radomir owned property.

"I'll let you know when we're close," Jasmine added, looking at me when I didn't answer.

"Okay, thanks." I forced a smile for her, but unease had crept into me. "You're making your case for having me be a reference for you on your résumé, by the way."

"Oh, good. What's changing your mind?"

"You're a good researcher."

"Because I looked up the squirrel population?"

"Among other things."

"I did also think to bring the *family*-size bag of Doritos instead of a small one. I'm good at shopping for snacks as well as recording werewolf battles."

When she'd mentioned bringing provisions, I'd envisioned sandwiches, not chips, but all I said was, "A prospective employer will be delighted by those skills."

"Well, maybe not, but I do know all about residential and commercial financing for real estate. If you ever need a loan, I can hook you up with a good rate."

"I'm not a fan of debt, but I'll keep that in mind."

"You're not buying that fourplex you talked about with cash, not in the Seattle area." Jasmine looked over at me. "Unless you're a lot richer than I think."

"I'm saving up money for a downpayment, but I'm definitely not rich."

"I figured not when I saw you pull gas money out of an envelope and debate whether or not you had enough to fill the tank."

"Observant, aren't you?"

"Yup. That's a bullet point on the résumé. Since I'm light on actual work history, beyond the stuff I do for Mom, I had to fluff it up a bit with adjectives. Five miles." Jasmine held up the phone to show me the map, then switched to the browser again.

I debated whether to ask about her music tastes—currently, a female rapper was spitting lyrics on my truck's tinny factory speakers—or her opinion on young druids enraptured with her beauty. But she spoke again first.

"There's nothing about potion factories on this list of things to do in Deming."

"The other building might have been the company's flagship location—until they listed it for sale."

"Racehorse Falls is a hike in the area. You can visit Nooksack Salmon Hatchery. Oh, if you're up here in June, you can go to the Deming *Log Show*. That's sure to be a good time."

"I'll put it on my calendar."

"You'd be a fool not to."

A few lights came into view ahead, a gas station and handful of other businesses along the highway.

"This is the town," Jasmine said.

"There's a coffee shop." It had already closed for the day. "Technically, a coffee *trailer*. You didn't mention that as a highlight on your things-to-do list."

"It's coffee. It's a commodity, not a to-do."

"Logs are a commodity too."

"A log *show* isn't. You know that's a good time. I bet they have that event where you balance on a log floating in a pool of water and try not to fall off. Have you put it in your calendar yet?"

"No, but only because I'm driving. My eagerness to enter the hot-saw competition can barely be restrained." We'd already left the commercial buildings behind, and I watched the highway for the turn-off.

"I bet Duncan would like to go," Jasmine said. "Europeans enjoy folksy American hobbies."

"He'd probably wander off and magnet fish under some of those waterfalls you mentioned earlier."

"That might be safer than wielding chainsaws." Jasmine grunted as we bumped through a pothole.

I turned onto a dirt road, the map promising it would wind and squiggle its way up a slope on its way into the foothills. A mixture of massive ancient stumps and new-growth Douglas fir grew to either side. As we climbed, I rolled down the window and turned off the music, listening over the rumble of the engine in case howls floated to our ears.

"Not a rap fan?" Jasmine gripped the oh-shit handle as the potholes grew more numerous.

"I enjoy listening to nature."

She rolled down her own window. "Do you think he's out there howling?"

"That *is* the specific nature I hope to hear."

"Do you think he's a prisoner at this place we're going?"

"Those guys—Radomir and especially Lord Abrams—have a magical device that can call and control him." I'd told her most of the story of our confrontation with them but couldn't remember if I'd included that detail.

"That's what drew him away the other night at Augustus's house, right?"

"I'm positive of it."

"He's pretty powerful to be controllable by someone else. Someone who doesn't like werewolves and is stealing our artifacts."

"That's why we have to get him away from them," I said firmly.

The truck groaned and bumped its way farther from the highway, the road turning to switchbacks as the slope steepened, and I grew skeptical that we were going to anything but an old logging area. Did this road even have a name? I hadn't spotted a sign when we'd turned.

"I thought it was because you were thirsty for his bod and wanted to smash," Jasmine said.

"Something that's easier to do with a guy who isn't magically controlled by someone else."

"Truth. Is that a building?"

I peered into the rain, skeptical of finding anything out here. I'd been looking for a place to turn around. But Jasmine was right. The slope had grown less steep, and the rectangular outline of a building stood out against the cloudy sky, the grounds around it cleared.

As we drove closer, a motion-sensing light came on alongside the road, the clouds heavy enough that it registered as nighttime. Before long, it would be.

The light was directed onto a sign: Selene Mushroom Farm.

I stopped the truck in front of it and scratched my jaw. "Tumwater Tonic Corporation has eclectic facilities."

"Mushrooms can be potion ingredients, can't they?" Jasmine asked.

"Oh, I guess that makes sense. The other facility was in the middle of a lavender field, and they were using that as an ingredient." My nostrils itched at the memory of all the floral scents in that potion factory. "You'd think they could have grown mushrooms in a building on the same property though."

"Maybe *special* mushrooms grow out here." Jasmine waved toward the trees.

I started to scoff, but I'd seen glowing fungi before when hunting as a wolf in the forest. As a human, I was oblivious to magical plants and mushrooms, but I knew they *did* exist. Further, some places had inherent power, enticing such things to grow. The cave in the gully behind my mother's cabin came to mind.

"Could be." I drove into a gravel parking area with room for three or four vehicles.

The odor of decay wafted through the open window, and I wrinkled my nose. Had something *died* out here?

Another motion-sensing light came on, gleaming from above a modern steel door. Made from rounded stones held together with crumbling mortar, the building itself predated Radomir's business ambitions, if not Radomir himself. What had once been a couple of high windows had been bricked in, the mortar much newer than that which held together the stone walls. The metal roof also appeared to be a recent upgrade, though whoever had done the renovation hadn't altered the old stone chimney that thrust up through it.

When I turned off the engine, we could hear the gurgle of water, a stream winding through the trees beyond the building. I sensed a hint of magic from somewhere inside, and my hopes rose. Maybe this was the right place. Might a werewolf-occupied dungeon hunker behind those walls? At the least, it did indeed seem to be one of Radomir's facilities. If Jasmine's *dad* ever needed a reference that vouched for his research abilities, I would happily give it.

"I think some of those special mushrooms are inside." Jasmine pointed, apparently also sensing magic within.

"I'm hoping for a special werewolf." I didn't sense Duncan, but he could be behind walls that insulated his aura.

"I do get the vibe of a living being as well as inanimate magic... somethings." Jasmine cocked her head, trying to puzzle it out.

I was too. I sensed something moving around inside. A mushroom wouldn't do that.

"You'd think if he was being kept a prisoner, there would be guards and a bunch of high-tech stuff to keep him in though." Jasmine eyed a few moss-blanketed flagstones making a path from the parking area to the door. "I don't think this place even has a tripwire."

"Yeah." Though I hoped I would be wrong, I doubted Duncan waited inside. Still, we might find clues.

Also, if we were close to where my half-sibling had sensed him, he might yet be in the area. Maybe I could *imbibe* the potion and locate him from here.

"Let's check it out." I pocketed my keys and slid out of the truck.

The scent of decay was stronger out here, and I half-expected to see a dead animal near the road. But maybe I was smelling mushrooms—or the compost they grew in breaking down.

I'd only taken a few steps toward the door when a scraping noise came from the roof—no, the chimney. I paused to eye the spot.

Daylight was waning, and the motion-sensing light didn't do anything to brighten the top of the building. More scrapes floated down from above. Unfortunately, whatever was making them sounded small, not like a werewolf climbing out of the chimney.

I pulled out my phone and opened the flashlight app, though it lacked the power to brighten much on the roof. A chittering heralded the chimney climber, and a raccoon scampered out, its dark outline visible for a moment, something in its mouth. A mushroom? With white speckles that were unnaturally bright?

Before I could get a better look, the raccoon skittered down the back side of the roof and disappeared from view. Had I also glimpsed faintly glowing eyes, or was that my imagination? Maybe the *raccoon* was the magical being we'd sensed inside. If so, that was disappointing.

"Your fearsome presence scared away the squatter." Jasmine slid out of the truck to stand beside me.

"Apparently. This place might not get visited often." I returned my phone to my pocket and drew out Rue's bag of potions but hesitated to open the one attuned to Duncan. Other than a family member *thinking* he'd sensed Duncan more than a day ago, did I have any reason to believe he was within ten miles?

"That door looks modern and secure." Jasmine tugged on the knob and found it locked. "Someone cared enough to spruce this place up to keep out the riffraff."

"But not the raccoons."

"Maybe they're not a threat to one's carefully cultivated magical mushrooms."

"It was *stealing* one."

"True. Do you think they eat mushrooms?" Jasmine poked the browser on her phone. "I'll check."

I walked around the building, finding more recently replaced doors and more bricked-in windows. Out back, another structure rose near the stream, which turned out to be a larger waterway than I'd envisioned. Almost a river. The wood structure looked like an old mill, but it was far more dilapidated than the stone building.

There was also another more modern building, a small barn or maybe a garage. Painted red, it had double wooden doors that would have been wide enough for a truck to pass through, and my flashlight app illuminated tire tracks. There didn't appear to be a lock, but when I tugged on one of the metal handles, the door didn't open. The building had a single window. I tried peering inside, but it was too dark to see more than a couple of tiny green indicator lights near a side wall.

Around back, there was another door, this one with a padlock on it. I returned to the front and considered the lack of a visible lock. Maybe there were boxes stacked in front of the doors. Or might a wood board or metal bar keep the entrance secured from within? An old-fashioned "lock"?

Whatever it was, it did an effective job. I eyed the glass window, debating if I wanted to engage in vandalism. Did I truly think a clue inside a detached garage would help me locate Duncan?

"You never know," I muttered to myself. "Besides, after tormenting me and especially Duncan, Radomir and Abrams *deserve* to have some stuff vandalized."

I returned to the truck and pulled the magnet out from under the seat. Hurling it through windows doubtless wasn't what Duncan had envisioned when he'd left it for me, but he wouldn't frown upon such actions.

"Not when it's to *save* him."

Still standing by the truck, Jasmine lifted her phone. "Raccoons are omnivores and *do* eat mushrooms."

"When I see Radomir, I'll be sure to let him know about the security hole in his facility."

"Hopefully, his whole mushroom farm got eaten by nocturnal visitors. That'll thwart his plans. What *are* his plans, anyway? Did he say why he's gathering artifacts related to werewolves?"

"He didn't share his plans before siccing his brute squad on us."

"Why are bad guys always so rude?"

"It's encoded in their DNA." I held up the magnet, which elicited a puzzled expression from Jasmine. "I'll be right back."

Back at the garage, I hefted Duncan's gift, intending to throw it through the window, but I paused.

"Just in case..."

I walked to the door and pressed it to the wood where a horizontal bar on the other side might be. Duncan's magnets were powerful enough to be potent through boards. I was certain. I'd seen him pull an entire rusty bicycle frame off the bottom of a lake.

And, yes, I did feel resistance through the door. When I moved the magnet up slowly, a slight scrape sounded, something on the other side brushing against the wood. When I lowered it, the object thunked back into place. Not sure how to dislodge what I couldn't see, I moved the magnet to the side. The object shifted with it. I pulled the magnet away from the door, and a clatter sounded as something inside hit the ground.

This time, when I tried the door, it swung inward.

"Hah."

"Are you breaking and entering, Luna?" Jasmine leaned around the corner of the other building to look at me.

"I haven't broken anything. I may enter something." I pointed my flashlight at the interior of the garage. "Do you still want a recommendation for your résumé, or do you now consider me a morally questionable person to associate with?"

"Nah, I was just wondering if I should get my Doritos to have snacks while I watch the show."

"This shouldn't take long."

My flashlight beam swept over stacks of coolers and insulated foam shipping boxes. The green lights I'd seen belonged to refrigerators lined up against one wall. I opened the door of one and found baskets of freshly harvested mushrooms, including the same speckled variety the raccoon had been enjoying. Others glowed green, blue, or yellow.

"I'm guessing these aren't on their way to WinCo for the produce aisle," I murmured.

I peeked in a few more refrigerators. More mushrooms. That was it. Nothing in the garage gave hints about where werewolves were kept prisoner.

"Just a place for growing potion ingredients," I said. "Like we thought."

Duncan might not have ever been in the area.

Disappointed, I headed back to the door but paused to eye the insulated boxes. Some of them had shipping labels already. When I poked through them, I recognized most of the addresses from the list Jasmine had sent me, other facilities that Tumwater Tonic Corporation—Radomir—owned. But one wasn't familiar. An address just outside the small town of Maple Falls.

My eyes snagged on the name because that was where Austin was staying for his vacation. That again made me feel uneasy, even though it all had to be a coincidence.

I took a photo of the address to check on later. It wasn't far from where we were, so we could drive up there, though it probably wasn't one of Radomir's facilities. It hadn't been on the list from Jasmine's father. Maybe it belonged to some alchemist who ordered glowing 'shrooms from this farm. Maybe Rue would recognize it as a colleague's address.

As I rejoined Jasmine, a howl wafted out of the night.

"Is that Duncan?" Jasmine asked.

My first inclination was to say no, but distance and trees muffled sound. I stepped away from the building, cocking my head and hoping the howl would repeat.

"If so, he doesn't sound like he's trapped in a dungeon," she added.

"If he wasn't trapped, he would have come home." Since Sylvan Serenity was home for me, not Duncan, I clarified. "Back to the apartment complex."

"Because he pines for you and also has smashing on his mind?"

"Yeah, but especially because his van is in the parking lot there. He would be bereft without all his fancy magnets and treasure-hunting equipment."

"I'd say he's kind of weird for a werewolf, but my dad would be bereft without his collection of Battlestar Galactica model ships."

"Quirky males are best. They're not as full of themselves as..." I held up a finger as the howl repeated. Or was that a different howl? Could there be a pair of wolves or even a pack out here? Lorenzo hadn't mentioned my half-sibling detecting anyone but Duncan in the area. "I don't think either of those howls came from him."

"Maybe they're werewolves who know where Duncan is."

The first howler answered the second.

"Is it my imagination, or do they sound peeved about something?" I asked.

Jasmine nodded. "To me, those sound like warning howls. They could be telling an intruder to beat it. Or telling their pack that there's an intruder around. We could turn wolf and go chat with them."

The next howl came across as more agitated than the earlier ones. Yes, those wolves were upset about something.

"They don't sound like they're in the mood to *chat*," I said.

"We could invite them to the coffee trailer."

"I have a hunch." I opened the potion bag and drew out the vial containing the wolf-gray liquid.

Jasmine shined her phone's flashlight on it. "What's in that?"

"Don't ask. If we're within a ten-mile radius of Duncan, this will help me find him."

"You said those howls aren't his, though, right? What makes you think he's out there?"

"He agitates almost every paranormal being who meets him. Because they can sense his power and that he's different from werewolves—at least *modern* werewolves."

"He's quirky. As established."

"Among other things." I removed the cork from the vial.

Hoping my hunch was right, I, per Rue's instructions, chugged the liquid inside. It tasted like rotten seaweed mixed with bat guano and had the viscosity of slug slime. My stomach and throat battled my tongue and lips as I struggled to keep it down. Tears came to my eyes as I fought down my gag reflex multiple times. Duncan had no idea how much I'd come to care about him, how much I would endure to help him.

"Are you okay?" Jasmine was watching my face—and the contortions it had to be making.

I shook my head and, with a final gulp, won the war against my upchuck reflex. Even so, tears blurred my vision by the time I could voice an answer.

"That was loathsome," I croaked.

"I guessed. You looked like you were trying to put out a fire on your tongue with your spit. We should have stopped at the coffee trailer for mochas to wash it down."

"By the full moon, *yes*."

If only the coffee shop had been open.

I wiped my eyes, drew a shuddering breath, and grabbed some of Jasmine's Doritos to get rid of the taste.

"Let's see if this works." I looked around the forest with determination.

In the distance, an agitated wolf howled again.

10

THE POTION GAVE ME HEARTBURN. *HORRIBLE* HEARTBURN. IT FELT like I'd drunk the free trial of Rue's blue-spider acid, the concoction she'd promised would eat through metal bars. I even double-checked the bag to make sure that smaller vial remained inside.

"Is true love worth this?" I flattened a hand over my breastbone.

Jasmine offered the bag of Doritos. We still stood in front of the stone building as full darkness settled over the forest. The irritated wolves had stopped howling. Now and then, a chilly breeze swept through, whistling across the old chimney.

"Love?" Jasmine asked. "I thought you just wanted to have sex."

"He's good company too."

"Because of the accent?"

"Just... because."

"Have you told him he's cool to hang out with?"

"Not in so many words. I'm usually busy threatening to have his van towed."

"Adults are weird about relationships."

"Bitter divorced adults are. But aren't you twenty-four or twenty-five now? You're an adult too."

"That can't possibly be true. I'm still living at my parents' place because rents in the real world are ridiculous." Jasmine said something else around the crunch of a Dorito, but my esophagus started to tingle, and I missed it.

At first, I thought the potion was trying to come up again, but the tingle didn't hurt. It caused the heartburn to ease and reminded me of the way magic felt under my skin when the wolf came over me. The sensation spread from my esophagus to my entire chest, and I had the urge to turn east, toward the snow-smothered Cascade Mountains. Even without the influence of the moon, I could see their white silhouettes between gaps in the trees.

Was Duncan off that way somewhere? Within ten miles? The wolf howls had come from that direction, so it made sense.

"My esophagus wants me to go that way." I pointed.

"Mine usually wants me to go to the grocery store."

"The snack food section?"

"Naturally."

Thinking of the wolves, I said, "Why don't you stay here?"

"Alone at the haunted mushroom farm?"

"Since when is it haunted?"

"The windows are bricked up, the light keeps flicking on and off, and the wind is paranormal creepy as it blows across the chimney." Jasmine pointed her chip bag toward the roof.

"Mushrooms like it dark, the light is motion-sensing, and the wind isn't *paranormal*. Besides, you're a werewolf. You're scarier than any ghost."

"You think so?"

"Yeah. You'll be even scarier if you wipe the Dorito cheese dust off your chin."

"Ha ha. Your heartburn is glad I brought them."

"It's turned into a warm tingle now, and it's guiding me in that direction." Again, I pointed toward the mountains, then grabbed the sword out of the truck. Most likely, if trouble found me, I would need to shift into a wolf, but Duncan might be tickled if I showed up to his rescue with it. Maybe I should have stopped to buy a superhero cape along the way, but that wasn't in the budget.

"Is it wise to go in the direction suggested by tingling heartburn?" Jasmine asked.

"Just stay here and call someone to help if I don't come back. Here." I handed her the keys. "Turn on the truck if you get cold."

"I'd feel guilty wasting your gas. I'll turn into a wolf if I get cold. Or spoon with the raccoon."

"Yes, they're into cuddling up with predators." I lifted a hand in parting. Not sure how long the potion or its tingle would last, I took off at a jog.

The movement kept me warm, but it wasn't long before the uneven ground and lack of a trail had me tripping in the dark, my human vision not up to traversing the forest on a cloudy night. I second-guessed bringing the sword and my clothes. This would have been easier in lupine form.

When the agitated howls sounded again, the same hunch that had told me Duncan might be out here told me to hurry. Whatever he was doing to irritate those wolves might escalate into an attack.

"He can take care of himself against a pair of normal werewolves," I told myself.

Of course, because I'd only heard two howling didn't mean there weren't more. I ran faster, accepting that stubbed toes and branches whacking me in the face were a fair byproduct of a heroic rescue.

Soon, I came upon an old logging road heading in the right direction and turned onto that. Was it the same road Jasmine and I had been driving up?

"Should have taken the truck," I panted, running on the packed earth.

Now and then, the gurgle of the stream reached my ears as I continued uphill, the snowy mountains visible beyond the trees.

The next time a howl sounded, it was close, so I slowed down, sweat bathing my face. It cut off abruptly, and I paused. Had Duncan or someone else attacked the wolf?

The howls didn't start up again.

Biting my lip, I continued on, veering off the road and in the direction I'd heard them, the direction the tingle in my chest kept leading me. It had faded slightly, and I worried the potion's effects wouldn't last long.

In the trees ahead, somewhere near the stream, two magical beings ran through my awareness. Werewolves.

Again, I slowed, this time holding the sword aloft in case I needed to defend myself. I didn't recognize the auras of those werewolves.

But they weren't coming toward me, instead running across the route ahead. They soon passed out of my senses. Palm damp around the hilt of the sword, I headed in the direction they'd come from.

Soon, I sensed more magic. There was a being—was that Duncan?—and more that I couldn't guess at. Artifacts? Magical beings? Whatever they were, they emitted more power than the mushrooms.

Something malevolent lingered about at least one of the things I sensed. It raised my hackles, reminding me of the magical security devices that my cousins had planted alongside Mom's driveway, the devices that shot beams at me.

Maybe Duncan was indeed a prisoner out here.

The warmth in my chest that had guided me in this direction had worn off, but I didn't doubt my own senses. He was out here. I just had to figure out how to reach him.

Again, I came upon the stream, ferns and thistle dense along its banks. I followed it toward a cliff with a waterfall tumbling down the face. Had there been a trail, I might have wondered if I'd reached one of the hikes on Jasmine's to-do list. But this was probably private land, maybe still a part of Radomir's mushroom farm.

I shined my phone's flashlight around the waterfall, debating if I could climb up the cliff to the top, but my senses believed Duncan was *inside* it. In a cave? The magical items were in that direction too.

Picking my way closer, I didn't see any openings, but my flashlight did glint off something metal among the ferns near the base of the cliff. As I approached, a high-pitched beeping started up, like a smoke detector in need of a battery change but louder. *Much* louder.

"That's definitely coming from the cliff," I muttered, wishing for earplugs.

If that had been going off earlier, it might have been what irritated those wolves. Another scan of the cliff face didn't reveal any cave openings, but... was that a gap behind the waterfall?

"Duncan?" I called. "Are you back there? Shackled to a stone wall and being tortured by that annoying beeping?"

I didn't receive an answer.

"There you are." I stepped over the ferns toward the gap. I was right; it led behind the waterfall.

My toe clunked into something. I'd almost forgotten the metallic glint. It was...

"One of Duncan's magnets?" I asked in confusion.

Attached to a rope, it appeared similar to the one Rue had wielded like a weapon in the parking lot. But Duncan hadn't had any of his magnets with him the night he'd helped me in Augustus's mansion. He'd brought some explosives but not a whole backpack. Even if he'd had more with him, once he'd changed into his bipedfuris form, he would have lost everything.

"Duncan?" I called again as I crept through the gap, the spray of the waterfall dampening my face. "You *are* a prisoner, aren't you?"

The beeping halted abruptly.

I paused, listening, but with the waterfall roaring down so close, I could only hear very loud noises. When I tried to illuminate the darkness ahead with my flashlight, all I could see was a narrow tunnel disappearing around a rock bend.

"Duncan?" I continued forward over bumpy, uneven ground. If he was here and awake, he ought to sense me approaching.

The beeping started again, startling me.

I slipped and banged my elbow on the rock wall, almost dropping my phone. High-pitched screeches sounded, followed by flapping. A *lot* of flapping. A swarm of bats flew at me, their bodies glowing green.

Wings brushed my head and shoulders, and I couldn't keep from screaming. This time, I *did* drop my phone as I crouched low, covering my head with my arms.

More and more bats sailed past, flying out of the cave for the night. The bodies of more than half of them glowed. It wasn't until they all exited through the gap behind the waterfall that I lowered my arms, my heart hammering against my rib cage.

"What *is* this place?"

The bats had been magical, but I sensed more magic ahead. Again, this reminded me of the cave behind Mom's cabin, some natural repository of power that had existed long before man— and werewolves—had entered the area.

Hand shaking after the scare, I took a deep breath and picked up my phone.

"Just bats," I told myself. "Heading out to hunt."

A thunderous grinding followed by a *clank* sounded. A roar came after and then a great wrenching noise.

"That's no bat."

The beeping intensified, trying to pierce my eardrums. It was a wonder the bats hadn't left a lot sooner.

The roar sounded again.

Was that... Duncan? In his bipedfuris form?

The roars came from deeper in the cave. I hesitated to rush back. If he was being controlled by Abrams and had changed into that form, he could be a danger to me. When he'd shifted into a wolf or bipedfuris of his own accord, he had defended me, but when that control device was in play, it was a different story. Since neither Abrams nor Radomir was inherently magical, they could be back there, and I wouldn't sense them. The device also had the ability to manipulate Duncan from afar.

A cry of pain made me jump. That also sounded like Duncan.

Reminded that I'd come to rescue him, I made myself continue forward. If he turned on me... Well, he'd given me the sword for exactly that reason. With silver a part of its magic-touched alloy, it had been made to fight werewolves.

Around another bend, the tunnel opened into a cavern with a hole in the center. My foot brushed something on the ground.

Expecting another magnet, I looked down. It *was* metal, but it appeared to be a piece wrenched off a robot or other machine, not one of Duncan's cylinders. More bits of metal littered the ground all around me. I spotted a couple of wheels as well, and...

"Is that a head?" I shined my light toward the edge of the hole.

It wasn't a human head but a metal dog-shaped one, and magic emanated from it. In fact, faint hints of magic came from all the pieces on the ground. And Duncan...

Was he down in the hole? Had he fallen? I sensed him, so he was still alive, but I didn't hear anything anymore, neither roars nor cries of pain.

When I eased closer to the edge of the hole, a pair of eyes on the metal head came into view. They glowed orange.

"I can't believe I teased Jasmine about this area being haunted." I skirted the head as I continued to the edge.

Haunted might not be the right word, but magic had doubtless been used to... I wasn't sure what. Booby-trap this place? Had the robot-dog thing been a protector? Left to guard... what?

Splashes came from below. Maybe the hole was a cenote, though I hadn't heard of them existing in this part of the world.

I peered over the edge into utter darkness. A grunt sounded, and the splashes stopped. I swung my phone downward, and the flashlight glinted on a pair of eyes.

"Shit," I barked, fumbling and almost dropping my phone again.

11

THE EYES STARED UP AT ME, UNBLINKING. A LONG MOMENT PASSED before I could pick out the rest of the furry form, waist-deep in water and... was that a chain hanging from its sharp claws? From *Duncan's* sharp claws?

As I'd suspected, he had taken his bipedfuris form. Nearly twenty feet down, he might have fallen or climbed down there after defeating the magical robot dog.

"Are you possessed?" I eyed his forehead, checking the scar there.

In this form, his salt-and-pepper fur wasn't as long and thick as when he was a wolf, but it did fully cover his muscular bipedal body, including his face. Only when the scar glowed was it noticeable. I did catch a slight hint of that glow, but it wasn't as bright, as strong, as when we'd been at the perfume factory and Abrams had been pointing the control device at Duncan's forehead.

An inquiring grunt wafted up, Duncan's short snout parted to reveal fangs. He didn't look menacing, despite the earlier roars. Maybe he recognized me.

"I came to rescue you," I said. "I expected a dungeon and shackles, not a bat cave."

He grunted again, probably not understanding me fully. I could recognize human words when I was a wolf but didn't always get their full meaning. And the bipedfuris... Well, I had no experience being one, so I didn't know how it worked, but that form seemed even more savage—more primal—than that of the wolf.

Duncan thrust his furred hands upward, the fingers curled, the claws long and sharp. Had we been closer, the gesture would have been alarming, but I realized he was showing me the chain. A square medallion hung on it, something silver with green gems— emeralds?—embedded in the center in a tree-shaped design.

"Please don't tell me I've been worried about you for days, and you've been treasure hunting," I said.

He roared and sprang out of the water, landing several feet up, claws finding purchase on the side of the hole. His powerful muscles flexed, and he climbed toward me.

Startled, and not sure if he was under our enemies' control or not, I skittered back. My heel bumped against the dog head, and it clattered away, its orange eyes flashing as it rolled. Duncan surged out of the hole and stood, his head almost brushing the roof of the cave.

Alarmed all over again, I backpedaled until my shoulder blades hit a stone wall. I still held the sword and tightened my grip, though I didn't point it at Duncan. I didn't want to fight him. I'd come to rescue him, damn it.

The bipedfuris stooped to face me, jaws again parted. In this form, he stood two feet taller than I did. When he'd been in the hole, his height hadn't been that intimidating, but now...

Chain still dangling from his claws, he bent forward, hands dropping to the ground. He lowered his head too. His tail—hell, I hadn't even noticed he had a tail in that form before—swished back and forth, and his brown eyes glinted. Even though that scar glowed faintly, he didn't look like he meant to attack. If anything...

"Is that supposed to be a play bow?" I asked.

The tail swished again, and he lay the medallion on the ground, as if offering it to me.

"I'm sure that's very nice, but it doesn't go with the collection." I pointed the sword toward the emerald tree on the front. Now that the medallion was only a few feet away, I could sense magic within it, but there wasn't any sign of a wolf head, which all the other artifacts Radomir had collected had.

Duncan issued a mournful noise, something between a groan and a growl, then sat back on his haunches. His aura shifted before his body changed and he grew more compact and less furred.

Soon, he crouched before me in his human form. His *naked* human form.

A pair of puncture wounds in the side of his thigh leaked blood. The robot dog must have bitten him before he'd gotten the best of it.

Sympathy welled in my chest, and I longed to spring forward and hug him, but the faint orange glow on his forehead was more noticeable without fur covering it, and I hesitated.

"It's good to see you, my lady." Duncan straightened and bowed. He took a step toward me, lifting his arms, but maybe he understood the reason for my hesitation, because he didn't come all the way forward. Instead, he stopped beside the medallion. "And you brought the sword."

He beamed a pleased smile at me.

"Yeah, I've had a single lesson with it now, so I'm pretty badass."

"I knew that to be true the day I met you." He winked.

"The day you met me, I was carrying a toilet."

"*Exactly.*"

"So..." I looked around the cave and waved at the destroyed robot-dog pieces. "I came to rescue you." I wasn't sure he'd parsed that in his other form. "I expected you to be more dungeon-based and shackles-adorned."

Duncan shook his head ruefully and touched his scar, as if to say the shackles existed in another form. "I understand the compound with the dungeon is for sale."

"It is. And the real estate agent was *extremely* rude about giving me information on it. You're lucky I found you. Though, ah, you don't look like you need rescuing as much as I believed."

"That's debatable."

"You *look* like you're here having a grand adventure." I waved toward the hole and the medallion.

Duncan touched his wounded thigh. "I've been perforated."

"I know you well enough now to be positive that doesn't negate my statement."

"It hasn't been an *unappealing* adventure, but I didn't start upon it of my own accord. I've been worried about you. I was fairly certain you escaped after your cousin died with his abode on fire, but I didn't see you before the call overtook me, the over-powering urge to obey and come to..." He sneered. Had he almost said something like *my master*? "That device," was what he finished with, pointing at his forehead. "You were right that I'm more susceptible to that call when I'm in the bipedfuris form. Maybe I didn't need to take it that night, but if you've ever tried to hurl demolitions as a wolf, you would understand my choice."

"I'm surprised you had the wherewithal to do something like that while in *either* form." As a wolf, I would find explosives a puzzling human thing and probably avoid them. As a wolf, *most* human things were puzzling.

"The bipedfuris is a little more clever than the wolf."

"So, you've been doing Abrams's bidding these past few days?

While I was worried about you and not sure if you were a prisoner or dead or what?"

"It's been Radomir's bidding actually. As I mentioned before, Abrams doesn't want much to do with me. He has a new werewolf to train up—" Duncan grimaced, probably empathetic to the boy, to the little *brother* he'd only recently learned existed, "—and he doesn't trust me for some odd reason."

"You did burn his castle down."

"Yes, including the library. I think I was as aggrieved about that as he was. I adore books, you know."

"Yes, you mentioned that they were responsible for your habit of calling twenty-first-century women *my lady*."

"Quite." Duncan bent and lifted the medallion. "These days, Radomir is the one holding the device and sending me off to do his bidding. Abrams is in their lair researching wolf artifacts. His work led me to check this place out, but I don't think this is what they hoped I would find." He pointed at the tree medallion.

"It's pretty, but it looks more like a druid thing than a werewolf thing."

"Yes. It has power, but I don't know if they or any of our kind could call upon it. Perhaps your intern could."

"I doubt those guys would want you to give it to Bolin to check."

"Likely not. I don't think this is technically on the land they purchased, ostensibly for mushroom farming but also because they'd heard rumors about this place." Duncan's wave encompassed the cave as well as the treed land out to the highway. "Even so, I'm sure they believe anything they send their... *minion* to find —" he touched his chest, "—belongs to them."

"Have you figured out yet *why* they're collecting werewolf artifacts?"

"I have not. Neither of them has confided in me."

"They sound as rude as their real estate agent."

"*Ruder.* Remember, Abrams ordered me to be dumped naked into a ditch."

"I do remember that. And that you, somehow, even in such a state, talked a female chocolatier into giving you caramel apples and truffles."

"Because of my irrepressible charm. It overrides any alarm ladies might otherwise feel about my nudity."

"Is that so?"

"*You're* here with me and not alarmed by my nudity."

"Because I'm holding a sword."

"And the single lesson infused you with confidence in your ability to use it?"

"Well, I now know which end goes in the werewolf, so there's that."

Duncan grinned and pointed at his chest—his *heart.* The amusement didn't entirely reach his eyes, and I shivered at the reminder of why he'd given the gift to me.

"Thanks for arranging for those lessons, by the way," I said quietly.

"You're welcome. Anyway, Radomir, it turns out, was irritated with Abrams for casting me into said ditch. *He* recognized my value and that I'm a true gem."

"Uh-huh. Do you call him *my lady* and kiss the back of his hand?

"I call him *my lord* and, when the magic compels me, drop to one knee in front of him."

"Gross."

"It is irritating to be forced to do so. Magic can be a vexing impediment to freedom of choice."

"I'll bet. Look. I drove up here in my truck. It's well-stocked with provisions—Doritos and chocolate-covered crickets that my son gave me for Christmas." I didn't mention that the latter weren't delicious and I'd only put them in my truck to serve as emergency rations in case I ran out of gas. "If I try to finish rescuing you—or maybe I'd be *kidnapping* you—would you allow it?"

"*I* have no objection to you kidnapping me. You could take me all the way to your bedroom in Shoreline, if I had my way."

"But you don't?" I raised my eyebrows.

"Well... I've chosen not to exert my willpower to its fullest to break away. Not yet."

I couldn't tell if that was a lie. Maybe he'd tried to escape their magical control and it hadn't worked, and he didn't want to admit it. Duncan had a history of being evasive with me.

"Are you waiting for a dramatic moment?" I asked.

"When Radomir explained this quest to me, I wasn't entirely against it. As you ascertained, that bauble isn't what he sought." Duncan pointed to the tree medallion.

"Yeah, an ancient artifact imbued with magic and embedded with emeralds. What a useless tchotchke."

"I'm sure it's not that, but it's not what he's looking for."

"Do you have any idea what it does?" I sensed magic in the medallion but couldn't tell anything about it.

"For all I know, it's a fancy paperweight."

"I doubt *that*."

Duncan flicked his fingers in dismissal. "What Radomir *hoped* I would find is the mate to your mother's medallion, the version your pack once held that was made for male werewolves to wear."

"My mom did mention that there is such a thing, but she thought it was lost a long time ago, maybe before the pack even came to America."

"Radomir believes it wasn't lost that many generations ago and that it's still in the Pacific Northwest."

"Are you *sure* he didn't tell you about his nefarious plans for the artifacts?" I asked.

It seemed like Duncan knew more than he'd implied about what those two masterminds were up to.

"I'm sure, but Radomir didn't deny that they're specifically seeking werewolf artifacts and also tomes written about and by our people."

"Were there a lot of books penned by werewolf scribes in the past?" Other than Jasmine's computer-geek father, I'd heard of very few scholarly-inclined werewolves in my life. Sadly, my cousin Augustus had been a more typical representative of our kind.

"Not that he's discovered. Hence the focus on artifacts. As I was saying, I would have been delighted to find the male version of your family's medallion. I don't know what it does, but I thought if I located it, I might then test and break the magic of the compulsion and come to you. Together, we could visit your mother and lay the medallion at her feet."

"I do need to visit my mother." Recalling Lorenzo's request, I felt guilty that I'd driven up the highway, passing not that far from Monroe on the way, and hadn't stopped in.

"If I was responsible for finding it, I figured she might think kindly of me and allow me to visit without siccing your pack on me."

Only my cousins had attacked him. Mom hadn't had anything to do with it.

"She already thinks kindly of you," I said.

"Ah, yes. She did bring up... the offspring." Duncan's expression didn't suggest he was into that notion.

"Yeah, sorry about that. She gets ideas in her head, and she's a stubborn woman. But you don't need to bribe her with medallions to visit. The ones who attacked you... They're all gone now."

"All? The brute who jumped me on the porch wasn't one of Augustus's followers, was he?"

"You mean Rocco? Whom you smashed face-first into the log wall? You couldn't have been disturbed by that ineffectual display of aggression."

"I suppose he wasn't egregious to deal with, but it would be nice..." As Duncan trailed off, looking past my shoulder, his expression grew wistful.

"To have a family?" I asked, aware that he'd never had that, not in his youth, growing up in Abrams's castle laboratory, and apparently not in the decades he'd been a nomadic treasure-hunter either. "A pack?"

"Over the years, I've occasionally found the notion had some appeal."

"It might, but I don't know if *my* pack is the one you'd want."

Duncan snorted softly. "Does anyone ever love the family they're born into?"

"I don't know. My sons are okay."

"Even the one who gave you chocolate-covered crickets?"

"*Especially* the one who gave me chocolate-covered crickets."

Austin, after all, had come home for Christmas. I hoped he had a good time snowboarding with his friends—and that Radomir and Abrams didn't know he existed. *He* didn't have any werewolf magic and wouldn't be able to assist in figuring out those artifacts, so he shouldn't interest them in any way. By now, they'd probably lost their interest in me too. It wasn't as if much had happened when they'd lured me up to their base so I could touch the wolf medallion.

"That's not a new preference for you, is it?" Duncan asked. "Because if you adore those chocolates, I could buy you a pallet of them."

"Don't you dare. I really would have your van towed. And as it was dragged away, I would pelt it with candy crickets."

Duncan grinned at me. Did he look... smitten? Nah, he probably had something in his eye.

"I've missed your snark," he said.

Huh, maybe that *was* a smitten look. I admit it touched me.

Most men I'd dated, including my ex-husband, had found my sarcasm unappealing. *Vexing* was a word I'd heard often.

"You should have called and invited me along on your adventure." I stepped closer to him, reaching a hand toward his.

"Would you have come?" Duncan wrapped his fingers around mine. "I believe you only joined me at the pond next to the convenience store because you were avoiding people."

Bolin's parents, yes. I tried not to think about the problem they represented, one that couldn't be solved with werewolf magic or anything else that I could imagine.

"The pond full of duck droppings didn't sound that interesting to me," I said.

"Such a strange woman you are."

"Says the naked guy standing amid the remains of a robot dog."

"It *is* a romantic setting, isn't it? Did you see the glowing bats?"

"Yeah, they really set the mood."

"Quite."

He must not have been dive-bombed by them.

He leaned closer, eyebrows raised. Asking for permission to kiss me?

The cave was magical and weird, the eyes still glowed on the robot's head, and the creepy bats might return at any time, but I nodded to him. The setting was *not* romantic, but he... he kind of was. And I was relieved to see him healthy, aside from the bite marks in his leg. After his help with my cousins, I owed him something too. Something more than a pelting with crickets.

I set the sword aside and leaned toward Duncan. Our lips met, perhaps with more eagerness than I intended. But I'd missed him, and I didn't mind in the least when he wrapped his arms around me and pulled me close. His taut naked body was hard against mine, his powerful arms protective and comforting.

As his lips and tongue teased mine, sending streaks of hot

pleasure through me, I shifted my grip to his shoulders, grasping him and thinking of more than kissing.

The hard cave floor littered with metal shouldn't have made me imagine getting horizontal, but it might be worth it to be with him in this private spot. Magically weird or not, we had the cave to ourselves. And despite his cocky arrogance, Duncan *was* charming. Charming, sexy, and hot. Even better, he thought *I* was hot, and he kept helping me with my increasingly chaotic and dangerous life. By the moon, I was falling for him. I—

A muffled honk traveled through rock and the waterfall to reach us.

Duncan broke the kiss and looked toward the exit tunnel. My grip tightened on his shoulders. I didn't want to stop kissing, but the way Duncan frowned in the direction of the honking made me believe he knew who it was—and didn't think it was anyone good.

"It might be Jasmine," I said, though I didn't want her interrupting our romantic interlude. Besides, I'd left her quite a ways back. I hadn't known I would end up more-or-less following the logging road to this spot.

"It might be Radomir or, more likely, his henchmen." Duncan sighed and released me.

"The overly muscled ones hopped up on potions?"

"Yes. We wouldn't want them walking in on us, and it's quite possible they could. If I'm not too far away, they can track me through the control device." Duncan waved to the scar on his forehead. It had stopped glowing, but that probably didn't negate anything.

"Better than through a burning esophagus, I suppose."

He looked at me.

"Rue made me a potion to find you. I can't recommend the taste. Or *aftertaste*."

"Worse than chocolate-covered crickets?"

"Much worse. I wouldn't pelt a van with it. It might be acidic enough to destroy the paint, if not eat through the frame entirely."

"Your willingness to gulp down such a thing on my behalf is touching."

"Well, there wasn't a warning on the label." Maybe I would suggest a pulsing red Mr. Yuck sticker to Rue.

More honks sounded. Insistent honks.

Sighing again, Duncan picked up the medallion and my sword, and clasped my hand to lead me toward the waterfall entrance. "Let's find out if we're in trouble."

"I usually am. Especially lately."

He smiled sadly at me and didn't disagree.

12

After we stepped out from behind the waterfall, Duncan paused to fetch his shoes and clothes from a log. He hurried to dress and also picked up the magnet I'd seen earlier. After stuffing the heavy cylinder into a jacket pocket, he grasped my hand again and headed up a treed slope. Maybe he knew the way to the road.

Another honk sounded.

As we climbed, I braced myself for truckloads of bad guys. If Duncan hadn't been holding my hand, I might not have headed *toward* the road. When trouble honked, it was a good idea to go in the other direction.

"Did you know there were werewolves in the area when you were in that cave?" I asked as we navigated through ferns and over logs.

"Yes. A bonded pair, I believe. I didn't recognize them but wondered if they claimed this territory for themselves. They didn't follow me into the cave to discuss it. They did start howling a lot whenever the guardian robot beeped."

"Is *that* why they were howling? I assumed you were irritating them."

"Moi?" Duncan touched his chest, the medallion dangling from his fingers. He'd given me back the sword after we clambered out of the cave.

"Yeah, you. You were at least irritating the robot. I trust you were the reason it was beeping."

"Yes, it guarded the medallion. Rather, I *assume* that was what it stood watch over. I doubt it was placed there to keep an eye on the bats." Duncan pointed at headlights now visible through the trees. Whoever was honking, their vehicle was stationary. "The beeping started after I lopped off the first of its wheels."

"It didn't like that? Weird."

"Quite. I think... That isn't one of Radomir's thugs."

No. As he spoke the words, we drew close enough that I could sense Jasmine's familiar presence. When my truck came fully into view, she stood outside it, the engine idling as she peered into the forest in our direction.

"Had I known one of your relatives was responsible for the honking," Duncan said, "we could have continued our most pleasant cave rendezvous."

"You would have been okay with my niece walking in on us?"

"I do prefer my cave rendezvous to be private, but *she* wouldn't have used a magical control device to force me—to *attempt* to force me—to attack you."

I caught his slip, and it wasn't comforting, but I didn't comment on it.

By the truck, Jasmine had shifted from looking toward us to back down the dark logging road. I couldn't see or sense anything in that direction, but more than a yearning for my scintillating company might have prompted her to drive up here.

"Hey, Jasmine." I lifted a hand as we stepped out of the undergrowth and onto the bumpy dirt road. "I didn't expect you to follow me."

"I got cold," she said, "so I decided to drive farther up the road and see if I could sense you."

"The raccoon wouldn't spoon with you?"

Duncan blinked.

"It didn't show up again," Jasmine said. "My fearsome were-wolfness probably scared it away."

"I'm sure that's it."

She looked back the way she'd come again. "There were also some headlights visible through the trees, a couple of cars that had turned off the highway and were coming up the road. I thought it was weird that someone would be visiting a mushroom farm in the rain at night. Or at all. And we hadn't seen anything else back here that would prompt visitors..."

"There's an enchanted cave formerly guarded by a robotic dog and bats with glowing bellies." Duncan waved toward the waterfall.

"You think that attracts a lot of visitors?" On the way to it, I hadn't stumbled across a trail, so I doubted many people knew about the cave—especially if it was on private land.

"It attracted *me*." Duncan flattened his hand on his chest.

"Yeah, but a lot of weird things attract you."

He smiled and gazed at me but didn't suggest that *I* was weird.

Two beams of light cut through the trees from down the slope, the direction of the mushroom building.

"Did they see you driving up here?" I asked Jasmine.

"They might have. I got out of there before they reached the raccoon den, but it was too dark to drive up without headlights, so they could have seen the truck. It's also quiet enough out here that they could have *heard* it." Jasmine spread her arms. "I didn't know if I would find you. I thought I might get lost or stuck in one of the crater-sized potholes. Congrats on rescuing Duncan, by the way."

"He didn't exactly need rescuing," I said.

"Except from my supreme loneliness and angst over not being able to visit you," he said.

"I thought there would be shackles involved."

"Intangible magical shackles, yes."

I tilted my head as I considered him. "Can you come back with us now? Or are you compelled to keep hunting for the medallion? The *other* medallion?"

Duncan looked toward the headlights. Whoever was driving had decided the mushroom farm held no interest and was continuing up the mountain. Toward us. Or toward Duncan, anyway. His forehead scar glowed faintly in the night.

"I'm not certain," he said. "As I mentioned, I haven't fought the control as hard as I have other times."

"Like when they tried to get you to kill me in that courtyard?"

"Yes."

"So, you'll fight them when they want you to murder a friend, but when they want you to go treasure hunting, you're all in."

Duncan winced. "I wouldn't say I'm *all in.*"

"You ripped a glowing-eyed robot dog to pieces, leaped into a twenty-foot-deep hole, and swam around in murky water to find a magical bauble that wasn't even what you were looking for."

"The water wasn't that murky."

I folded my arms over my chest.

"I don't think my priorities are wrong," Duncan said.

"You shouldn't be working for them, not willingly."

Not at all.

"Whatever they want those artifacts for," I continued, "it can't be anything good. Those aren't the kinds of people who are out to do *good* in the world."

"I'm certain they are not."

"But?"

Duncan extended his arm in the direction of the water, fingers flexing. Still called by the hunt? The *treasure* hunt?

"Come back with us." I patted the truck door. "We'll give you a ride to your van. It misses you."

"I also miss it—and the equipment carried within."

"Uhm, Luna?" Jasmine turned her face as a Jeep rolled around a bend toward us, headlights shining in our eyes. A larger vehicle followed right behind, something that looked like a mix between a tank and an SUV.

With a start, I realized I'd seen it before. It had been in the garage at the lavender farm in Arlington.

"Get in the truck," I told her.

"There's not much room to turn around and go past them," she said.

"They're here for me," Duncan said with certainty.

"I don't doubt that, but they wanted *me* at one point too." As I'd been thinking before, I hoped Abrams and Radomir had lost interest in me, but I couldn't count on that.

"They won't get you." Duncan held out the medallion he'd found and walked into the road, arms spread.

"Come back with us," I tried again. "We'll find a way past them."

Duncan shook his head, not looking back, and took a few more steps, as if he might keep the vehicles from running him over to get to our truck. Of course, if he turned into the bipedfuris, he would have that ability. I'd seen him rip steel doors off their hinges. The tank-SUV looked armored, but he could tear into that Jeep; I had little doubt.

The vehicles rolled to a stop, and I could sense magical beings inside. Or, if Radomir had the same army as before, those were normal humans amped up on potions that enhanced their strength.

"Duncan, if you abandon your treasure hunt and come back to Shoreline with me, to help me fight crime in the neighborhood, I'll reward you with the finest of cacao-nib and bacon-bit dark chocolate."

He looked wistfully over his shoulder at me. "That *is* very tempting."

But not tempting enough, his resolute expression said.

I thought about promising him an invitation to my bedroom if he returned, bribing him with a more carnal pleasure. But the continuing glow of his scar left me uncertain about whether he could disobey that control device, even if he truly wanted to, and I didn't voice the offer.

The passenger-side door of the Jeep opened, and a brute got out, a rifle in his grip. He squinted at Jasmine and me before looking toward Duncan and whispering something to the driver. He also glanced at the tank-SUV, though nobody had stepped out of that yet. I could just make out the driver, another brute with a similar magical aura to the other, and he nodded and pointed at us. Or... at me?

I couldn't tell if these guys were among those who'd been at the compound the night Duncan and I had fought our way out. After turning into the bipedfuris, he'd killed a lot of those security guards. But even if these men hadn't been there, they might have been given a photo of me, and they might have orders to collect me.

Duncan held up the medallion he'd found. The small emeralds glinted, reflecting the headlights.

The brute opened a back door and pointed for Duncan to get in.

"Turn around first," Duncan said. "Both rigs."

"We've got something to collect." The brute looked at me.

I stepped behind the truck, waving for Jasmine to duck low. I didn't want my ride to be shot up, but I wanted my niece shot up even less. And I would prefer not to end up bullet-ridden myself. If the men were supposed to *collect* me, they might not shoot me, but I wouldn't bet a stick of gum on that.

Two doors on the tank-SUV opened, and another pair of muscled riflemen stepped out.

My stomach twisted with unease. If those firearms were loaded with silver bullets, the men might be a match for us, even if I turned wolf and Duncan shifted into his more powerful form.

"Nice of her to join you out here," the first speaker said, "so we can get both at once."

"Radomir doesn't want her anymore," Duncan said.

"Oh, he does. We just confirmed that." The man nodded toward the driver of the Jeep. Maybe the guy had called their boss to ask. "We'll even get a reward for finding her."

"If you want this, what your boss *really* sent you out to collect, you'll leave her alone." Duncan swung the medallion in the air.

He and I knew it wasn't what Radomir wanted, the match to my mother's medallion, but Duncan had to believe the thugs wouldn't know one magical artifact from another.

"We'll have it *and* her." The first rifleman pointed his firearm at Duncan's chest.

My skin heated, magic tingling through my veins as the desire to protect him tried to bring forth the wolf. Maybe it wouldn't be a bad idea. Even if they had silver bullets, we would have a better chance of dodging gunfire and fighting the men as wolves.

"Oh, I can ensure you *won't* have it." Duncan drew the magnet out of his other pocket and held it close to the medallion, as if it were an old hard drive, and he could wipe its data. The dangling artifact didn't stir, which I assumed meant it wasn't made from anything magnetic, but Duncan's confident expression implied he could do something to it. "This'll steal the magic and make the bauble useless. It won't help Radomir's plans, and he'll be very angry about losing it. There'll be a punishment, not a reward." His eyes narrowed. "And I know you've felt his punishment before... and how unpleasant it is."

The men exchanged looks.

"I'll get into the Jeep with you," Duncan said, "but you leave the women alone, or I'll destroy this."

Faint murmurs came from the back vehicle. One of the men speaking on a phone to someone? Radomir?

If so, he might think to ask one of the brutes to get a good look at the medallion and describe it. He might also know that a *magnet* wouldn't do anything to a magical artifact. At least, I doubted it would. Maybe Duncan truly did have something that could affect the medallion.

During the call, the riflemen kept their guns pointed at his chest. One of them continued to eye me as well. None of them were paying attention to Jasmine, who was doing as I'd asked, staying low behind the cover of the truck. But her jaw was clenched, her eyes determined, and I suspected she also felt the pull to change, to deal with a threat. She was, after all, a werewolf.

"All right. Fine." The thug who'd opened the door for Duncan lowered his rifle. "We don't need her. But, you, get in."

Duncan gazed at all of the riflemen. They put their weapons in the vehicles and climbed in.

After giving me another look over his shoulder, Duncan tucked the medallion and magnet into opposing pockets in his jacket and headed for the vehicles. As the tank-SUV drove in reverse until the driver found a spot wide enough to turn around, Duncan got into the back of the Jeep. It also turned around, the headlights finally out of our eyes.

"Why do they want *you*?" Jasmine asked as the two vehicles bumped down the road, heading back toward the highway.

"I'm not sure. When I met their bosses before, they had me touch some wolf artifacts, including my mother's medallion and a chalice that gave me a vision, but I don't think they knew about that."

Actually, I had no idea about if they did. Wasn't it possible the chalice had shared that vision with the whole room? In it, a bipedfuris—it might even have been Duncan—had been standing next to a waterfall and holding the cup aloft. If Radomir and Abrams had seen that vision, maybe it had prompted them to call Duncan and start sending him to check waterfalls in the area. Especially if they'd scrounged up some other research that had offered similar clues.

"Well, they seemed to want you back. I guess I'm glad nobody wanted *me.*" Jasmine waved to herself. "Even if that's kind of insulting."

"It's better *not* to be wanted by bad guys. Trust me. You can focus on being wanted by prospective employers instead."

I waved for her to get into the passenger seat and opened the driver-side door, but I couldn't help but gaze wistfully down the mountain, wondering when I would see Duncan again. At least he wasn't in a dungeon. He was doing what he loved. I did worry, however, what would happen when he returned to Radomir and Abrams without the werewolf medallion, especially after he'd implied to the thugs that he had it.

I shook my head. Duncan had chosen those actions of his own accord. What befell him wasn't my fault. It bothered me, though, that he'd done it to protect me. It also bothered me that I had no idea how to rescue him if he was willing to go along with that magical compulsion and not fight it as much as he could. I didn't think that was a good idea. My gut told me we didn't want Radomir and Abrams acquiring any more werewolf artifacts. It also told me that they might get rid of Duncan once they had no use for him. Abrams had already had him dumped in a ditch once. Next time, he might have Duncan shot with a silver bullet.

"Are you okay?" Jasmine looked over at me.

I'd slid into the driver's seat and gripped the wheel but was staring out the windshield without putting the truck in gear. Too lost in my grim thoughts.

"Yeah," I said, even if I wasn't. I forced a smile for her and started the truck down the road.

"You're a crappy liar, Aunt Luna."

"Yeah," I repeated.

13

LOST IN MY THOUGHTS, I DROVE DOWN THE BUMPY LOGGING ROAD, winding toward the mushroom building. I wanted nothing more than to get back out on the highway and head home. Or should I visit Mom tonight? It was getting late, but I had promised Lorenzo I would talk to her.

Worried about her and Duncan, I wasn't paying attention to my senses or surroundings as I drove. Jasmine was the one to grip the dashboard and say, "Wait. Someone's up there."

She pointed toward the silhouette of the mushroom building.

Under the cloudy night sky, it stood in the dark, and I didn't see anyone near it. Radomir's vehicles had passed by long enough ago that the motion-sensing lights had gone out. But, now that Jasmine brought my awareness to it, I could sense magical beings. Not raccoons. Men. A couple of those thugs we'd just encountered?

Had their drivers dropped them off at the building? To lie in wait for us?

The front door remained shut, the windows bricked in, so it

wasn't as if they could fire at us from inside. It was, however, possible they were lying on the roof with their rifles pointed at us.

"We'll go by quickly." I hit the accelerator.

If I'd thought there was another way back to the highway, I would have turned around and taken it, but these logging roads tended to head deeper and deeper into the mountains, not the other way around.

"Hang on," I added.

We hit a bump, and, even with her seatbelt on, Jasmine's head thumped against the ceiling of the cab. "You think?"

She gripped the oh-shit handle.

"Sorry," I said but didn't slow down.

I sank low in the seat in case guns fired and I needed to duck below the windows.

"My wolf keeps almost coming out." Jasmine also sank low.

"You think it can help with potholes?"

I eyed the building as we drew even with it. If there were people on the roof, I still couldn't see them.

"It could nibble on the hands of the person driving us *into* the potholes."

"That's not a good way to get a reference for a résumé. I wouldn't be able to write kind things about you without my fingers."

"There's voice dictation."

I started to smile, but as we passed the building, an engine roared to life. Headlights came on, almost blinding me.

Startled, I nearly veered off the road. It was the damn tank vehicle. The men had been hiding in it behind the building, not on the roof.

Even as we tilted and wobbled on the uneven road, driving far too fast for all the bumps and bends, the tank-SUV roared after us. Something told me that vehicle was made for off-roading and would have a lot less trouble than my old truck.

As we whipped around a bend, a branch smacking the windshield and making Jasmine curse, the passenger-side window rolled down on the tank-SUV. A gunman leaned out, his rifle poised to fire.

"Shit." I drove faster.

If we could make it to the highway...

The tank-SUV hit a bump hard enough to gain air. It came down right behind me, and I pressed the accelerator harder, worried about them shooting up my truck or outright ramming it. They might well shoot *us* too. I stayed low, even as the bumps and rocks in the road threatened to toss me into the ceiling.

A rifle fired, but I didn't hear it hit. Hopefully, the road made it hard for them to aim, though it was possible the bullet had pierced my tire.

I growled, tempted to halt, jump out, change into a wolf, and attack them. But if I stopped, that armored bully of an SUV might hit my truck in the rear and launch it into the next county.

"Is there anything I can do?" Jasmine peered over the seat's headrest and out the back window.

"Got anything you can throw at them?"

Visible in the rearview mirror, the rifleman hanging out the window was trying to steady himself enough to shoot again.

"Uh, Doritos?"

"Unless they have points like throwing stars, those aren't going to help."

"In this climate? Are you kidding? They get soggy five seconds after you open the bag." Jasmine opened the glove compartment as the truck bumped through another pothole, tilting alarmingly.

Something thunked out onto the floor. My first thought was that it was Duncan's magnet, but I'd put that under the seat, not in the glovebox.

"What the hell?" Jasmine bent, clunking her head as we whipped around a bend, the tire catching momentarily in a rut before the truck jerked free. She picked something up. "Is this... It looks like a grenade."

"I don't have anything like that in the glovebox."

"Are you sure?" Jasmine poked her hand into it. "Because there are three more in here."

"They're *not* grenades."

"Luna, they have pins and look like the military ones in the movies." Jasmine held one up, the lights from the tank-SUV flooding our cab to make it easy to see.

Shit, that *did* look like a grenade.

"Duncan had to have put them in there at the same time as the magnet." I shook my head. "But he said he was out of them. That's why he was using underwater demolitions at Augustus's place."

Maybe he'd picked some up on the way out there. We'd taken our separate vehicles, so it was possible. And then he'd tucked them into my glovebox at the same time he left the magnet gift?

Jasmine rolled down the window. "I'm going to—"

The tank-SUV rammed into us with a wrenching of metal and a great jolt that knocked the wheel out of my hands. The truck lurched wildly. We veered straight toward a tree.

Cursing, I grabbed the wheel and turned us back into the road. "Those *bastards*!"

Rage flooded my veins with adrenaline. Adrenaline and magic. The wolf in me wanted to roar forth, to attack those who were threatening us.

But I couldn't *drive* in wolf form. And were those headlights visible through the trees ahead? We were close to the highway. I had to hold it together. If we made it to the flat pavement, I'd stop and *then* we could turn wolf and attack these assholes.

"I've got this, Luna." Jasmine yanked the pin out of the grenade, leaned out the window, and lifted it. "Wait, do you have to count before throwing?"

"No," I blurted, sure she'd already waited too long. "Throw it!"

She did before my words got out. Her aim was accurate, and the grenade struck the windshield of our pursuer.

I was afraid it would bounce off, but it exploded right after hitting. White light flared, far brighter than their headlamps, and I squinted, barely keeping from driving off the road. As close as our two vehicles were, the shockwave struck us, my truck shuddering violently.

Broken branches pelted us. Something clattered and flew away, hitting a tree. Part of their vehicle? Part of mine?

Since theirs was armored, I feared the latter, but the truck kept running, taking us down the road. More headlights flashed through the trees. Yes, that was the highway.

"That was fun," Jasmine announced and grabbed another grenade.

Blinking and trying to clear my eyes, I peered into the rearview mirror. The brilliant light had faded, but their headlamps were still visible. The driver had slowed down after the explosion, and I hadn't, so there was more space between us, but they were still coming. If their windshield was cracked, I couldn't tell.

"Who the hell has an *armored* SUV?" I demanded.

"Bad guys, Luna. Duh."

"Can they order that out of a *catalog*?"

"The *bad guy* catalog."

I gave her an exasperated look, but she was leaning out the window again, another grenade in hand.

"Don't," I warned. "That hurt us more than it hurt them."

If we could just make it to the highway...

"They're picking up speed again," Jasmine said. "I have to—"

We passed a huge cedar, moss blanketing its bark, and an idea popped into my mind.

"Aim for some of those big trees. Or even the ground. To make a pit they won't be able to drive out of."

Jasmine issued a skeptical noise—understandable, since that

beast of an SUV could probably navigate out of a ten-foot-deep crater—but she did throw the second grenade toward the trees.

Fingers tight on the wheel, I was ready this time and squinted to protect my eyesight. Fortunately, the grenade landed farther back, and the shockwave didn't affect the truck as badly. A thunderous crack came from behind, followed by a chain of snaps, then a thud that made the earth tremble.

Before going around a bend, I glanced in the rearview mirror. A huge tree had fallen across the road, branches and trunk blocking the way.

The tank-SUV came to a halt, and a broken branch from above landed on its hood. It didn't damage the armored vehicle any more than the first grenade had, but it didn't matter. For the moment, the driver couldn't continue down the road. It would take some time for them to navigate around the downed tree.

The rifleman in the passenger seat leaned out the window again. He fired at us, but we were already tearing around the bend.

Ahead, the dark pavement of the highway came into view. Bullets slammed into trees behind us. I accelerated, peeling onto the highway and heading south toward home.

Something clattered behind us. My fender falling off?

I sighed, glad we'd escaped but lamenting the repair bill for my truck.

"That was handy," Jasmine said.

"What's that?"

"You're my only relative who keeps grenades in the glove compartment."

"Are you sure that's true? You're a werewolf, and we have a big pack full of belligerent members." I wouldn't have been surprised if Augustus had kept explosives in his vehicle. After all, he'd had a suit of armor holding a *poisoned sword* in his living room.

"Some of them have guns. *You're* the only one with grenades. I'm positive." Jasmine beamed an approving smile at me.

I didn't mention that Duncan must have stashed them there for me. As a gift. Normally, I would prefer fine dark chocolate, but, in this case, the explosives had been handy.

I looked back at the dark highway in the rearview mirror, wishing he had come with us. It was not, I told myself firmly, a betrayal that he hadn't. He was being magically compelled to work for Radomir.

Even so, it was hard not to feel a hurt tangle of emotions because I was driving south, and he'd headed off, seemingly of his own accord, in the other direction with those thugs.

14

Due to pieces falling off my truck, and fatigue after the harrowing chase, I didn't visit Mom that night. After dropping Jasmine off at home and checking the grounds of Sylvan Serenity to make sure Radomir's men hadn't been by and the police weren't staking out Rue's apartment, I went to bed and slept for ten hours. Fortunately, on a Sunday morning, nobody pounded on my door early.

After drinking two cups of coffee and wolfing down toast and scrambled eggs—I was still working on the cartons Duncan had purchased for me—I visited my truck with duct tape to engage in a few temporary repairs. That done, I headed north to make good on my promise to Lorenzo.

It was still early enough that there wasn't much traffic, and I made it to Mom's cabin in good time. Numerous trucks and cars were parked out front, suggesting a meeting was going on. One that I hadn't been invited to? Or maybe the pack had gone on a hunt the night before. Several of my relatives were sleeping in the backs of trucks or on Mom's porch. A couple of them were naked, looking sated after feasting on whatever they'd caught as wolves.

One of the trucks I passed on the way to the porch had antlers attached to the grill, a gun rack in the cab, and coyote tails tied to the radio antennae.

"Jasmine is delusional if she doesn't think any of our other relatives have explosives in their gloveboxes." I climbed the steps, looking around to see if Lorenzo was on the grounds before I realized I sensed him inside with Mom. They both seemed to be in the bedroom. I paused before approaching the door.

What if they were engaged in post-hunt amorous activities? Did Mom still have urges for that? In her condition?

"Hey, Luna," came a male voice from the end of the porch.

Emilio sat against the railing, his naked butt pressed to the boards. The nudity made it easy to see the scar on his lower abdomen, a gift from one of Radomir's men who'd shot him with a silver bullet. Emilio was lucky to be alive.

"Hello, naked relative."

"You'll have to be more specific." He grinned and waved at a couple other snoozing nudes. "Did you bring any salami?"

"No, sorry. I thought only Mom would be here." I dug into my pocket and held up a bag of midnight-chocolate-covered goji berries, something I'd picked up for her. They were more tart than my tongue preferred, but goji berries, also known as *wolf berries*, were supposed to have health benefits. Mom could use health benefits.

"You don't think she craves salty cured meats?"

"Not as much as she craves chocolates." I pointed at the closed front door. "Do you know if she's..."

"Home? Yeah, she's in there. She came on the hunt last night."

"I meant do you know if she's *busy*?"

Emilio looked blankly at me.

"With Lorenzo," I added.

My clarification didn't help with the blankness. Emilio only tilted his head.

"Having *sex*," I whispered.

"*Oh.*" He drew back, clunking his head against the railing. "I'm sure they're not doing *that*." He lowered his voice and raised his hand to his mouth to whisper, "She's injured, and they're *old*."

"Old people can have sex."

"No way. I'm sure they can't even—" he made a gesture that prompted me to roll my eyes, "—you know."

"Apparently, Mom can still hold her own against a bear. I'm sure she can *you know* if she wants."

Whether she wanted to was what I didn't know. Being ill had probably sapped her of her libido. Still, I knocked quietly, not wanting to disturb them if they were being intimate.

"They're probably in there rubbing liniment into each other's achy hips," Emilio said.

The door opened in time for Lorenzo to hear that. He was shirtless—thankfully, not *pantsless*—and looked quite fit and not in need of liniment.

"Thanks for coming, Luna." Lorenzo shot Emilio a dark look before stepping back and waving me into the cabin. "I'll let you two talk."

"Okay."

I thought Lorenzo might stick around, waiting in the main room, but there was a haunted look in his eyes, and he stepped outside soon after I entered. Not much had changed in the last day, I suspected. Or maybe Mom had gotten worse.

Uneasy, I stepped into the doorway to her bedroom. I smiled and rattled the bag of chocolates. Only when Mom glared in my direction did I realize it sounded like someone rattling a bag of dog treats to entice good behavior from a hound.

"I'm fine." Mom sat in a chair at the end of the bed, working on the corner of a puzzle stretching across a piece of plywood set up to act as a table.

Despite her proclamation, there were bags under her eyes, her skin was pale, and a bandage wrapped her left hand. To cover one of the wounds Lorenzo had mentioned not healing as quickly as usual? A scar on the side of her neck, half-hidden by her white hair, was also new, though it had sealed up and didn't need a bandage.

Ah, was that a jewelry chain around her neck? Maybe Lorenzo had given her the longevity talisman.

"And I don't need a *talking* to," Mom added. "If you try to lecture me, I'll boot you out faster than a fox in the smokehouse."

Lorenzo must have admitted that he'd invited me up—and why. Or she'd sussed it out on her own.

"I came for advice, not to give a lecture." I sat on the edge of the bed and groped for something I could ask that wouldn't make that a lie. "And to deliver these chocolate-covered berries."

"If my chocolate is going to cover something, I prefer it be bacon."

"The berries have health benefits." Reading off the back of the bag, I said, "They promote immune function, better sleep, and protect cells from damage caused by free radicals. They may even engender a feeling of wellness and calm."

Judging by the baleful look Mom sent me, she didn't put much stock in candies promising calm or wellness. And she thought I was an idiot for falling for the marketing hype.

"They sound like they'll taste awful." She picked up an edge piece to find a spot in the puzzle for it. That seemed to imply she would only half-heartedly pay attention to me if I brought up her solo bear hunt. Maybe she would ignore me altogether.

"They're tart," I said. "Not horrible. I would put them at the same notch on the delight scale as chocolate-covered crickets."

"Those sound like they'd be better."

"Do you want me to bring some up next time? I have a new supplier." I almost mentioned Austin and that he had come to visit for the holidays, but Mom barely acknowledged that my human children existed.

"No. What advice do you want?" She looked balefully at me again, seeing through that story. "And what the hell is a *free radical*?"

"Something malevolent that swims around in your bloodstream."

"You have no idea, do you?"

"Not really. I'm trying to figure out how to get Duncan back from the artifact thieves."

Mom put down her puzzle piece to look fully at me. Jasmine must not have mentioned our previous night's adventure to the family yet. I couldn't remember exactly what I'd told Mom about Duncan's past before, so I summed up the magical control device, his scar, and his relationship with Abrams.

"They're using him for his treasure-hunting skills," I said to finish. "For some reason, they want him to find the male match to your medallion." I waved to the bedside table where she'd been keeping it the last time I'd seen it. "They probably still want your medallion too."

"Oh, I know they do. Now and then, their thugs drive slowly past the property and peer in this direction. I'm sure they're waiting for an opportunity to attack when there isn't much family present, but Lorenzo has pack members visiting around the clock to keep an eye on things. And on *me* now." Her mouth twisted.

Ah, maybe it hadn't been a hunt that had prompted all the visitors outside. Or not *only* a hunt.

I wondered if her sneaking away to confront a bear had been as much about what she perceived as overprotection and smothering as a desire to die on her own terms. Maybe some of both.

"We also have more of those booby traps that you triggered," she added.

"*I* didn't trigger them. My cousins triggered them on me. There was a remote that Orazio used to zap me while I fought Augustus."

Mom waved away the details. "Yes, yes. I know." She lowered her arm and smiled slightly. "Though it was a shame to lose fit pack members, I'm glad you got the best of them. I knew you had the power to do so, if only you'd untether it."

"Duncan helped," I said.

"Have you mated with him yet?" She looked hopefully at my abdomen—my *womb*.

I rolled my eyes. Not this again. "No. That's hard to do when the bad guys have him. I'm sure they wouldn't allow conjugal visits."

"You'd think that sex would invigorate him so that he would treasure-hunt better. But that medallion was lost long ago. I doubt it's in this area."

"I guess their research suggests otherwise. You don't know anything more about it than what you've told me? Anything that could be helpful in finding it?"

She shook her head. "I can ask the family archivist if she knows anything."

"Okay, good." I hadn't *known* the family had an archivist, but that sounded promising. "I want to get Duncan away from those guys, but I would also prefer to keep them from acquiring more werewolf artifacts. It worries me that they want them. They've got to be *up* to something."

"It is strange that someone would put so much effort into stealing them. Men with money and means."

"But who aren't magical themselves. Most of these artifacts regular humans wouldn't even be able to use, I don't think."

"Perhaps if you get Duncan back," Mom said, "they'll be handicapped and unable to find any more of them."

"That's not the main reason I want him back, but it would be a perk."

"I'm sure." She smiled at me, looking smug.

"If you start talking about mating and offspring again, I'm going to pelt you with these berries."

"Is that how the health benefits are delivered? Through physical contact?"

"That's how the free radicals are knocked out of your body, yes."

Mom shook her head and gazed out the window in the direction of the road. "Those men have been attacking us and stealing from our kind and others for weeks now. They deserve to have their throats torn out."

"Probably, but I haven't had the opportunity to do so yet." I shifted on the bed, worried she would suggest I plan their murder. Maybe they *did* deserve that after all they'd done, but it still disturbed me that I'd lost control of the wolf and killed the underlings that had attacked me at Sylvan Serenity.

"Perhaps you should seek that opportunity out. You said you have a list of their addresses?"

"I have a list of properties that Radomir's company owns. Whether he and Abrams live at any of them..." I tilted my palm toward the ceiling.

"Search them. You need to find those men and deal with them before they deal with *you*."

After the previous night's attack, it was hard to deny that logic.

"And if you could take or destroy that control device, you wouldn't need to worry about Duncan turning on you or working for them."

I blinked. That hadn't occurred to me. Of course, it wasn't as if I'd had the opportunity to take it—I hadn't seen it since the night I'd escaped the potion factory, and I'd been busy staying alive then. Still, it might make as much sense to try to find *it* as Duncan. Assuming they sent him out again to search for the werewolf medallion, he could end up anywhere in the state. Or anywhere at *all.* Those guys would presumably be at one of their facilities around Puget Sound.

"Probably not destroy it," I murmured, "since I don't know what that would do to *Duncan.* He's linked to it through some magic embedded in that scar of his." I touched the spot on my forehead where it existed on his.

"But if you took it, they could not control him."

"Yeah."

"*You* could control him, though he is a strong werewolf and would not appreciate such."

"No, I wouldn't do that. I could just... hide the device in the heat duct under my bed."

Mom's eyebrows twitched.

"Or in my sock drawer next to my hormone cream. That would ensure no guy would ever touch it."

"Your time among humans has made you odd, my daughter."

Out front, someone let out a sound similar to, "Yeehaw!"

Emilio yelled, "That was a fat one."

"Varmint hunt!"

Thuds sounded on the porch as my family leaped off to chase whatever had stirred their wolf blood.

"You think it's humans that made me odd, huh?" I asked.

"Absolutely." Mom smiled.

Her curved lips warmed my heart, even though the gesture didn't last. She looked sternly at me and said, "You're welcome for the advice. Now, go find him. And don't come harass me if I choose to hunt on my own again. I can still handle myself when the magic infuses me." She didn't admit, as she had done before, that the wolf sometimes evaded her now when she reached for it.

"Don't do yourself in, please, Mom. Taking on a bear alone is unwise. And Lorenzo—"

"Is a nag," she said firmly.

"Then why are you spending time with him?"

"Most of the time, he's decent company. And he's good in bed."

I groaned and dropped my face in my hand. "I knew Emilio was naive about that."

"He's naive about a lot. I bet he would fall for the hokum on the label of that bag. Why don't you give him those berries?"

"He prefers salami."

"Go home, Luna. I'm fine. Make some plans, and go retrieve your old-world wolf. And the device that controls him. Perhaps he'll be so grateful that he'll—"

"Don't say it." I jerked my hand up, palm toward her. "No more talk about offspring. Please."

"He'll be a loyal protector and companion going forward," she finished, though I believed I'd guessed right about what she'd *intended* to say.

"He's already that," I said softly. Then, because she looked tired, I rose to take my leave. I left the chocolate-covered berries. Just in case.

"Another reason he would be a good father to werewolf pups then," Mom said softly.

I heard the words but didn't look back, not wanting to argue further.

Besides, I had something else on my mind. The beginnings of a plan to find Radomir and Abrams and steal that device from them.

15

Afternoon approached as I returned to Sylvan Serenity. My stomach grumbled, requesting lunch. Bolin's fancy SUV was in one of the staff spots, his inflatable protective bubble around it. He didn't usually come in on the weekends, and I hoped he hadn't brought his parents with more prospective buyers.

Logically, I knew the sale of the complex was inevitable and that I should prepare myself to accept that fate. Emotionally, I wanted to roll around on the grass, throw a temper tantrum, and demand to know why the world kept hurling so much crap at me.

Only Duncan had been a good thing in my life. On the drive back, I'd mulled over possible ways to find Radomir and Abrams so I could help him.

Why hadn't I asked Duncan where they were staying now? Would he have told me? Or would he mulishly *not* have told me? For my own good?

The only idea I had was to drive around Puget Sound and check all those addresses. It wasn't a great plan, but it was a starting point.

When I leaned into the leasing office, Bolin sat at the computer, scowling and typing.

"Are you being assailed by spam emails?" I asked. "Or applicants with low credit scores and histories of evictions?"

He looked at me. "Are those the kinds of things that disgruntle you at the computer?"

"On a regular basis, yes."

"My parents have tasked me with putting together marketing materials for the complex. They're determined to list it. It'll take a while to find a buyer since the market is slow right now, and apartments with this many doors cost a lot of money. Did you know there are more than two-hundred units?"

"Of course. I've lived and worked here for more than twenty years. I've replaced the faucets in most of the units. Showerheads. Toilets. Water heaters. Door locks. Flooring."

"Is there anything you don't do?"

"Mold. I hire druids for that."

"Ha ha."

I peered at the computer screen, my Duncan quest momentarily diverted by this other problem. "I don't suppose I can talk you into making the place sound dingy and unappealing with a horrible cap rate?"

"You want me to lie?"

"What's the opposite of exaggerating to make something sound good?"

"Meiosis?"

"My-what?"

"Meiosis means understating something when you present it. However, it's usually employed to achieve a greater effect rather than a lesser one."

I'd never heard of the word. "Can you spell it?"

"Of *course*. M-E-I-O-S-I-S. That's not even hard."

"Huh." I still hadn't heard of the word, but it amused me to challenge Bolin's spelling-bee skills.

"The original meaning refers to chromosomes in gamete-producing cells being reduced by one half. It's kind of the opposite of mitosis."

"I don't think I asked." By now, I'd forgotten what we were talking about. Oh, right. Marketing.

"Your puzzled expression conveyed a need for knowledge."

I scratched my cheek. "Does it do that a lot?"

"Yes, but I try to refrain from explaining every time. Bullies beat up pedants, you know."

"I'm concerned you categorize me as a bully." I smiled, but it might have been a sad smile. Before the incidents in the parking lot, I doubted *anyone* would have thought of me that way. At least they hadn't during the years I'd taken the sublimation potion. A part of me rejoiced in being a werewolf again, and a part of me felt I'd lost something. My humanity, maybe.

"Oh, I don't. But you're tough and strong and... lycanthropic."

"A word I don't need you to define." I waved at the screen, hoping the need for marketing material meant the first prospective buyer hadn't made an offer. "How long until the listing goes live?"

AKA, how long did I have before I had to find a new job and relocate my life?

I grimaced, imagining returning victorious with Duncan and the control device only to have to move into his van with him. That had to be cramped for even *one* person.

"My parents are shooting for next week." Bolin shrugged apologetically. "If it helps, they'll be happy to provide a reference for you. Assuming the new owner doesn't want to keep you employed. Which they should. You're a big part of why the returns are so good here."

"Yeah." I couldn't manage any pride or gratitude. This sucked. I hadn't realized how much I liked this place until I was in danger of losing it.

"You're also more like a paladin than a bully. You protect people."

"Thanks. Paladins aren't the ones who have to be celibate, are they?"

"That's clerics, and even then, I think it depends on the gaming world. But, by the way, ew."

"Ew that I like sex?"

Bolin drew back. "Yeah. You're... a mom."

He'd been about to say *old*. I was sure of it.

Maybe my grays were showing. I hadn't had time to dye my hair lately, and those buggers stood out against the usual black. Still, I hadn't seen any grays in the mirror when I'd looked last. Since I'd stopped taking the potion that squelched my werewolf magic, I'd felt more vitality. *Younger*, even. Maybe Mom was right that our kind could be fertile longer than humans.

"You haven't been talking to my cousin, Emilio, have you?"

"Not unless he turned in a leasing application."

"I don't think he needs an apartment. Middle-aged people can and do have sex, FYI. Retired people too."

"I was going to say something helpful and encouraging about how quickly you'll find another job as a property manager, but you've distracted me with unasked-for knowledge."

"It's because you had a puzzled expression that begged for an explanation."

"That *can't* be true," he said without acknowledging that I'd turned his words on him.

"Do you know what your parents are going to ask for this place?" I knew how much came into the coffers in rents each year, and it was such a large number that my mind boggled at the idea of some multiple of that.

"Millions."

"A lot of millions, right? It's over a million for even a fourplex around here."

"Yeah." Bolin probably knew the number and didn't want to tell me because his parents would be the ones getting that insanely fat check in their bank account.

It was possible—likely—they had a loan and maybe other backers that would need to be paid, but after all the decades the Sylvans had owned this place, I still deemed a fat check likely. I didn't need that kind of wealth, but I couldn't help but feel wistful. If I'd had a husband who'd been more of a partner in finances than an impediment, maybe I could have gotten on the property ladder years ago.

"You're pricing fourplexes?" Bolin probably wanted to change the subject.

"Always." I thought I'd told him about that, but maybe he'd forgotten—or I'd forgotten. When prompted, I tended to wax nostalgic about that long-term dream/goal. "I'm saving for the downpayment on one. It's my retirement plan. Live in one unit and have the rents from the other three pay down the mortgage until I own it outright. Then the rents can pay for my coffee, chocolate, and medical needs in my doddering old age."

"Do lycanthropes dodder?"

I hesitated, thinking of Mom and how I hadn't talked her out of anything. Instead, she'd been the one to lecture me. I couldn't help but feel I'd failed Lorenzo.

"Not usually," I said. "They go off alone on a moonlit hunt, pick a fight with a stronger foe, and die on their own terms."

"This conversation got grim." The old rotary phone rang, and Bolin pounced on it. "Sylvan Serenity Housing."

I turned for the door, reminded of the quest I needed to plan for, but paused when Bolin frowned at the phone.

"You try that, and I'll unleash a paladin and all her hellhounds on you. We've upped the security here and hired private guards. They'll personally drag you to jail."

I tried to make out the response, but the hum of the computer fan and people talking on the walkway outside thwarted my attempt. All I got was that the speaker was male and had a menacing voice. I thought of the motorcycle riders who'd threatened me and lifted a hand.

Bolin handed me the phone.

"This is one of the hellhounds," I said. "What do you want?"

"You're the paladin," Bolin whispered.

"If you don't want to lose the kid and your tenants, you keep your fangs out of this town's business." The speaker hung up before I could respond.

I hadn't recognized the voice but had a hunch it belonged to one of the motorcycle thugs. And I wasn't surprised they'd figured out that I was the werewolf around town. After all, I'd changed right in front of them.

"Sorry, Bolin." I handed him the phone to put on the cradle. "I need to get Duncan back, and then I'll figure out a way to deal with the miscreants troubling us—and Shoreline. You might want to dawdle a bit on the marketing material and the listing. Until I get rid of that problem."

Duncan could help me. He was the one who'd suggested I turn into a crime-fighting superhero. He'd offered to turn my blanket into a cape and mask.

"I thought you wanted the problem to be rampant when prospective buyers were here," Bolin said.

"A part of me does, but a bigger part of me knows I need to be responsible and deal with the problem I've inadvertently created."

"Noble."

"Like a paladin?"

"Absolutely. Have you gotten a chance to ask Jasmine about her interest in... things?"

"Things like you?"

"Well, in activities and hobbies that I might also arrange to share. I'm working on my violin rap songs."

"I'm sure your neighbors appreciate that."

"I'm talented. They don't mind."

"Are you sure? Should I poll them?"

Bolin frowned at me. "No."

"She played Lil Wayne and Cardi B on the way up to Deming, and she's hunting for a new job in real-estate finance right now. I don't think she's got time for hobbies."

"Hm." A slightly scheming look entered his eyes. "If I could help put her in touch with people who are looking to *hire* someone with her skills, she might think favorably of me. Right? She might be so pleased that she would want to get mochas with me."

"You aspire to lofty goals."

"I... just want a chance. She remembered my name. Did you notice?"

"I did. I don't think you need to get her a job though."

"I don't have that kind of power. It'd just be introducing her to some of my parents' colleagues that I've known a while. Like... while we're on the way to the mocha place."

Bolin was scheming so hard smoke was coming out of his ears. I was on the verge of pointing out that my geeky twenty-two-year-old intern probably couldn't help anyone with networking, but that wasn't true, was it? His *parents* certainly had to be connected and know a ton of real estate bigwigs in the Seattle area. Maybe he could introduce Jasmine to someone who was hiring.

"It could work," I offered.

"Oh?" His expression cheered. Maybe he'd expected me to crush his idea. "I'll practice my violin beats too. Just in case."

"I would."

"Uhm, do you need any..." Bolin glanced out the open door,

waiting for the couple who'd been chatting to pass by before continuing in a lower voice. "I could make you a few helpful items if you're going on a jailbreak."

"More bath bombs?"

He mouthed the words.

"The little spheres that made the floor sticky," I clarified.

"Those were Orbs of Entanglement."

"Yeah, they were helpful. Though I entangled my own paw a couple of times. It's hard to keep track of floor stickiness when you're fighting."

"I can make some more for you. And some anti-stick powder for your, uhm, feet."

"Good. I'm going to need everything I can get."

Bolin turned back to the computer, shaking his head and muttering, "*Bath* bombs."

16

BEFORE DINNER, I HAD ANOTHER SWORD-FIGHTING LESSON WITH Yuto. With so much going on, I had been tempted to skip it, but who knew what expertise I would need to steal the control device?

I was back home now, packing for the attempt, and had a pile of weapons and tools on the dining table. They included the two remaining grenades from the glovebox, the magnet on a rope, and the magical sword.

What else would be useful? Aside from locating Radomir and Abrams? Too bad I didn't have an Elixir of Locus for one of them. Though I didn't know if I could stomach swallowing another of those concoctions. Nobody's esophagus deserved that kind of torture.

"I'd need to pack Pepto Bismol."

To think I'd made fun of the werewolf bartender, Francisco, for serving his paranormal customers a drink made with the stuff. Maybe *most* potions upset one's stomach.

A knock sounded at the door. Before I could answer, Jasmine strolled into my apartment with a backpack slung over her shoulder.

"I heard you're storming another castle and need help."

"Where'd you hear that? My mother?"

"You were chatting with her next to a porch full of werewolves."

"There were logs in between us."

"You know our kind have good hearing."

"Emilio was probably hoping to learn where I get my farm-sourced salamis."

"Oh, no doubt."

"Is your truck still drivable?" Jasmine waved in the direction of the parking lot.

"Yes." The back end now lacked a fender, and the tailgate was so mangled that it wouldn't open, but the truck had made it up to visit Mom. "Some parts have just fallen off."

"Comforting. We can take my car if you want."

"Don't you have a twenty-year-old hatchback?"

I'd seen it before. The tiny car looked like it would crumple in a stiff wind.

"It gets good gas mileage," Jasmine said.

"I'm sure, but you can't storm a castle in a hatchback. You need something badass. Like whatever that vehicle was that tried to run us off the mountain."

"A Rezvani tank. I looked it up. It was pretty dope."

"It's an actual car that you can buy?" I'd assumed it had been custom-made and that only evil overlords could afford it.

"Yup. I bet they had the military edition. It's got ballistics armor, a ram bumper, electrified door handles, and night vision."

"We felt that bumper firsthand."

"I'm a little sad we didn't get to see the electromagnetic-pulse protection and smoke screen."

"How much does all that cost?"

"It's a steal at three hundred thousand."

"Is that all? I'll put one on my grocery list."

"I would." Jasmine waved toward the window. "Oh, I forgot to ask. Did you know there's a police car in your parking lot?"

"Again?" I groaned. Were those same officers back to question me? Or Rue? Maybe they'd gotten their warrant.

"Don't you feel bolstered knowing the authorities are spending so much time keeping an eye on your complex?"

"If they had succeeded in stopping a single crime, I would."

Leaving my gear on the table, I stepped outside. Since my apartment didn't face the parking lot, I had to go around the corner of the building to check on it. I spotted the police car right away, but it was empty.

Groaning again, I headed for the building toward the back of the complex where Rue's apartment was located. Jasmine trailed after me, the walkways well-lit as twilight descended.

"You don't need to come," I told her. "I'm just checking on someone."

"There might be adventure, excitement, and a chance for me to prove myself worthy of your heartfelt recommendation for my résumé."

"After all we've been through, I'll give you one."

"Oh, good. Will it be heartfelt?"

"Aren't you just going to type my name and number on a list? How could that be heartfelt?"

"I could use a fancy font. Maybe with curlicues."

"Nothing says you're a professional like curlicues and hearts on your résumé."

I thought about mentioning Bolin's offer to help her network with real-estate moguls, but he could bring that up to her himself.

"It says I have personality. People like that in colleagues and subordinates."

"You think so, huh?"

I peered around the corner of the back apartment building

and sighed. The male and female officers stood at Rue's door. No, they'd *opened* Rue's door. Or she had.

Worried for her, I picked up my pace. If she got arrested because she'd been standing next to me when I'd turned wolf to defend the complex...

Damn it, why was everything my fault these days? Or at least happening because of me?

"Can I help you?" I called.

They were already stepping into the apartment. It was dark, and I didn't sense Rue inside.

"Good evening, Ms. Valens," Dubois said, no emotion on her face to suggest she'd been caught doing something shifty.

Before she held up a digital copy of a warrant, I knew she had one.

"Do you know where Rue Thepnakorn is? We've been issued a warrant allowing us to search her apartment, but we would prefer to let her know we're doing so before barging in."

"You've already barged in," I said as her partner turned on the lights.

"Only because she's not here."

"What do you expect to find? She's eccentric and has an eclectic collection of stuff, but nothing is illegal." I hoped not anyway.

Rue had objected to making potions using ingredients like livers from recently deceased women, so I gathered she had ethical lines she didn't cross in her field.

"A wolf." The male officer halted inside and sneezed three times. "What *is* this place? A mad scientist's laboratory?" He sneezed again.

Dubois looked upward to twists of herbs and baskets of tubers dangling from the ceiling. The lease forbade making holes in the walls and mentioned sticky hooks that could be removed. I would have to have a chat with Rue about using those.

"She's into botanicals and chemistry." I doubted they would believe me if I told them she was an alchemist. "But I've never seen her with a wolf, a coyote, or even a mouse. We have a no-wild-animals-for-pets rule here."

Dubois sniffed. "I can smell a cat box."

How could she smell anything over the pervasive incense odor?

"We allow those." I'd yet to see Rue's feline familiar, but she'd mentioned having one several times.

The male officer walked into the kitchen and lifted a frying pan on the burner. "Looks like she was making dinner. This is still warm." He gave his partner a significant look. "She might have seen us coming and hidden on the premises."

"Does your warrant allow you to search this entire place?" I folded my arms over my chest, certain it didn't.

"Is there a reason you're protecting Thepnakorn, Ms. Valens?" Dubois asked.

"I'm protective of all of my tenants."

"Even the criminals?"

"Nobody here is a *criminal*. I do background checks. You can't get an apartment if you've passed bad checks, much less trained a wolf to attack people. And that *hasn't* happened. You can't even do that. Wolves aren't dogs. They don't sit for treats."

That probably wasn't true. I could imagine Emilio sitting for salami. And Duncan for chocolate-covered bacon. Hell, *I'd* offer a perky sit and a tongue loll for a bar of quality dark chocolate.

"We're not sure what's possible in that area." Dubois exchanged a long look with her male partner, then eyed something slightly magical that was glowing on a shelf.

There were a lot of objects and ingredients in the apartment with magical vibes, but I didn't think the mundane police officers would be able to sense them. Of course, if the objects insisted on *glowing*, it didn't take someone with paranormal senses to detect magic. And these two... looked like they might be on the verge of broadening their horizons on what was possible.

"Let's check the woods. That's city land." The male officer eyed me. "We don't need a warrant."

I rubbed my face, hoping Rue *wasn't* hiding out on the property, but the warm pan did suggest she had been here recently.

"They look like the kinds of people who are going to keep turning over rocks until they find a worm," Jasmine said after the police officers left.

She lingered outside the doorway, eyeing some of the items in the apartment but not stepping inside.

"Unfortunately." I joined her on the walkway. "It would be helpful about now if a crime wave would start up in Lake Forest Park or Edmonds, and the police would be distracted by other work."

"Maybe if you put an end to all the crime in Shoreline, they'll stop feeling the need to visit your property." Jasmine smiled at me.

Maybe I shouldn't have told her about the convenience-store owners' wish that I do that. And Duncan's willingness to make me a superhero cape.

"If I could keep crime from happening *here*—" I pointed to the ground, "—that would be a start."

"Likely so."

I pulled out my phone and debated calling Rue. If she *was* skulking in the woods or behind a rhododendron somewhere on the property, I didn't want ringing to give her away. One should silence one's phone when hiding from the police, but one didn't always think of such things in the heat of the moment.

My phone rang, startling me. A number I didn't recognize popped up. I eyed it warily. It might be Rue contacting me from someone else's phone. More likely, it was the troglodyte who'd called the leasing office and threatened Bolin.

"Hello," I answered.

If it *was* the troglodyte, it might be useful to answer on a phone that would store the number.

"Ms. Valens?" The male voice was familiar, but I groped to place it.

"Yeah."

"This is Minato." Ah, the store owner. "I'm here with my wife."

Uh-oh.

"Did someone try to rob you again?"

"No. A few black vehicles have driven by, those inside peering in our direction, and there was a knife fight earlier in the parking lot, but nothing that threatens our business or persons has happened yet today."

"Yet today? Are you expecting a mugging or murder tonight?"

"Nighttime is always more dangerous," Minato said grimly.

I wished I could retract my sarcasm. With their store on a busy intersection, those two had likely witnessed the deterioration of the neighborhood firsthand. I felt guilty that I wasn't, even now, doing something to help.

"You may also find it increasingly so," he added. "We heard from a man who purchased beer and is associated with the dubious criminal element that you are being targeted."

"Yeah, the motorcycle thugs threatened me. It's okay."

Minato hesitated. "You are not concerned? Because of your... paranormal powers?"

"I'm not *unconcerned*. I'm just..." I didn't know how to explain that I was too busy to spend time worrying about those guys. Further, I'd battled werewolves and supernaturally powerful thugs shooting silver bullets. Purely human enemies didn't concern me as much. "I've been taking sword-fighting lessons," I offered as an explanation.

"Is that necessary? When you have a powerful... alter ego?"

A flashlight beam slashed through the woods. The police were wandering around out there.

"Sometimes, it's inconvenient for one's alter ego to come out," I said. "Trust me."

"Had I that power, I would bring it out always." Minato sounded wistful.

"Even when shoppers are browsing in the beer aisle?"

"Hm, perhaps not at work."

"Exactly."

"Is there any chance you are cogitating on a solution for our mutual problem?" There was that wistful tone again.

"It's a priority. Trust me."

Right after dealing with Radomir and Abrams and getting Duncan away from their clutches.

"Thank you," Minato said earnestly. "You are our only hope. I've mentioned you to others, and, if you change your mind about accepting financial compensation, many in our community are willing to chip in."

"That's not necessary." I said goodbye and hung up.

Jasmine arched her eyebrows.

"I miss being nothing more than a mom and a property manager." I thought about calling Austin to see if he'd had his first snowboarding lesson yet and was having fun, but would he want to hear from his mother while hanging out with a bunch of his friends? Probably not.

"Sounds boring."

"You say that because you don't have kids. They keep things interesting." For that matter, my tenants did too.

"My mom said Aurora and I were pains in the ass growing up."

"But interesting, I'm sure. Werewolves are by default."

The flashlight beam in the woods had disappeared from view. Hoping the police were giving up and returning to their car, I headed back toward my apartment. I stopped ten feet from reaching it. The door was ajar.

"Did you leave that open?" I asked Jasmine.

"No. I didn't know how long we would be gone, so I turned off the lights and closed the door."

"Hell." I ran for the entrance, thinking of the magical sword, the wolf case, and other valuable things inside—like my espresso maker, damn it.

I halted one step inside the apartment. Furniture was tipped over, blankets and clothes strewn about the floor, and plates that had been yanked from cabinets and hurled across the living room lay shattered by the wall. The table I'd placed my gear on was upended. I picked my way through the mess toward it, afraid...

The sword was gone. I swore again.

The grenades were missing too. Only the magnet on the rope lay tangled on the floor, cast aside as something worthless.

"How am I supposed to storm a bad-guy lair with only that?" My fists balled in frustration. I hadn't even figured out where the lair was yet, but I would have. I still would. I just—

"Did you see this, Luna?" Jasmine stood by the overturned coffee table, pointing at the faux wood floor.

With anger and frustration tightening my muscles, I joined her. Heat warmed my skin from within, my magic offering to bring forth the wolf. But with the police officers loitering, that was the last thing I should do. Too bad. Whoever had done this had done so recently. We hadn't been out of the apartment for long. With my lupine nose, I could have tracked them by scent.

Jasmine pointed at a message written in red paint. It was probably supposed to pass as blood, but my nose told me otherwise.

Don't interfear. Don't attack again. Or die.

"Nice spelling on interfere," Jasmine said. "You're dealing with some real masterminds."

"Unfortunately, it doesn't take a mastermind to rob an apartment or deliver a threat." I headed for my bedroom, worried they might have found the wolf case. Maybe I'd been foolish to underestimate the local thugs.

"That's not blood... right?" Perhaps not the paint connoisseur that I was, Jasmine eyed the damp red writing with more unease.

"Nope. Sherwin-Williams. Trust me. I buy it often. Evergreen Fog is a staple here." I paused in the doorway, able to sense that the artifact remained in the heat duct under the floor. It was a good thing the robbers hadn't been paranormal, else they might have sensed its presence and hunted for it.

"Is that a color?" Jasmine asked.

Stepping back into the living room, I waved to the soft gray-green paint on the walls. "2022 Color of the Year."

"Fancy."

I shifted my fingers toward the writing. "That looks like Beetroot. Maybe Sun-dried Tomato."

"Is it weird that you know their whole line-up of paint colors?"

"Nope. I've done a lot of painting."

"Is it weird that you're not visibly creeped out by this?" Jasmine waved to indicate the writing and the vandalized apartment.

"I'm too busy being frustrated that they stole Duncan's gifts."

"Oh, man, they took the grenades?"

"And the sword." That had to be a lot more valuable than the explosives Duncan had picked up at a military-surplus store or wherever one could purchase such things. "It was an antique."

"The grenades were super handy." Jasmine sounded more distressed by the loss of them. Maybe hurling them out the truck window had been exhilarating. "What bastards." She shook her head. "What kind of thugs steal a woman's *grenades*?"

"The kind that are pissed that she's determined to drive them out of Shoreline."

"When are you going to do that? You've got a lot on your plate."

"Tell me about it." And with these brutes gunning for me, it was going to be hard to focus on my number one priority.

I sensed someone approaching from outside and turned toward the door, no weapons nearby that I could grab. But my blood was hot, anger making my magic rise to the surface and sweep through my veins. If I needed to, I could call upon the wolf.

17

I RECOGNIZED THE MAGICAL BEING APPROACHING MY APARTMENT AND didn't call upon the wolf.

"Duncan?" I asked in wonder.

After our last parting, I hadn't expected to see him again for a while. With his scar glowing to remind everyone of his magical tie to the device, he hadn't implied that he would return for visits.

"Maybe he can get you some more grenades," Jasmine whispered.

I stepped outside to greet Duncan on the threshold. Though delighted to see him, I realized I would have to admit that I'd lost his sword. The smile I offered him held mixed emotions.

Fully dressed in jeans, boots, and what was probably one of several black leather jackets that he owned—he lost his clothes in changes almost as often as I did—he looked as handsome as on the day I first met him. At the moment, the scar looked perfectly normal, like a relic of a childhood sports accident, not an indicator that a bad guy with a magical device could control him.

"Good evening, my lady." Duncan stopped in front of me to bow, but only for a moment before making it a hug.

When I returned it, he rumbled a pleased, "Ah," and looked like he might shift the embrace into a kiss.

The door remained open, however, and he noticed Jasmine. His jaw drooped, and he lowered his arms. He'd also noticed the huge mess inside my apartment.

"What happened? Were you robbed?"

"Robbed and threatened," I said, thinking of the phone call. "It's been an eventful day."

Jasmine pointed toward the message on the floor again. After giving me a concerned look and an arm squeeze, Duncan stepped inside to look at it.

"Is that the American spelling for interfere?" he asked.

"It's the ignoramus spelling," Jasmine said. "Bolin would be appalled."

I lifted my eyebrows. I hadn't realized Bolin had managed to speak with Jasmine for long enough to bring up his spelling-bee background. Even if he had, it surprised me that she had listened to him on the subject.

"*I'm* appalled." Duncan touched his chest. "For many reasons." He turned his concerned expression back toward me. "Are you all right?"

"Fine, but..." I grimaced. "They got your sword."

"*And* the grenades that you left Aunt Luna in her truck."

"Egregious," Duncan said. "I'm relieved neither of you was hurt."

I wasn't surprised that he cared as much—*more*—about us as the sword, but his utterance of *egregious* hadn't sounded that heartfelt. As if he wasn't that worried about losing a priceless centuries-old magical artifact. I couldn't imagine that.

"Did this just happen?" Duncan crouched and touched the paint. A smear came off on his finger.

"While we were checking on Rue—Rue's apartment," I said. "Yes."

He sniffed the air.

"It's paint, not blood," Jasmine said. "Beetroot."

"Possibly Sun-dried Tomato," I said, though I doubted paint taxonomy was what prompted Duncan's air sampling. He would have recognized the paint scent without waving his nostrils about.

"I can catch a whiff of them." Duncan straightened. "There were two men, I think."

"Probably some of the bikers who have been threatening me of late," I said.

He frowned at me. "I see I've missed important things by being away."

"What brought you back?" I asked. "I'm glad to see you, but I didn't expect to for a while. Did you miss your van?"

"*Terribly.*"

"And me?"

"Even *more* terribly. But at least you visited me in the woods. The van..."

"Doesn't have that self-driving feature so you can summon it for a reunion?"

"It does not. Perhaps I need an upgrade." Duncan removed his jacket. "I'll shift and go after those chaps. The trail is still hot. Do you want to join me?"

"I was tempted, but the police are around, and they're specifically looking for a wolf."

He paused, not removing more clothes. "Did they figure out our kind were responsible for the deaths in the parking lot?"

"They already knew that, but now they think Rue trains wolves and was responsible." My words spilled out quickly, influenced by a mixture of frustration, bleakness, and worry.

Duncan blinked. "What led the police down that back alley?"

"I shifted to fight some of the thugs in the parking lot, and Rue was there. One of the ghost hunters got a photo of her patting my back. My *lupine* back. Now, on top of everything else, I have to worry about the police arresting her." I bent forward, the night's events—no, the whole last *month's* events—surging to the surface and making me emotional. Needing support, I gripped my knees. "She was in the wrong place at the wrong time. It's all me, and the police don't even know it. Unless I confess. Would they believe me if I did? I can't let her take the fall. But I... don't know what to do."

Duncan came around to my side and rested a supportive hand on my back. "We'll address our problems one at a time."

"We? You're *one* of my problems."

"Are you still trying to rescue me?"

I straightened to say an exasperated, "*Yes*," to his face.

"You're a lovely woman, do you know that?"

"I may punch you."

He grinned. "And have my van towed?"

"This very instant, yes."

Jasmine watched us and glanced toward the door, like she didn't know if we were about to fight or have sex. Or both.

"Do you want me to give you privacy?" she asked.

"Just for a minute." I waved her out, though I didn't have fighting or sex on my mind. I wanted to ask Duncan a few things that he might be less likely to answer with an audience present. Half the time, he didn't even answer *me* when I questioned him.

"Not for long," Duncan told her. "I'm going on a hunt soon."

"The police..." I warned.

"Won't spot me. I'm swift, like a cheetah on the savannas of eastern Africa." He winked.

"Have you treasure hunted there?"

"Off the coast, yes."

After Jasmine stepped out, closing the door behind her, I said, "Do you know where Radomir and Abrams are now?"

"In one of their lairs, I'm certain." Duncan waved vaguely. Because he didn't know? Or he didn't want to tell me? Perhaps sensing the unspoken questions, he added, "I believe they know you're thinking vengeful thoughts about them. They haven't been staying in one place."

"I bet a lot of people have vengeful thoughts about them. They've enslaved you, had their thugs steal from my mom, shoot her and Emilio, and they're still staking out her property, like they think she's going to go on a vacation and they can sneak in and steal the medallion back."

"Then their itinerant choices make sense."

"I'm ready to kick their asses across the ocean. Maybe all the way to the savannas of eastern Africa."

"A few islands and continents in the way would make it difficult for you to punt them to that destination from here."

"I've got a strong free kick with a lot of clearance."

"Goodness, an American using football terms? I'm falling in love."

"My kids played soccer. We do have it as a sport over here."

"An improperly named sport."

"*Duncan.*" I gripped his hands. "This isn't the time for banter. If you don't know where they are..."

"Finding them won't help with this problem." He pointed his chin around the ransacked apartment.

"Oh, I know, but I want to free you. *Completely* free you." I looked at his scar and almost spoke about my plan to steal the control device, but what if they called him back and could coerce him into sharing whatever I told him in confidence? I hoped that couldn't happen, but I kept that plan to myself.

"I do also desire that," he said, his voice and eyes more serious. "But I'm here now. Let me help you."

"I thought you were hunting for the other wolf medallion."

"I was, but... as you requested, I came to help you put an end to your local crime problem. And anything else that I can assist with."

"Does that mean you're at a dead-end and can't find the medallion?"

"No. It means... I regretted that I disappointed you by going with Radomir's thugs."

"Oh." My snark faded, emotion tightening my throat.

"I have the sense that you've been disappointed a lot in your life," he said softly.

"Just the normal amount, I think."

"That's too much." Duncan hugged me.

I leaned into him, glad for his support, glad he'd come. He rested his hand on the back of my head, fingers gently stroking my hair.

"I *am* at a dead-end with the medallion," he said, his tone dry, "but that alone wouldn't have made me leave. I'm quite the determined treasure hunter."

"I have no doubt."

After a minute, Duncan lowered his arms. "I do wish to go after the men who robbed you. While the trail is still warm. If we don't get that sword back, you'll never get an opportunity to prong me with it."

"That *would* be lamentable."

The smiles we shared were more grim than pleased. We both knew that if I had to *prong* him, it would be because Radomir had control of him. The blade, with silver mixed into the alloy, would be the only thing that might allow me to stop a powerful bipedfuris.

My phone rang, and I grimaced. What now?

Duncan stepped back and removed his shirt while I turned to check it. I didn't recognize the number and waffled over whether to answer it. I didn't need more heavy breathers threatening me. Unless I could get clues from them about where they had taken my sword. As good a nose as Duncan had in wolf form, he would be out of luck if the men had gotten into a car or on their motorcycles, and I assumed they had.

"Hello?"

"Luna? It's Lorenzo."

Worry made me forget about the theft. "Is Mom okay?"

Duncan, naked and ready to shift, paused near the door.

"She is no worse than when you saw her. After you left, she decided to reach out to her Aunt Concetta."

"I didn't realize she had any aunts left alive."

"Concetta is ninety-eight and doesn't go on hunts or do much with the pack anymore, but your mother visits her in her home on the edge of town from time to time. Concetta has kept records for the family for decades and is the closest the Snohomish Savagers have to an archivist."

"Oh, Mom did mention her, just not by name."

"After you spoke of Duncan's quest, your mother asked Concetta about the lost medallion. She located a book that had been kept by the *last* archivist. It's handwritten in ink that has faded, but most of it is apparently still legible. In it, there is mention of a werewolf named Tommaso who left the pack after losing his mate. Sometime after his departure, what the archivist called the male version of the Medallion of Memory and Power was found to be missing. Nobody had any proof, but the archivist believed Tommaso stole it. Some of the pack members went after him to find out. They chased him up to the forests west of Mount Baker, but he disappeared near a lake up there. Neither he nor the medallion was ever seen again."

I rubbed the back of my neck. Since Duncan had been hunting along waterways in the forests in that direction, maybe Radomir and Abrams had found similar information.

"The archive just referenced *a lake*?" I asked. "No name?"

Since this was the rainy side of the mountains, there were

thousands of lakes about. Even saying west of Mount Baker didn't narrow it down as much as one would hope.

"That's all that the archivist recorded, yes. It may have been too small a lake to have a name. Or it may not *yet* have been named by anyone other than the native tribes. This all would have happened a hundred years or more ago."

"Okay. Tell her thanks for checking. I know Mom has other things on her mind."

"It would please her to see the matching medallion returned to the pack so that a rightful male alpha could wear it again and protect our kind."

"Yeah. I just wish... I'm sorry I don't have a solution for her more permanent problem." It would be wishful thinking and nothing more to imagine the medallions, once reunited, would have the power to cure her of her cancer. My experience thus far with these magical items was that the mushroom-shaped artifact in the wolf case was closer to something that might heal a person.

The thought made me look toward the doorway, reminded that I'd intended to ask Duncan if he could try changing next to the case and we could see if his bipedfuris aura could open it. What if we did that near Mom? Maybe her illness would activate the artifact inside and prompt it to heal her.

But Duncan had left, his clothes draped over the upturned couch. He'd only just arrived, and he was already off, trying to solve one of my problems. I hoped it didn't get him into trouble—more trouble.

"I don't think there's a solution for that," Lorenzo said sadly. "Even for those with magical blood, our time in the mortal realm must have an end."

"Unless you get bitten by a vampire." I tried to make my tone light, but the night had left me grim and somber.

"I do not believe your mother would care to be beholden to a vampire master. There are some prices that one doesn't pay, not even for immortality."

"Yeah. She doesn't even like being beholden to her nephews for fixing her internet."

"True," Lorenzo said fondly. "She's a proud woman."

"Did Mom mention where her aunt lives?" I wondered if I could learn more if I spoke to the woman personally. "Or if she has a phone number?"

"I believe Concetta eschews modern technology and that her home is off the grid."

"Does that mean no address?"

"Or modern amenities like power and plumbing."

"Are you telling me that my ninety-eight-year-old great aunt doesn't have an indoor toilet?"

"As I said, she eschews modern technology."

"Some modern technology is worth adopting. Like refrigeration, electricity, and toilets."

"Your mother says she can draw you a map to her home."

"Tell her that *she* could stand to adopt some modern technology too."

"I will relay your message."

"Thanks. I'll see what I can do about the medallion. If it would bring Mom peace to have it returned to the pack, I'd like to make that happen." Because my to-do list *needed* more entries.

At least I knew Duncan would help with that quest. What I didn't know was if, when we found the medallion, he would return it to the pack or he would hand it over to those who controlled him.

18

JASMINE WAS HELPING ME STRAIGHTEN THE MESS IN THE APARTMENT
when someone knocked on the door. I didn't sense anyone paranormal and grimaced, having an inkling of who it was before I
opened it. Yes, Dubois stood outside.

She started to speak, but her gaze snagged on the living room
behind me, the painted message visible from the door now that
we'd righted the couch and coffee table. We hadn't yet swept up
the broken plates and the rest of the carnage.

"Someone vandalized your apartment?" Dubois asked.

"While robbing it, yes. I'm missing—" I broke off, realizing
grenades probably weren't items one should admit to a police
officer that one had. Even a sword might be considered an odd
thing for a property manager to own. "A valuable family heirloom
is missing."

Surely, that sword had been *some* family's heirloom.

"I'm sorry," Dubois said, more sympathetic than I expected.
"This place is quite the magnet for crime, isn't it?"

Her gaze didn't seem suspicious, not of me, when she met my
eyes. That made me feel guilty. She suspected Rue, not I, was at

the center of everything. How could I set the record straight without landing myself in jail?

"Lately, some weird stuff has been happening, yes," I said.

"I'll see if I can get an unmarked patrol car down here to stake out the apartment complex for a while." Dubois waved toward the street beyond the parking lot.

"To stop robberies or to catch Rue when she comes back?"

"Maybe both." She smiled as she lifted a hand and departed.

Poor Rue. She never should have moved from her apartment in Seattle. All she'd had to deal with there were bible-toting grannies who'd called her a heathen while leaving graffiti on her door.

Even as I had the thoughts, I hoped she would return. As vile as her concoction had tasted, I could use a potion to help me find Radomir and Abrams. Of course, I didn't have any of their cells or *essences* to give to her.

"Too bad I didn't get a chance to bite them in their asses," I muttered, though I doubted Rue could collect a blood sample from my canines weeks after the fact. "Alas."

"Are you going to be okay?" Jasmine knelt by the wall, picking up shards of broken plates.

"Fine." I was about to step inside when the phone rang, Bolin's number popping up. Before answering, I checked to make sure the police officer had disappeared around the corner. "Hello?"

"Hi, Luna. I've made or acquired a few items that you may find useful."

"Great. I'll take whatever they are as soon as possible. I'm hoping to use them before long."

"Are you planning to infiltrate a fortress of evil?"

"As soon as I can find it."

While I stood with the door open, a salt-and-pepper-furred wolf trotted between two rhododendrons and toward my apartment. Duncan had returned.

He sniffed the air and looked in both directions along the walkway before changing back into his human form.

I leaned into my apartment to grab his clothes. "Did you learn anything useful about those men?"

"One doesn't shower regularly and left the scent of his powerful body odor on every grass blade between here and the street four blocks that way."

"Does that mean you found him, pounced on him, and forced him to say he would never bother me again?" Under other circumstances, I might have admired Duncan's physique as he pointed off toward the neighborhood, but I offered him his clothes, not wanting the female officer—or any officer—to return while he stood naked on my threshold.

"I followed the men to that street, but cars picked them up, and I wasn't able to track them farther."

"I was afraid of that."

"One had slashed a Z into a tree trunk near where they were picked up. I'll assume that means they're the ones who took the sword."

"A Z? Did he think he was Zorro?"

Duncan spread his arms, then accepted his underwear and bent to put it on. Three apartments down, a door opened, and one of the tenants stepped out, a twenty-something woman with a couple of canvas grocery totes in her hand. She glanced in our direction, gaped at Duncan's bare ass, and stepped back into her apartment, shutting the door firmly.

As I handed him his T-shirt, I wondered if naked Duncan was a more alarming thing to find on the walkway than furry Duncan.

"Guess I should have brought you inside before asking you to dress," I said.

He glanced over his shoulder, but the woman hadn't reappeared. Unless she was peering out her window.

"This won't take long." He took his trousers from me. "And

then... I'm yours insofar as seeking out crime goes. Or anything you wish really." After tugging up his trousers, he bowed deeply. "I'm here to lend my support in any capacity."

"Your fly is down."

"As I said, I'm here to lend my support in *any* capacity." He waggled his eyebrows at me.

I wished we could enjoy a night together—the moon knew I could use a release, and I would also be entertained by pillow talk with him afterward, I suspected.

"I don't suppose you'd like to visit my mother?" I asked instead of inviting him inside.

"Er, that's not the kind of support I imagined giving you. Don't you want to go after the sword thieves? You said you have a potion, right?"

The thought of swallowing another elixir prompted me to make a sour face. If I'd dwelled on the taste longer, I might have gagged.

"I need to talk to my mother, and I was hoping you could try opening that case to see... to see if the artifact inside could help her."

"I don't believe *I* have the power to open it."

"I'm fairly sure the taller, furrier version of you does."

His skeptical expression said he was less sure about that. "It might have been the poisoned sword that prompted the lid to release."

"I don't think so. Anyway, this will be a chance to experiment."

"I'll go, but you had better also bring a rattlesnake incase the bipedfuris isn't enough."

"Sure, we'll stop at the pet store in Monroe along the way."

He wiggled his fingers to dismiss my sarcasm. "I'm willing to do anything that might help your mother, but I want to remind you that I am more susceptible to the call of the control device when I'm in that form. After coming all the way back down here on foot, I would hate to be called away again when you need me."

"Maybe I can put a leash on you, and then you can lead me to them if they call." I'd meant it as a joke, but as soon as the words came out, I realized I *could* find Radomir if I could follow Duncan back when the control device summoned him.

"A leash?" He drew back in horror. "I'm not a pet poodle."

"No, the bipedfuris might not appreciate being constrained either." I tapped my chin thoughtfully. "What we really need is a GPS tracking collar."

"You're being serious."

"Actually, yeah. I might be able to follow you if I shifted into my lupine form, but if I had a tracking device, I could stay human and bring the truck. Or even your van. My truck had a little mishap and needs repairs."

Duncan lifted a hand to his neck, as if imagining the indignity of wearing a collar.

"They're not that bad," I offered. "I've seen them on hunting dogs. Other than the radio antenna sticking out like a black flag, they hardly look any different from normal collars." Never mind that the collar I'd seen had been fluorescent orange.

Duncan propped his fists on his hips. "I see what you're getting at, that you think following me back to Radomir would be a good idea—I don't agree with that, by the way—but my dignity as a man and a wolf will not allow me to wear a *collar*. How ignoble."

"Sacrifices must be made for true love." I smiled winsomely at him. Maybe this would be the time to promise him an invitation to my bedroom if he complied, but I would prefer our first time having sex not have any strings—or bargains—attached to it. Besides, I didn't want to manipulate him. This was just... important.

"Can you imagine how I'd feel if I led you to them, and you ended up shot? Fatally?"

"Don't worry. I have a plan." I almost told him that I wanted to steal the device but hesitated, again worried that he would either feel compelled to warn them or that they would get the gist of his thoughts through it and learn about my plans.

"Does it involve druid concoctions again?"

"It might. We need every advantage we can get."

"I'll go with you to see if we can help your mother, but I'm going collar-free." Duncan squinted at me.

"Are you absolutely positive? You'd look good in fluorescent orange. There's a Walmart in Monroe. Maybe they sell them."

"From what I've seen, they're hundreds of dollars. Is that in your budget?"

I grimaced. "No."

I took out my phone to research the collars and see if he was right. Looking a little smug, or at least satisfied, he folded his arms over his chest.

When the price came up on the collars, I grimaced again. "I'll just turn into a wolf to follow you."

"I thought you might decide on that."

"Will you let me?" I looked into his eyes, again debating whether to tell him everything. If he knew what I intended and that I would bring some potions and whatever else I could find to help, he might have more faith that I could handle Radomir and his thugs.

"*I* won't attempt to thwart you." Duncan flattened his hand on his chest. "I'm less certain about the bipedfuris. In that form, well, it's like in the wolf form. Sometimes, other instincts come into play, and he may see you as a threat if you're trailing along at his heels."

"I'll take my chances." I would follow from a distance, tracking by scent. If there was one thing I could be sure of, it was that the bipedfuris wouldn't have a pickup car waiting for him, at least not until he reached Radomir. And even if Radomir had the control device, I doubted he would pat the seat and invite an eight-foot-tall clawed and fanged werewolf to hop in next to him.

"As you wish, my lady." Duncan looked wistfully in the direction he'd tracked the men, looking like he would prefer to help me with my local problem instead of dealing with Radomir.

Too bad. I needed him to be free of control before I could fully trust him. I also needed to make sure those guys wouldn't harass my mother—or worse—anymore.

"If you don't need anything else tonight," Duncan said, "I'll reestablish my relationship with my van and my bed."

I sniffed. "Maybe reestablish a relationship with a shower too. You've been in the woods a long time."

Duncan pointed his nose toward his armpit. "Hm. Yes."

As he headed off, Bolin's voice came from my phone. "Luna?"

"Sorry." I lifted it to my mouth. "I didn't realize you were still on the line."

"I'm packing up your druid supplies to drop off."

I lowered my voice. "Can you find me an inexpensive GPS tracker too? Like something that could be used to find a car?"

Or a werewolf, I thought, but kept to myself.

"I don't have a spell book for GPS trackers," Bolin said dryly.

"I'm sure you can get one at a store on the way. I'll pay you back."

"Okay, fine. When do you need me to drop everything off?"

"You could come along with us once you've got *the* everything." I didn't know how I was going to manage this, but if I had to shift into wolf form to follow Duncan, I wouldn't be able to carry potions and grenades. Hell, *I* might have to wear the GPS tracker.

"You want me to come with you to a huge fortress of evil?"

"It might only be a small compound of dubious intent."

"I'll pass."

"Jasmine is going."

"I'll go," Bolin said. "When are we leaving?"

In the living room, Jasmine arched her eyebrows.

"Can you be here at dawn?" I was tempted to head out that very night, but Duncan needed some sleep.

"My phone says that's 7:56 am tomorrow."

In the winter, it was hard to get an early jumpstart on villains. "Yeah, work usually starts at eight, so it shouldn't be that hard for you to make it then, right?"

"I'll bring extra coffee."

"Good. I think we'll need it."

19

I woke up in the dark, the clock promising dawn wouldn't arrive for hours, but my heart was hammering. I'd heard—or *sensed*—something. Was that the roar of a motorcycle in the distance?

When I'd had allies around, I hadn't been that worried about the threats from the local thugs, but, alone in the night, with that painted message on the living room floor and my apartment still in disarray, unease crept into me. I might be a werewolf who'd learned to once again embrace her powers, but I was far from immortal. And, once again, I had no weapons with which to defend myself.

Another distant engine roar sounded. I didn't sense anyone magical nearby, but that didn't mean no danger lurked.

While hurrying to dress, I checked my phone to see if anyone had texted or called. The night before, Jasmine had gone home, but Duncan might be nearby, sleeping in his van. Knowing that bolstered me as I stuffed my feet into my shoes.

When I pushed aside the curtains, moonlight trickled through the window, wakening the magic in my blood. This problem might be better dealt with as a wolf, but after getting Rue in trouble, I hesitated to change into that form, at least here at home. Besides, I didn't know what had woken me. With busy streets nearby, roaring engines weren't *that* uncommon, even before dawn.

I texted Duncan to see if he was up, then slipped outside to listen for trouble. The shattering of glass greeted me, followed by a car alarm wailing.

Jaw clenched, I took two steps, intending to run to the parking lot to defend my territory as a human, but a surge of anger and annoyance with the ongoing situation swept into me. My skin heated from within as magic pricked at my nerves.

My first instinct was to try to tamp down the wolf again, but I was too frustrated. No, I was *pissed*.

Yanking the clothes I'd donned back off, I stepped back into my apartment. I kicked off my shoes, threw my pants and shirt on a chair, and left my phone on the table by the door. As I ran out and around the corner of the building, I dropped to all fours, fur sprouting as my magic turned me into a wolf.

Feeling protective, territorial, and irritated, I raced toward the parking lot. More glass broke. The car alarm continued wailing, the high-pitched noise hurting my sensitive ears, but I kept going. As I rounded the buildings and ran across the lawn toward the parking lot, gunshots fired.

Maybe that should have made me pause and approach slowly to assess the situation, but frustration continued to be my overriding emotion. It propelled me forward, making me run faster.

When I spotted the first man, one of the leather-wearing brutes who'd threatened me the day before, I sprinted toward him. He crouched behind a car with a gun in his hand, but he wasn't looking at me. He pointed it toward the side of the parking lot near the street, at a target I couldn't yet see.

Duncan? The one I wished to be my mate?

His rolling den was in that direction.

Worried he had come out and was the man's target, I sprang.

My snarls must have been audible over the wailing alarm because my target turned before firing. Eyes bulging, he whipped his gun around to point at me. Faster than he, I struck his chest with my body as my jaws snapped for his throat.

He jerked his arm up quickly enough to protect his vulnerable neck. I sank my teeth into that limb instead, biting deep. Crying out, he stumbled back and struck a car as he tried to pull free.

We tumbled to the pavement together, and I released his arm, but only so I could aim for a more vital target. Big and strong for a human, he flailed wildly, kicking and shoving at me. I didn't manage to reach his throat, but I clamped down on his shoulder. His collarbone snapped under my powerful jaws. He screamed.

Elsewhere in the parking lot, more shots fired from several different positions. His allies.

My instincts told me I would be in danger if I stayed in one place. Reluctantly, I released the man, though the savage part of my magic that I couldn't control was trying to rear up, trying to get me to finish him off.

The human world kept intruding upon my sanctuary and those I protected. I wanted to end the threat once and for all.

As I backed away, staying between the cars for cover, the gunshots continued. A bullet slammed into a car, but it was many yards away. That surprised me. Wasn't I the target of these intruders? No, I remembered Duncan. I could sense him on the far side of the parking lot. He must have drawn their ire.

I loped down the walkway and around a set of large metal boxes, trying to circle the men to reach Duncan without crossing through the gunfire. When I glimpsed him, also in wolf form with his fangs bared, he faced a big brute in dark clothing. As I raced toward them, intending to fight at Duncan's side against the threat, the man fired at him. Immediately, the intruder jerked his handgun to the side to shoot over a car at someone else.

In the distance, sirens wailed, a new obnoxious noise in addition to the car alarm. My human side would have understood its significance, but, as a wolf, I knew only that the loud sounds hurt my ears. I longed to escape this place and run into the woods.

Duncan sprang upon the gunman while our foe was busy shooting at someone else. I'd almost reached Duncan's battle, intending to help, when two motorcycle riders roared in from the side and turned down the lane. Their headlamps flashed blindingly in my eyes.

With little time to react, only instinct guided me. I leaped for one of the men, clearing the handlebars and slamming into his chest. I knocked him backward, and he yelled and flailed as we flew to the pavement. Unguided, his motorcycle smashed into a car. I landed on top of the man, his breath whooshing out as his back hit the pavement hard. That didn't keep him from yanking a gun free and pointing it at my face. Before he could fire, I bit his hand. Hard.

He cried out and dropped the gun.

Sensing another threat behind me, I spun. The other rider had jumped off to face us. Instead of pointing a gun at me, he lifted his palm and aimed a magical oval that glowed purple in my direction. Five silver rings on his fingers were linked to it and each other by slender chains, and sparks flowed between them and glinted in the oval. Mesmerized, I paused to gape at it, momentarily forgetting the fight.

The sparks intensified, flowing from the rings and into an oval-shaped gem. I took a step toward the device.

A growl from farther up the car lane broke into the trance I hadn't meant to enter. I crouched, realizing I was still in danger, and prepared to spring at the man. But the purple glow brightened, and a knife of pain erupted in my skull, as if something had struck me between the eyes.

The intensity of it shocked me; the agony made me cry out.

"Shoot her," someone said.

The man I'd knocked down found his hands and knees and crawled toward the gun he'd dropped.

I struggled to move, to stop the man—or, better, to attack the person with the pain creator. But my limbs responded jerkily, that purple glow not only driving agony into my skull but affecting my ability to move.

Abruptly, something hit the man from behind. Duncan.

Our foe pitched forward, dropping his arm. The magical tool didn't fall out of his grip, but when his arm dropped, his palm no longer faced me and the pain lessened.

I whirled, snapping at my nearest foe, the one I'd bitten earlier. He'd picked up his gun with his left hand. I sank my fangs into that one too, determined to end the threat that he and that weapon represented. My head throbbed, the pain still there, but that only made my bite harder and more effective. The man screamed, released his weapon, and jerked away. I let go, and he rolled to the side, then leaped to his feet and ran.

A gunshot fired from the lane next to ours, a bullet slamming into a car window not far from Duncan. He'd been about to bite the man with the magical tool, but he leaped away instead, doubtless fearing more bullets.

These weren't made from silver, not that I could sense, but that didn't mean they couldn't hurt us. Enough mundane bullets striking in the right spots could *kill* a werewolf.

Duncan leaped behind a car for cover, and I rushed to join him. The man with the magical tool took advantage of our distraction and ran away.

More guns fired, but the bullets didn't land near us. Had the first been a stray round? Who else out here could our enemies be shooting at?

On the other side of the parking lot, a woman yelled in pain. One of the tenants that I protected?

Snarling, I left the protection of the car and ran to check. Duncan didn't hesitate to lope beside me, his powerful strides matching mine.

We ran around cars and into another lane where a man lay on the pavement, not moving. Unlike the thugs dressed in black baggy clothes, he wore different attire, dark and crisp with buttons and metal bits, but the significance was lost on my wolf mind.

A woman in matching attire knelt behind a car with flashing lights on top. She was not one of the tenants, one I felt compelled to protect, but there was something familiar about her. My human side knew her. Was she the one who'd yelled in pain?

As Duncan and I approached, two men fired toward the vehicle the woman knelt behind. When they paused, she leaned out and fired back. It was difficult for her because she gripped her shoulder. Was she injured? The scent of blood hung in the air, blood from many sources.

Without consulting each other, Duncan and I ran toward the men shooting at the woman. Maybe he also recognized her and believed we should assist her. Oh, but how I longed to run into the woods, to leave this place and all this noise. The sirens I'd noted before had grown louder. Closer.

The men behind the car noticed us charging at them, but they didn't have time to switch their targets. Running fast on strong legs, we reached them before they could fire at us, and our jaws tore into their flesh.

They shouted words at each other—orders to depart? With my wild instincts controlling me, I wasn't certain. Unlike the man who'd hurt me, they held no magical weapons.

Duncan and I tore their firearms from their grips, crushing the metal with our powerful jaws and flinging the weapons away. With his great strength, Duncan also flung one of the *men* away, sending him crashing into a nearby car. When his head struck the door, he didn't rise again.

Our other foe backed away, his hands bloody as he raised them. In surrender?

I crouched, tempted to continue attacking. These men had assailed my territory before. They refused to learn to leave it alone, and if they could not learn, they should be punished for their obtuseness.

But movement to the side distracted me. The woman had come out from behind the car. She gripped a handgun as she stared at me.

I tensed, not certain if she would prove an ally or turn into another enemy.

Duncan brushed my shoulder and pointed his snout toward the woods. The cars with the wailing sirens were turning into the lot, lights flashing. Yes, leaving would be best. This was too much for a wolf's senses, and I... I had an inkling that something significant had happened, that this woman had seen us change and knew what we were. Nothing good would come of that. Any moment, she might try to shoot us.

After giving me a significant look, Duncan ran between two cars, then angled across the lawn and toward the woods. I followed him into the vestiges of the night.

20

"Luna?"

The distant call woke me, and I blinked in confusion. I was not in bed. Instead, I shivered as frosty fern fronds came into focus scant inches from my eyes. The only reprieve from the cold was a warm body pressed against my back.

"Luna?" That was Bolin. "Are you out here?"

He stood at the edge of the woods, shining a flashlight beam around the trees, and I remembered where I was—and what had happened. And I groaned.

"Does that mean we're *not* out here?" Duncan murmured, stirring against my back.

After the fight in the parking lot, we'd hidden in the woods in our wolf forms, vaguely aware that we should avoid the human woman and her allies that had arrived. But, despite peering in our direction a few times, they hadn't come out to search for us. They'd been dealing with the death of one of their officers, and they'd also dragged one of the injured intruders to an ambulance. This time, neither Duncan nor I had lost ourselves completely to the savagery of our magic, and we hadn't killed any of our enemies. But it wouldn't matter. The female officer had seen us fighting, and she might have seen me change. I feared she would figure out that we were werewolves—and that we'd been responsible for the previous deaths.

"I came *more* than four minutes early for the dawn excursion," Bolin called a little tartly as he swung the flashlight around again. The police must have departed before he'd arrived because he wasn't keeping his voice down; his tone didn't warn that I might be in trouble. He didn't yet know...

"Dawn excursion?" Duncan asked.

"I recruited help to storm Radomir's castle—wherever it is." I pushed myself to my bare feet, brushing fir needles and dirt off my skin.

"And you're not in your apartment," Bolin added. "*Or* Duncan's van. I checked."

"I'm here," I called back, "but meet me at the office, okay? I need to get..."

"Breakfast?" Duncan suggested. "Supplies?"

"Dressed. I doubt my young intern wants to be subjected to my naked mom bod."

"Your mom bod is fabulous and in wonderful shape."

"Were you examining it while I slept?"

"No, I was sleeping while you slept, but I enjoyed being snuggled up to it, and you've been naked often enough in my presence that I've imprinted the memory. I believe I mentioned that."

"You did."

Bolin swung his flashlight—maybe that was only his phone's light—in our direction, but he jerked it away when the beam illuminated us. He lowered it to the ground and looked away.

"I'll wait at my car." Bolin turned and walked toward the parking lot.

"See, he was traumatized by our middle-aged nudity." I looked around the apartment complex before stepping out of the trees. A cloudy dawn was lightening the grounds.

"My nudity is magnificent, not traumatizing."

"You've a high opinion of yourself." I led the way toward my apartment.

"I occasionally look in a mirror. I see what I see."

"I wouldn't have guessed you could fit a mirror in that van."

"It flips down from the visor above the driver's seat."

"I have that same kind of mirror in my truck. It's only good for seeing your eyes. Maybe whether you have nose hairs that need to be trimmed."

"Nothing on me needs to be trimmed. I keep myself impeccably groomed."

I glanced back as I opened the door to my apartment, though I pointedly looked at his face, not the rest of his body. That didn't keep him from posing in an invitation to admire his physique. Like a magazine model, he put one hand behind his head and one on his hip as he tilted it for a shameless display.

A damp leaf was stuck to the back of his thigh. I plucked it off. "I've never seen someone so eager to have their trimmage looked at."

"Only by certain people." Duncan stepped past me to enter the apartment first, peering around to check for trouble.

"You wouldn't pose for Bolin, then?"

"Certainly not. *He* wouldn't be impressed."

"I barely even looked."

"And yet... you're impressed. I'm certain."

"Yes, I'm on the verge of swooning right now."

Nobody had come through to clean my apartment in my absence. Too bad. It also wasn't cordoned off by warning tape and staked out by police officers, so that was something.

While I showered and dressed, Duncan made sandwiches with bread and deli ham in the fridge. Lots of sandwiches. Either he was hungry, or he was making extra for Bolin and me. I didn't comment on his nude food preparation. One couldn't be picky when someone else was making lunch.

In the bedroom, I grabbed a towel and plucked the wolf case out of the heat duct under the floor. After all we'd been through together, it still zapped me, its defenses active. At least the towel somewhat insulated my hand.

On my way to the kitchen, I looked sadly at the corner where I'd leaned the sword that I hadn't stopped thinking of as *his*, despite Duncan giving it to me as a gift. Its absence made me feel bleak, like I'd failed by allowing myself to be robbed. After I freed Duncan from Radomir's control, I would come back and find it. I couldn't stomach the idea of taking that awful elixir of location again, but the motorcycle thugs came by regularly. They couldn't live that far from here. I only hoped they hadn't sold the sword at a pawn shop. I also worried about that magical artifact the man had used on me.

All along, I'd thought of the local thugs as annoying but normal and not as dangerous as those who courted the paranormal. But if they had acquired magical items, they could prove more deadly going forward.

"Do you want to shower before we go, Duncan?" I waved to the bathroom.

"Another time, I would accept that offer, but your interns await."

"Interns? I only have one."

"Your niece knocked on the door. She mentioned working for you to earn your heartfelt recommendation for her résumé."

"I told her she's already got that. We even discussed fancy fonts with curlicues to convey that heartfeltness."

Duncan spread his hand. "She believes she must do more."

I *had* invited Jasmine to come along, so I didn't say more. When offered a sandwich, I accepted it and also raided the kitchen for coffee, bottles of water, and two salami logs—in case I needed to bribe any family members to get in to see Mom. Once packed, we headed toward the parking lot, Duncan finally hopping into his van to put on new clothes. As a werewolf herself, Jasmine wouldn't have thought anything of him answering the door naked, but I was glad nobody else had come by the apartment.

"As I told you, my weapons were taken in the robbery," I said when he rejoined me. "Do you have anything we could use?"

"For the discussion with your mother?" Duncan asked. "Is it likely to get spirited?"

"You know what else I hope will happen while we're visiting my mom." I held up the wolf case.

Duncan sighed but didn't say he wouldn't change. The wariness in his eyes did make me wonder if he knew something I didn't know—and wouldn't like. Such as that he might, in biped-furis form, mercilessly attack someone who followed him?

"You lost the grenades as well as the sword, right?" Duncan asked. "I'm afraid I haven't had a chance to buy more."

"Yeah, sorry. I do still have the magnet you gave me."

"Well, those come in handy. That's good."

"I used it to open a barred garage door."

"Oh?" His eyes gleamed with pleasure. "That's excellent, my lady."

"Some people would chastise a woman for breaking and entering."

"I'm not that kind of a people. One never knows where treasures might be located."

"I found freezers and shipping containers."

"Were there treasures *in* them?"

"Smelly mushrooms."

"Maybe you'll find something better the next time you use my magnet."

"I'll cross my fingers." The control device I hoped to steal came to mind.

My phone rang as we walked out to the parking lot, and I paused, my son's name popping up.

"Hi, Austin." I strove for a casual tone, but I'd been worried about him since we'd learned Radomir had factories—or mushroom farms—not far from where he and his buddies were staying for their trip. "Everything okay?"

"Why, did you hear something?"

"Uhm, no."

"You didn't check Oakley's socials, did you?"

"I can't even remember which one of your friends Oakley is."

"Ms. Valens," came a young male voice from the background. "I'm offended."

An image of a freckled red-haired kid came to mind to match the voice. "Okay, I remember Oakley, but I don't follow him on the social-media sites, no." I kept from scoffing aloud at the idea.

"Okay," Austin said. "Then my lesson went *amazing* yesterday. I'm hardly bruised at all."

That prompted laughter in the background from more than one mouth.

"As long as you didn't break any bones," I said.

"I didn't."

"The *tree* broke bones," Oakley said. "Or branches. When Aussie hit it."

Duncan had been walking at my side but stopped to wait, his eyebrows raised.

"I told you to avoid trees and cliffs," I told Austin.

"There aren't any cliffs on the Heather run. But there are trees everywhere. It's a forested mountain, you know."

"Are you okay?"

"Fine. I just called to say... Well, the guys said... I mean, it's okay if you come up for Christmas morning if you want."

Even if I doubted Austin and his gaggle of freshman friends wanted a mother there, the invitation touched me. I hadn't meant to make him feel guilty enough to ask his buddies if I could join them, but the fact that he had, probably risking ridicule to do so... meant something.

"Thanks. I've got some work stuff keeping me busy, so I might not be able to make it, but we'll do our own celebration when you get back, okay?"

"Oh, yeah, that would be great." Austin sounded more relieved than disappointed.

I was glad I'd read him right.

"Are you sure you don't want to come, Ms. Valens?" came a call from the background. "Aussie needs someone to rub Icy Hot on his bruised bits."

"Shut up, Davenport. You almost hit that tree too."

"*Almost* is not the same as *smacked* right into it. With your entire body. Like you wanted to make love to it."

Austin sighed. "I gotta go, Mom. Bye."

I said goodbye and hung up.

"Am I work?" Duncan asked dryly. "Or were you referring to Radomir?"

"Oh, you're *absolutely* work."

We crossed the parking lot and found Bolin and Jasmine standing near his SUV. Bolin plucked nervously at the hem of his shirt while Jasmine poked at her phone screen, neither of them looking at each other or speaking. It was hard to imagine Bolin successfully serenading Jasmine. Had he even managed to mumble a *good morning*?

When our eyes met, Bolin looked away, though I was now fully clothed, even wearing a parka in the nippy morning air.

"Do you want me to drive?" Bolin waved at his Mercedes SUV, though he also looked warily at the missing fender and smashed rear end of my truck. "Four people won't fit in there unless they ride in the back, and it's... been violated."

"That's one way to put it," I murmured.

"We can go in my van," Duncan said. "It's sturdy, and I've missed it."

"How does it navigate during low-speed car chases on old logging roads full of potholes?" I asked.

"Like a champ," Duncan said. "Remember, it has off-road tires."

"It's not armored," Jasmine said. "Aunt Luna's enemies have an armored SUV with electrified door handles."

"If we come face to face with her enemies, I'll deal with them another way. With the power of my physique, not my automobile."

"At least it's trimmed," I murmured, heading toward his van.

"I knew you were impressed."

"Oh, wait," Bolin blurted before following us.

He unlocked his SUV and pulled a violin case out of the back seat.

"Are you going to thump my aunt's heinous enemies with that?" Jasmine asked.

"Not exactly." Bolin managed a quick smile, but he didn't meet her gaze.

This might be a long car ride.

"Did you bring *me* anything?" I asked Bolin, reminded of why I'd invited him.

"Yes." He dug into a pocket, pulled out a felt pouch, and placed it in my hand. Two compressed-powder spheres followed.

"Do those work like the others?" I resisted the urge to call them bath bombs again. He'd found that insulting.

"Yes, they're also Orbs of Entanglement." Bolin nodded firmly, then patted another pocket. "I reserved a couple for myself, should self-defense be necessary."

"So I should send the bad guys straight at you?" I asked.

That prompted an aggrieved look. Bolin glanced at Jasmine, probably reminding himself why he'd volunteered for something so far out of his wheelhouse, then hugged his violin case to his chest.

"I'll send them at Duncan," I said.

"Good. I'm sure he'll appreciate them more." Bolin nodded, then held up a finger and pulled out a small metallic circle.

Having an inkling of what it was, I drew him aside and stood so that we would block Duncan's view.

"Is that the GPS tracker?" I whispered.

"Yeah. It's magnetic, so you can stick it to a car."

"What about to a werewolf?"

"Uhm, not unless they've been drinking water from ferrous pipes recently."

I got the joke but didn't laugh. How would I convince Duncan to carry a magnetic tracking device? It was less obvious—and dignity-destroying—than a collar, but I had a feeling we would have to go with my backup plan. I would have to change into a wolf and follow Duncan, somehow remembering to carry the tracker in my mouth so Bolin and Jasmine could trail us with our gear.

Bolin glanced toward Duncan, who was waiting for us by his van.

"He's a nonferrous werewolf, I'm pretty sure," I said.

"Well, if you can figure out a way to stick that to your target, I've got it set up with an app on my phone."

"Okay. Thanks." Not wanting to rouse Duncan's suspicions by delaying longer, I tucked the tracker into the bag of items that Bolin had given me.

"To your mother's cabin?" Duncan asked when we were all in the van, me in the passenger seat with my knees to my chest and my shoes propped on boxes and bags where one's feet would normally go. Bolin and Jasmine found places to sit in the back.

I nodded. "It's where all hunts begin."

He gave me a wary this-is-a-bad-idea look again, but he put the van in gear and didn't object to my plan.

21

Since we were taking Duncan's Roadtrek, I didn't object to him driving, but when we were cruising along on the highway, and he leaned forward, grunting and grabbing his forehead, I second-guessed that choice. His scar lit up, a faint orange glow seeping out between his fingers.

I lifted a hand, worried I would have to take the wheel to keep the van from veering off the road.

Duncan clenched his jaw, squeezed his fingers into a fist, and lowered his hand. He seemed to get control of himself, though the glow continued to be noticeable.

"Is that going to be a problem?" I asked quietly.

Outside, dark gray clouds had rolled in, and fat snowflakes wafted down. If they started sticking, the roads would turn slick. A distracted driver would be a bad idea.

"He's calling me back. *Trying* to call me back."

"That didn't quite answer my question."

"It's what you wanted, isn't it?" Duncan frowned and returned both hands to the wheel, but his peevishness didn't last long.

"Sorry. Having to fight it makes me testy." He managed a quick smile for me before returning his focus to the highway—and keeping Radomir from affecting him, I had no doubt.

"It *is* what I was hoping for today, but not while you're driving, ideally. Unless the call would prompt you to roll us right into Radomir's garage."

"With the wolf case that he's been trying to steal nestled in the glove compartment?"

"It's nestled between my feet. I looked in your glove compartment, but I wouldn't be able to fit anything else in there. You have it stuffed with tools."

"Stuffed. Really. The tools are neatly organized."

"They're covered with dust, and there was a Queen *tape* in the mix. Does your van even have a tape player?"

"*I* have a tape player. For nostalgia."

"Back there among the underwater demolitions?"

"No, you don't keep your music in your armory." Duncan looked at me like I didn't know anything, though a more relaxed smile accompanied the expression. Maybe the magic trying to compel him to Radomir's lair had faded. If so, I had no doubt the guy would try again. "It's in the little cabinet for bathroom supplies."

"Silly me," I murmured. "I'd assumed extra rolls of toilet paper would go in there."

"When you live in a van, there's no room for extra rolls of toilet paper. You have to be conservative."

"But using storage space for eighties cassette tapes is okay."

"One has to prioritize."

"I might prioritize bathroom necessities over that, but it's your van."

"They *do* sound like a married couple, don't they?" came a whisper from the back. Jasmine.

If I hadn't had enhanced hearing, I might not have heard the words over the rumble of the engine and the road noise.

"I told you," Bolin replied softly. "Luna keeps saying they're not, you know, but they *act* like they're, you know."

"Having sex?"

"Yeah." Bolin's cheeks were probably red.

Duncan, whose hearing was as keen as mine, slanted me a look. "I thought when your intern brought the violin case, he would play music, not gossip about us."

"I think he's going to use it to thump bad guys." I didn't mention the serenading plans. Jasmine also had keen hearing, and I didn't want to spoil the surprise in case Bolin went through with it.

"Some druids have magical staffs they use as weapons," Duncan said.

"He's kind of a neophyte."

"I can hear you two," Bolin said sourly.

Apparently, it was okay for them to talk about us but not vice versa.

"It's not a very big van," I said.

"Tell me about it." Two thunks sounded as Bolin opened and closed a cabinet door. "There's SCUBA gear stored with the crackers and Spam."

"Just don't ask about extra rolls of toilet paper," I said.

That earned me another look from Duncan. "I was going to tell you what I know about the location of the other missing medallion, so we could compare notes, but you've been teasing me a lot this morning. I might withhold."

"If you knew the location, you wouldn't have been battling a robot dog over a druid doohickey."

"Radomir had a list of possible places he wanted me to check. That was one."

"Druid doohickey?" Bolin asked.

"A medallion with a tree on it," Duncan said. "I had to give it to Radomir. He wasn't that pleased, since I'd implied I had the *wolf* medallion, but it was valuable enough that he said a collector would be interested, so he forgave me."

"A collector?" I asked. "Not him or Abrams?"

"A collector. Abrams and Radomir are only after werewolf artifacts."

"But you have no idea why?"

We'd already discussed this, so I didn't expect a new answer, but Duncan didn't always tell me everything. Maybe something pertinent would slip out this time.

"Werewolves are magnificent." He lifted his chin.

"You're not going to bring up trimming again, are you?"

"No. That's a personal choice. Not all werewolves keep themselves tidy. Some are quite..."

"*Au naturel*?" I suggested.

"Indeed." Duncan took the turn off the main highway to head through town and toward the forested lands that held my mother's cabin. As we traveled into the foothills of the mountains, the ground grew snowy. At the higher elevation, it had been sticking for a while. "Radomir had a map with lakes, ponds, streams, and rivers circled. He'd come across some rumors or lore about the medallion last being seen near a waterway."

"Mom's aunt said a lake specifically."

Duncan nodded. "That's possible. Back in the days before goggles and SCUBA gear, a relatively deep body of water might have been considered a decent place to hide something."

"So if the wayward wolf who stole it from my pack knew he was being pursued, he might have thrown the medallion in?"

"Even if those trying to retrieve it could sense the magic," Duncan said, "diving down and getting it out would have been difficult."

"It would have been difficult for the thief to get it out too."

"Maybe, at that point, he simply didn't want to be caught with it and didn't hope to find it again. Or he was naive about his ability to do so in a lake."

"I guess it's a good thing you've got a van full of SCUBA equipment."

"Absolutely."

"You should probably let Radomir call you to his garage, so you'll have easy access to it." I waggled my eyebrows. That would be a lot easier than trekking after a bipedfuris with a GPS tracker in my mouth.

"With you and your well-armed brute squad—" Duncan glanced back at the violin case, "—ready to jump out and attack him when we arrive?"

"Naturally."

Duncan gave me a longer look. "Are you planning to kill him? Both of them? So they can't harass your mother again?"

"I'm not a murderer." I winced, well aware that I *had* killed before. But that had been in self-defense, damn it. "And I'm more worried about keeping them from harassing *you*." That wasn't entirely true. I *did* want to end the threat to my mother, ideally to the whole pack. "From controlling you anyway."

"I'd prefer they not harass *or* control me," Duncan said wistfully.

"Good. I've wondered how hard you're fighting them... or at least their quest."

"As I admitted, this quest isn't unappealing, but I would be happier searching by your side, with the intent to give the medallion to *you*, rather than having anything to do with *them*."

"I believe you. I'm going to make sure *they* leave the picture." I set my jaw and looked out the window as we drove deeper into the forestlands, snow dusting the boughs of evergreens.

Duncan looked like he wanted to ask more, but he fell silent as we continued up the road. A for-sale sign that hadn't been there before caught my eye. It was past the beaver pond and not far from Mom's property, though it was on the opposite side of the road.

"Is that a bite taken out of that sign?" Bolin asked from the back.

"That happened the day it went up," Jasmine said. "The *night*. Some of the pack members like to dissuade people from buying and developing the land out here, and normal humans aren't dissuaded by the usual ways wolves mark territory."

"Does that mean one of your family members..."

"They've been known to pee on such real-estate signs, yes."

"I can see where humans wouldn't really notice that."

"Yeah, they're obtuse. You should see what one of my cousins did to a land-development notification a little ways back down the road."

"I'm not sure I want to imagine," Bolin said.

"The pack knows those lands don't belong to us, not in the legal, human sense of these things, but when you're in wolf form, you know how it is." Jasmine shrugged. Maybe she'd forgotten that Bolin wasn't one of our kind and *wouldn't* know that. "You think like a wolf, not someone aware of property lines. At least the family still owns quite a bit of land back here. Your mom specifically, I think, Luna. My parents mentioned that once. Apparently, more than one real estate developer has approached your mom about selling. None of those meetings went well for them."

"Were signs not the only thing bitten?" I asked.

"I think not."

When we turned into Mom's driveway, I sensed other werewolves about. None of the family had attacked me since Augustus had passed and his cronies had been asked to leave the pack, but I gripped the case through the towel. Others would sense its magic and be curious. They might be *more* than curious.

Only a couple of cars were parked in Mom's driveway. At the moment, there weren't any werewolves, naked or otherwise, snoozing around the cabin. With the temperatures dropping, and snow blanketing the ground, maybe the family wasn't inclined toward that hobby.

After Duncan parked his van, I opened the door and rearranged the towel to fully hide the case.

"Should we... stay inside?" Bolin peered out one of the van's side windows, one that wasn't blocked by equipment, and into the trees beside the long driveway.

I didn't see anyone but sensed a couple of pack members in that direction, likely in wolf form. Was that Rocco? He was a young upstart who might interfere.

"You'll be fine here," Jasmine said.

"Because you'll protect me?" Bolin asked.

"Because the family hates Duncan and focuses their animosity on him."

"I thought that was only Luna's cousins." Duncan slid his keys into his pocket. "And they're gone now."

"Oh, everyone gets concerned when you're around," Jasmine told him. "It's the uber powerful old-worldness that clings to you."

"I should have taken you up on your offer to shower this morning," Duncan said to me.

As if that would wash away his power.

Still, I smiled and said, "Yes," before getting out, a half inch of snow squishing under my shoes. It dusted the ferns and rocks to either side of the driveway, though it hadn't yet filled in under the trees.

None of the loitering wolves intercepted me on the way to Mom's front door. They were probably here as protection in case Radomir's men showed up.

Inside, Lorenzo sat at the table, looking worried.

"Are things... okay?" I asked him, holding the door open for Duncan to follow me in.

"Last night, while many of us were gone hunting, one of the

enemy's trucks came by and presumed to come halfway up the driveway. A magical security device blew out one of its tires and knocked the fender into the trees, and the driver retreated. The vehicle parked down the road until several of us returned home. Also..." Lorenzo looked toward the open door to Mom's bedroom. "Your mother didn't snip or snark at me this morning."

"And that's... unusual?" I guessed, knowing my mother's personality well, despite my long absence.

"It is. I would have deserved it. During the hunt, I was distracted and failed to bring down a buck." Lorenzo shook his head sadly.

"Do you want *me* to snark at you?" I looked toward the front door.

Duncan stood at the threshold and hadn't yet presumed to come in.

"It wouldn't be the same." Lorenzo considered the towel I held, the case bundled within, occasionally zapping me through the thick material.

"It's an artifact. I'm not sure if we told you about it."

Mom might have told him about it. I unwrapped the towel enough to show him the ivory case, the fanged wolf head carved into the lid. I also shared the translation and that we'd seen it heal Duncan after he'd been poisoned.

"It may not do anything for Mom," I warned when a glimmer of hope entered Lorenzo's eyes, "but I doubt it'll hurt to try."

"It felt quite delightful, actually." Duncan rested his hand on his side in the spot where the poisoned sword had slashed him.

"You're welcome to make the attempt." Lorenzo nodded toward Mom's room. "Assuming she'll let you."

"She might snark about it," I said.

"I *hope* so." He smiled wistfully.

I waved for Duncan to follow me but realized that Lorenzo and the others would sense it when Duncan changed into the powerful bipedfuris form. Would the whole pack run in, believing my mother threatened?

"If you sense something," I told Lorenzo, "Mom won't be in trouble. We need to summon the magic of the artifact."

I looked at Duncan, hoping that was the truth, that Mom wouldn't be in any danger. I didn't *think* so. When Duncan had turned in my presence, without the control device nearby, he had defended me.

"They can't make me attack anyone from this far away," he said quietly, as if reading my mind.

"What do you mean by *sense something*?" Lorenzo asked.

I held up the case. "It only responded before—opened to let the artifact inside come out—when a werewolf was present. A real bipedfuris." I extended a hand toward Duncan, certain Lorenzo knew by now that he could change into that form.

The flat, cool look that Lorenzo adopted implied he knew... and wasn't thrilled about it. Maybe Mom hadn't told him that she wanted Duncan to be my mate and produce powerful offspring.

"Perhaps we should have stopped at that pet store for a rattlesnake," Duncan murmured to me when Lorenzo's cool look continued.

"I was being sarcastic about that. You can't buy rattlesnakes at pet stores."

"Something else venomous then?"

"I don't think so. They don't want parents to sue them when scorpions sting their little kids."

Lorenzo looked back and forth between us. What he took from our banter, I didn't know, but he gestured toward Mom's bedroom door. "Do what you must. I trust Umbra will let you know if she objects."

"Oh, I'm positive."

I walked to her bedroom, knocking lightly on the open door. "Mom? Are you awake?"

"Awake enough to sense your artifact and your old-world werewolf." She rested in bed, propped against pillows, a book closed beside her.

Her left hand was still bandaged. That was odd. Werewolves usually healed quickly—our kind were known for that. Even if age and illness had diminished her power, I wouldn't have expected a wound she received several days ago to still need bandaging.

More, there were not one but two chains around her neck. The witch talisman and... was she wearing the female version of the family medallion under her shirt? Because she felt the need for more protection? Or hoped their power would help her feel better?

"That's pretty awake," was all I said, forcing a smile though worry knotted my stomach.

"I sensed him before you turned up the driveway. He's like the sun."

"Radiant, warm, and delightful?" Duncan stepped into the doorway and bowed to Mom, though he didn't call her *my lady*. That probably would have elicited the snark Lorenzo had missed.

"Blinding," Mom said. "But since you're using your power to help my daughter, I won't object to it. Or to you." She gazed between us.

Willing her not to bring up fertility, I raised the wolf case. "We want to try something."

I wanted to try something, I amended silently. Duncan kindly did not object to my phrasing, though he did look pensively out the window. His scar wasn't glowing at the moment. I was glad. That might have worried Mom, and I would have had to explain it.

Her gaze lingered on his forehead when she looked him over. Maybe she sensed something magical—something *binding*—in the scar even without the glow.

"That is the artifact you've spoken of?" was all she asked.

"Yes. When it opened at a timely moment, it healed a poisoned wound." I hesitated to describe in detail the night I'd battled and killed my own cousin—even if Augustus had been a douche, he'd been family. But I wanted her to know why I'd brought the case, so I explained those final moments, the way the mushroom-shaped artifact inside had saved Duncan's life. "There's nothing in the translation on the case that suggests it would cure a terminal illness, but... why not try?"

I forced a smile, though tears threatened, brought up by thinking of Mom's end, of what would happen if the artifact couldn't do anything. Not for the first time, I regretted all the years I'd stayed away. Maybe she wouldn't have accepted me as I'd been, but I'd missed knowing her as an adult.

"I admit when you walked in holding an artifact, I hoped it was the lost family medallion, the male version of mine." Mom's hand strayed to the chains around her neck. "Did Lorenzo tell you all about what Aunt Concetta said?"

"He did, and we are indeed on a quest to find the medallion. Duncan already battled a robot dog and bats with glowing bellies in an attempt to locate it."

"The bats didn't bother me," he said.

"They dive-bombed me," I told him. "And did I tell you how some of Radomir's thugs stayed behind in that tank-SUV to try to run Jasmine and me off the road?"

His eyebrows rose. "I did wonder what happened to your truck, but I'd assumed it was the motorcycle hoodlums who keep assailing your home."

"We do get assailed a lot there." I sighed, reminded that I'd left *that* problem unfinished. Dubois might even now be knocking on my door.

Mom cleared her throat, probably not caring about the assailing of a human apartment complex.

"You will become the bipedfuris in an attempt to open the case?" she asked Duncan.

There weren't any tears in her eyes. Maybe she'd come to terms with her fate. If she'd hoped to end her life the night she'd picked a fight alone with a bear, she must have.

"We think that's what triggered it," I said.

"You can take that form at will? Even with the full moon not near?" Mom waved toward the window, more focused on Duncan than me or the case. "And no threat leaping upon you?"

"It's more easily bestirred by those things," he said, "the same as the wolf, but I can call upon it at will."

"I would like to see that. A bipedfuris. When you changed in my driveway before, I only glimpsed it. I would love to see it up close. Before you came here, I'd only heard the tales from those who were old when I was young."

"So you're game to try this?" I lifted the case.

Mom flicked dismissive fingers. "There are no artifacts that can heal the Taint. Rosaria, the wise wolf, confirmed that. But I would be delighted to see a bipedfuris before my time passes. What a gift."

Duncan smiled and bowed.

"He already thinks highly of himself," I told Mom. "Don't stroke his ego."

"Some stroking is usually required when one wants to win the favor of an exceptional mate," she said, holding my gaze, making it clear she thought *I* should be stroking something of Duncan's.

"She called me exceptional." Duncan waggled his eyebrows at me.

"She's buttering your buns because she wants to see you get tall and furry."

"Men do love to have things buttered."

"Oh, I know." I refused to do that, but I pulled out a bar of fine dark chocolate infused with hazelnut liqueur and dusted with chopped hazelnuts. Slowly—tantalizingly—I peeled open the wrapper and offered him two squares.

"Ah, delightful." He popped one into his mouth.

"Chocolate rewards for good behavior also work," I told Mom, then laid two squares on her bedside table in case she was in the mood.

"We all have our ways." She waved as if in dismissal, but she also picked up a square to eat.

"If you don't mind, I'll disrobe." Duncan looked around, as if he might find a dressing screen or a walk-in closet in my mom's two-room log cabin. There hadn't even been indoor plumbing when it had originally been built.

"We don't mind." Despite her age and weakened state, Mom managed something of a salacious smile.

"Ah." Duncan scratched his jaw and looked around again. Were his cheeks a touch pink?

I knew he wouldn't mind getting naked in front of me—in fact, I hadn't noticed that he minded getting naked in front of many people—but maybe a friend's mother was a different story.

"Show her how well trimmed you are." I swatted him on the chest but also nodded toward the doorway, in case he would prefer to undress in front of Lorenzo and then make a dramatic entrance. "She'll be impressed."

"As so many ladies are." Duncan recovered his equanimity enough to wink and bow to me.

"He's a little full of himself," I told Mom as she watched with a bland expression.

"Those with power always are."

Duncan issued a disgruntled sound, then started removing clothing, apparently deciding that doing it in front of Lorenzo wouldn't be any better than in front of us.

To give him privacy, I turned to look out the window past Mom's headboard. She didn't. She openly scrutinized Duncan as he undressed. She was probably assessing his power and fitness to father offspring rather than ogling him out of sexual interest, and I was positive she didn't care if he trimmed himself.

She didn't say anything aloud, but, after finishing her perusal, she did give me a significant look, as if to say, *This one will do.*

I sighed and shook my head.

After kicking off loafers and draping his clothes over a chair, Duncan walked naked to a corner and stared at the floor. He'd made it sound like summoning the bipedfuris was easy, whether the moon or a threat bestirred the magic or not, but he probably had to concentrate, perhaps imagine himself running through the forest in his furry form, hunting enticing prey.

I unwrapped the case from the towel and placed it on the bedside table near Mom. If I'd known any words I could use to entreat the magic to come forth, I would have chanted them.

"It can be difficult to call upon the beast without an inciting event causing strong emotions," Mom said, watching Duncan, his muscled back toward us.

"I could get Rocco in here to threaten him," I offered.

"That pup is no threat," Duncan murmured, not looking back at us.

"Maybe Emilio could beat you with a salami. That *has* to be threatening."

"Do not distract him," Mom murmured to me. "I am most curious."

"About the case or Duncan?"

Since she'd barely looked at the artifact, I didn't need to ask. She smiled at me.

The power that always emanated from Duncan increased, fluctuating like an energy field rippling over his skin. His muscles thickened, his torso broadened, salt-and-pepper fur sprouted from his skin, and he grew taller, his head almost brushing the ceiling as his face also changed, teeth sharpening and a snout half as long as a wolf's forming.

The bipedfuris turned toward us, fingers flexing, showing off sharp claws, and his brown eyes were no longer entirely human. Though they remained sharp with intelligence, their ancient depths spoke of power and the savagery of the wilderness.

Even though I'd expected this—I'd *requested* this—uncertainty swept through me. What if he attacked instead of helping? Neither Mom nor I had the power to stop him.

22

IN HIS POWERFUL BIPEDFURIS FORM, DUNCAN TOOK A STEP TOWARD us. Tense muscles flexed under his short salt-and-pepper fur, and his jaws parted, revealing racks of sharp teeth.

I tensed, shifting to stand in front of my mother's bed, afraid this had been a mistake. That feeling intensified when an orange glow grew visible through the fur on Duncan's forehead. Had Radomir and Abrams already somehow sensed that he'd changed? Duncan had said they wouldn't be able to manipulate him into attacking, not from afar, but was that the truth? Did he know for certain?

Even if they couldn't make him attack, they could call him away from us. I'd wanted that so I could track him to their hideout, but I'd hoped we could help Mom first.

Power throbbed in the air beside me, and I jumped, startled. It was the case. The lid tilted open, and brilliant silver light flowed out.

Duncan paused to peer at it before squinting and looking away. The mushroom-shaped artifact lay within the case, but the light made it too bright to more than glance at.

"It looks like you do activate it in that form." Keeping my gaze on Duncan, I lifted the artifact out of the case, the mushroom shape warm, smooth, and with heft. The silver glow from the case lessened. "Probably better than a rattlesnake."

Mom stirred in her bed but didn't move to rise. She was watching Duncan. While I'd been worrying about being in a confined space with a bipedfuris under someone else's control, she'd been studying him without fear.

"A rattlesnake?" she murmured.

"That's what I could have pulled into the bedroom with you." I placed the artifact next to her on the bed, hoping it would sense her disease and know what to do.

"Less appealing than a werewolf." Her gaze shifted from Duncan to the artifact. In the face of a bipedfuris, she might have been fearless, but her expression held unease as she eyed it.

"You think so?"

"Snakes are cold and scaly. He's strong and lush."

"Oh, he knows it." I didn't think Duncan would react much to the words he heard while he was in that form, but his short snout came up, as if with pride. I snorted. Maybe he recognized an acknowledgment of his appealing *lushness* in any form.

I debated what to do—how to call upon the artifact's magic. Before, it had reacted automatically, sensing the poison in Duncan's wound, and it had known how to heal him. Now, it emanated power, but it wasn't growing intensely bright as it had before. It didn't seem to be doing anything. My hope started to fade.

"I sense that it has protection magic," Mom said. "I would be interested to consult other elders and maybe our wise wolf about it. There's great power bound up within it. Maybe it can send its magic out across many miles."

"We only need it to use it across the bed."

Mom flexed her bandaged hand, lifting a finger to prod it. I opened my mouth to warn her it might zap her, but its power flared, and the silver light I'd hoped for came from the mushroom cap.

My hope surged back to life. Maybe it *would* cure her.

Behind me, Duncan paced. Distracted by the artifact, I'd forgotten to keep an eye on him.

Faint magic whispered into the room, raising the hair on the back of my neck. One of Duncan's clawed hands rose to his forehead. Using his heel, he cupped that scar. His hand blocked the orange glow, but I doubted that gesture could negate the power of the call. Radomir knew the bipedfuris was out and wanted Duncan to return to his quest, to serving him.

I clenched my jaw, wanting to find Radomir and put an end to all that.

The silver light intensified, pulling my gaze back. It flowed from the artifact and toward... my Mom's hand. The one wrapped with a bandage. Its power poured into the spot.

"It tingles," Mom said with awe. "Such power."

Feeling defeat rather than awe, I sank to my knees beside the bed. Unless Mom had *hand* cancer, I didn't think this was going to be the answer.

She sighed with some relief, letting her head fall back against her pillows.

Something stirred under her nightshirt, startling me. A glow that matched that of the artifact seeped out through the material. The talisman? Or her medallion?

The slender chains around her neck shifted, and both medallion and talisman, the two chains entwined, slipped out from under her shirt. I couldn't tell which was responsible for the new glow. Maybe both were, their magic activated by the proximity of the artifact.

They lifted into the air, defying gravity. I gaped as they were pulled across Mom's nightshirt and toward the glowing mush-room, somehow drawn to it.

Mom noticed and tried to tuck the jewelry back into her shirt. "Is that thing magnetic?"

She tilted her chin toward the mushroom artifact, its glow now fading.

I started to shake my head but remembered Duncan experimenting on the case. He'd used one of his magnets to attract what had then been an unknown-to-us object inside.

"It might be," I said. "It's at least got some metal in it that's attracted by magnets."

"These must too." Mom released her medallion and the talisman, no longer fighting their attempt to be pulled toward the artifact.

Something else distracted her. Her hand.

She flexed her fingers, then marveled, "It doesn't hurt anymore."

I smiled and murmured, "That's good," though I had a feeling the artifact hadn't done anything to heal the greater issue. Maybe it didn't have the power to do that. Even though nothing in the translation had suggested it could cure disease, it was hard not to be disappointed. "That was from the bear fight, right?"

I'd assumed that, but she hadn't told me anything about the wound.

"From the *trap* I fell on during the bear fight." She grimaced. "It was hidden in the leaves, and I didn't see it, an old-fashioned metal trap with teeth."

When she gestured in the air, as if to draw it, my mind conjured something from a cartoon. I hadn't thought anyone used traps like that anymore.

One-handedly, she tugged at the knots on the bandage. I helped her remove it, though I was aware of Duncan pacing behind us, the claws on his feet clacking whenever he stepped off the rug and onto the bare wooden floorboards. Tension knotted his body as he fought the call of the control device. Any second now, he might lose that battle.

Mom, more interested in what the artifact had done than Duncan's pacing, held up her hand to the daylight coming in the window and rotated it. The scars appeared to be old and faded, even more so than the one on her neck that I'd noticed the other day.

"Huh," Mom said. "That's amazing. We put a new bandage on my hand last night, and wounds were still weeping blood. Lorenzo thought the trap had poison on the teeth, and that was why my werewolf regeneration wasn't working well on the wounds. I admit I didn't wash the cuts after I got them, not until later. My whole life, wounds have healed easily and nothing has ever gotten infected, so..." She shrugged.

"If there was poison lingering, that might be why the artifact worked."

A grunt came from behind, and Duncan lunged for the door. He jerked to a halt before reaching it, the heel of his hand pressing to the scar again.

"What's happening?" Mom asked.

"The one who raised him bound him to a control device that can call him across miles." It could do a lot more than that, but I didn't go into details.

My gaze drifted to the talisman and medallion, the chains still entwined, a faint glow still coming from them. They clung together as if their magic had fused them. Or had the artifact changed something within them, giving them magnetism that they hadn't had before? I shook my head, not certain of the science that might account for this. Or even if science could explain *magic*.

Mom said something, but I didn't register the words. An idea had popped into my head, and I snatched the bag that Bolin had given me out of my pocket. I dug out the small GPS device, the *magnetic* GPS device.

Before I held it toward the artifact, I felt a pull. It was also drawn to it. Until I flipped it over. Then it was repulsed.

"Guess we know where the poles are on this." I pointed to the talisman. I wouldn't ask to take the medallion from Mom, but maybe that would do. "May I borrow that?"

Grunts and straining sounds came from Duncan. He wouldn't be able to fight the call much longer. It was as if he, too, was made from metal and being magnetically drawn.

If only the magic were that innocuous.

"It's yours," Mom said dryly as she untangled the two chains and reached for the talisman's clasp behind her neck. "It does help soothe my pain, by the way. I didn't thank you for that."

"I'll bring it back."

"Okay."

As I pulled the necklace away from her, a tiny beam of silver light shot from Mom's medallion to the talisman. It disappeared so quickly that I wasn't sure I'd seen it, but the mushroom artifact hummed faintly. For an instant, I sensed more than magic from it. I sensed... *emotion?* That it was pleased? The feeling faded as quickly as the beam of light had, and I shook away the thoughts. I'd probably imagined it all.

Another grunt from behind reminded me to focus on my new idea, my *mission*.

Mom watched as I held the GPS tracker to the back of the talisman.

Though the mushroom-shaped artifact had a greater pull, the tracker did click to it.

"Duncan." I turned, holding the chain up and trying to show him the talisman while hiding the GPS tracker now attached to it. That was a challenge since it was larger. But, maybe in his were-wolf form, he wouldn't be as observant—or wouldn't quite know what the flat black disc was. "They're trying to call you, aren't they?"

He grunted, his eyes locking with mine. They continued to look more animal than human, the power of werewolf magic within them, but there was recognition too. He knew who I was. And maybe he understood me.

"Do you remember when we found this locket? You said it was a longevity talisman. It's lucky, too, I think." We hadn't spoken of that, but maybe he wouldn't remember the details while in this form. "If you get called up by Radomir and Abrams, you're going to need luck."

He grunted again, but it sounded more suspicious than agreeing, and squinted at the locket. Then he snarled, clutching his forehead once more.

"Wear this, okay?" I stepped forward and lifted the chain, my heart hammering in my chest. Not only was I trying to trick a great bipedfuris much stronger than I, but I was getting close to him, close enough that he could tear into me with a sweep of his claws.

When he jerked his arms down, I jumped, afraid he would attack. Tension radiated from his body, from his every taut muscle. He looked like he wanted to slash into his enemies with those claws.

But he stared at me through the chain I held up, meeting my gaze. Again, I noted the intelligence in there. Could he remember the plan to follow him that I'd spoken of? The one he *hadn't* approved of?

I smiled encouragingly and lifted the chain a little higher, trying to indicate that I wanted to put it on him. Too bad it wouldn't fit over his head. I would have to clasp it behind his neck. Talk about walking into the lion's den... the werewolf's maw...

"Let's put this on you, okay?" Damn, my mouth was dry. "For luck."

Duncan's gaze shifted toward the locket and his eyes narrowed.

A bead of sweat ran down my back. Tricking him wasn't going to work. I had to tell him the truth and hope he would go for it. That he wouldn't be pissed.

But his eyes opened a little wider, and he cocked his head as he regarded the locket. As if he'd sensed something new about it.

Appearing almost contemplative, he met my eyes. I opened my mouth, groping for a way to sell him on the locket.

He surprised me by lowering his head. It took me a moment to realize he was offering his neck, that he would let me put it on him.

With a tremor in my fingers, I lifted the chain. When I tried to operate the clasp, I fumbled it and almost dropped the locket. I half-expected Duncan to come to his senses and spring away, but he remained utterly still. I fastened the clasp, and the locket fell against his furred chest, the GPS remaining attached.

When I stepped back and lowered my hands, he sprang into motion.

Startled, I scrambled away, but he didn't come toward me. He rushed out the door.

In the other room, Lorenzo grunted in surprise. The front door banged open. I lunged for the window in time to see Duncan leap the railing and run to his van. Claws scraping the metal, he flung open the door and jumped inside. A couple of seconds later, he leaped back out, carrying a big black case over his shoulder. Still inside of the van, Jasmine and Bolin gaped out the window.

I stared. What the hell?

Without glancing back toward me, Duncan charged into the woods, heading north.

Toward those with the control device? Those calling him? Of course. What else could it be? But why was he taking... whatever was in that case?

"What happened?" Mom asked. "Where's he going?"

"He's going to lead me to the ones with the control device, and

I'm going to take it from them so they won't be able to command him any longer."

Assuming the tracker didn't fall off. I hoped that magnet was strong.

"Oh, good," Mom said. "Nobody should command a werewolf, especially not one as powerful as he."

"I agree." I grabbed Duncan's clothes, fished his keys out of his pants pocket, and headed for the van. "Time to see if this plan will work."

23

"GOT HIM," BOLIN SAID FROM THE BED IN THE BACK OF THE VAN AS we headed away from Mom's property. "He's moving fast."

Jasmine sat in the passenger seat while I drove faster than recommended on the dirt road, the snow making it sketchier than usual. At least the Roadtrek had good shock absorbers, something Duncan had probably upgraded, the same as the tires. Treasure hunting wasn't always done on paved streets, after all. I was glad we didn't have to slow down much for the potholes. I had no idea how great of a range the tracking device had, but even if it had worked from across the world, I would still have felt tense with urgency. It could fall off the locket at any time.

"Heading north," Bolin added.

"This road doesn't go north, does it?" Jasmine waved toward the route ahead.

"No. I think we have to go all the way out to the highway and head east, then turn north." At least we could gain ground on him once we reached pavement. As a bipedfuris, he would be fast but not sixty-miles-per-hour fast.

"Do we have a plan for if it works?" Jasmine asked. "And he leads us to those guys?"

"I have a pocket full of potions and bath bombs."

Bolin made an aggrieved noise. "Orbs of Entanglement."

"But the sword and grenades are still missing, right?" Jasmine peered into the glovebox but only found the tools and cassette tape.

"Duncan might have some weapons in the back if you want to search." I didn't take my eyes from the road. When the dirt ended and we turned onto asphalt, I picked up speed. "I figure we'll have to go to fur-and-fangs at some point."

"Uh," Bolin said, "I don't have that option."

"I hope you have a pocketful of potions," I told him.

"I have... *some*."

"Aren't you going to beat people with your violin?" Jasmine looked back at Bolin. She'd made that comment earlier but couldn't know why he'd *really* brought it.

"No. That's for, uhm. I'm going to play us some battle music to get us in the mood."

"Oh, yeah?" She sounded curious. "Now might be a good time for that."

"I'll start when I don't need to watch the tracking app so closely. And when you're not— I mean, it's easier if you're not looking back at me."

Jasmine snorted. "Shy, huh?"

She looked forward.

"Didn't you do recitals in front of an audience?" I asked Bolin. "You said something about singing at church too."

"Yes. I don't have stage fright. It's... something else."

Girl fright. I didn't say that out loud.

"He's still heading north," Bolin said. "He's already past Lake Stevens."

"Does it look like he's paralleling Highway Nine?" I wondered which of the addresses on the list Radomir was staying at.

It was hard to imagine him and his thugs living in the window-less mushroom building outside of Deming, and we hadn't seen evidence of another residence. That was the only address that had been that far north though.

"For now, yes."

"Good. We'll be there soon." I clenched the wheel, annoyed that we'd entered a more populated area, and I had to slow for traffic. And was that a *light* ahead? I cursed. *Duncan* didn't have to deal with this.

The image of a bipedfuris stopping because a red traffic light dangled from a tree branch deep in the woods only briefly amused me. Mostly, I bared my teeth in frustration.

"Didn't your mom ever tell you that your face will get stuck like that if you hold that pissed-off expression?" Jasmine asked lightly, though she eyed me with concern.

Maybe my driving was alarming my passengers. The light turned green, and I forced myself to loosen my grip on the wheel.

"No," I replied. "As a good werewolf, my mother encouraged fearsome expressions. To scare one's enemies."

"That was less fearsome and more I-can-barely-hold-my-pee-any-longer."

"That disturbs enemies too."

"Especially when you're in their lair?"

"Absolutely."

Finally, we turned onto the highway. I floored it.

"Are you worried about the police at all?" Bolin had taken his violin out of its case, but that didn't keep him from creeping close enough to eye the dashboard.

"Yeah, but not for speeding." I didn't mention the previous night's debacle.

Bolin slid his phone, the map with the GPS tracker location

open on it, into a holder that Duncan had attached to the dash. I could see the dot moving, still paralleling the highway, though it was much farther north than we were. Before long, Duncan would be even with that mushroom farm.

"You'd better play something soothing," Jasmine told Bolin, probably noting my expression again.

"I was thinking of 'Ride of the Valkyries.'"

"Maybe save that for right before the storming," she said. "I'm prescribing relaxing and mellow music."

Even focused on the road, I saw Bolin's grimace. Maybe twenty-something guys didn't do mellow.

"I had to play 'The Lark Ascending' for a recital once. It's sleepy, boring, and fifteen minutes long. Not only did it threaten to put me into a coma, but it was so long that the grandpas in the back row kept leaving to go to the bathroom."

"We don't want a song that encourages that. Not until we're in the villain's lair." Jasmine smirked at me.

"Funny." I shot her a glare, then said, "Play the Valkyrie thing."

"Okay."

Reminded of Bolin's original reason for bringing his violin, I added, "Or rap. My niece likes rap."

"Oh, really?" he asked as if that were new information.

"Not violin rap," Jasmine said. "That's not even a thing, is it?"

"That sounds like a challenge, Bolin." I glanced at him, hoping he appreciated my help in setting him up to fulfill his dreams. Or maybe his *schemes.*

As he sat on the bed to play, he gave me a discreet thumbs-up. Soon, notes flowed from the back of the van.

Jasmine cocked her head, probably trying to recognize a familiar song. As Bolin had promised, it *was* challenging from just the beats—the violin version of the beats.

I eyed the GPS map as he started singing—or rather, rapping.

"Oh," Jasmine said with delight. "That's what that is. 50 Cent.

'In da Club.'" She clapped her hands together and started singing to the music.

I watched the dot on the map and decided this was the weirdest army anyone had ever gone into battle with. Maybe I would leave Bolin and Jasmine in the van.

Fat snowflakes hit the windshield. The sky had grown darker. Enough traffic had traveled on the highway that the lanes remained free of snow, but it blanketed the forests and farmlands that we passed. This wasn't the best weather for storming a villain's lair.

"He's going past Deming," I murmured, though nobody heard me.

The violin and the singing had gotten loud as Bolin and Jasmine shared their enthusiasm for the song. When it ended, they shifted to 'P.I.M.P.' and other rap songs I couldn't name. I was almost relieved when my phone rang.

Austin's number popped up. As I thumbed the screen to answer, I noticed the date—Christmas Eve—and wondered if he was calling again to invite me up in the morning. We were more than halfway there now. I snorted, imagining his reaction if I brought this strange crew to his friend's cabin. But my amusement evaporated when I noticed that Duncan had angled to the northeast. Toward the little town of Maple Falls.

A coincidence? All along, I'd been worried that Radomir was up to something in the same area where my son was vacationing.

"Hey, Austin." I waved for the singers to pause for a minute. "What's—"

"Mom, we're in trouble," my son blurted before I could finish the question.

"Did you hit another tree?" I asked, though my stomach knotted, certain something far worse had happened.

"No." He was whispering.

"What happened?" I also caught myself whispering.

Was there someone there with him? Someone he didn't want to hear the call?

Jasmine and Bolin fell silent and watched me—and listened.

Austin didn't answer.

What the hell was going on? It couldn't be anything minor. He was a grown-up now. He wouldn't call his mother over something small.

"Austin?" I struggled to keep my voice calm. My fingers tightened on the wheel again.

"Where is he?" Jasmine whispered. "At your apartment?"

I shook my head. "A cabin near Maple Falls. Either that or he's up snowboarding at Baker right now." The fresh powder would make that appealing, but it was late enough in the day that they might have finished up and returned. "Where are you, Austin?" I asked into the phone again. "What's wrong?"

The line went dead.

"Shit."

"We're about to pass the address for the mushroom farm." Jasmine pointed at the GPS on Bolin's phone. Our dot—Duncan— was well past the area and had continued to the northeast.

Worry for my son made me want to abandon our quest to get the control device. Duncan shouldn't be in any immediate danger. But Austin...

I tried calling him back, but he didn't answer.

"You're doing a good job of freaking your mom out," I told the phone with a scowl.

A text popped up. It was from Austin but contained only an address. A Maple Falls address.

Did he want me to drive up and rescue him from trouble? If burglars had broken in or some other crime was being committed, wouldn't he have called the police instead of his mother? He didn't know that I was a werewolf and had any power. I'd done my best all during his childhood to ensure that.

Watching the highway and not slowing down, I pasted the address into my phone's map program. I'd already decided to divert from chasing Duncan to find Austin.

"Looks like it's north of town by... whatever that lake is called. Silver Lake."

"Town?" Jasmine asked. "Doesn't Maple Falls just have a tiny grocery store and a gas station? It's even smaller than Deming."

I shrugged. I hadn't been up that way in ages.

"Population two hundred forty-seven," she read off her phone.

"That ought to make it easy to find Austin then." Which I was determined to do.

Again, I called him back. Again, he didn't answer. Had a kidnapper or robber taken his phone? Or hurt him so that he *couldn't* answer?

"Do you think someone forced him to call you?" Bolin asked.

Jasmine looked over at me.

"I don't know," I said.

I hadn't thought that, but I immediately latched onto the idea. That made more sense than my eighteen-year-old son calling his mom for help that didn't involve cooking, cleaning, or laundry.

"But... I need to go there and figure out what's happening."

"Yeah." Bolin put his violin away.

Too bad. I needed some battle music now.

I took the turn for Maple Falls. Even though this was the main route through the area, the weather had caused people to retreat, and there was little traffic as twilight descended. Now, the snow stuck to the road as well as the ground.

I kept glancing at the phone for another call or more texts. To say I was a distracted driver was an understatement, but I couldn't help it. At least the traffic map didn't show any accidents ahead. Fifteen minutes, and we would be there.

"Uhm." Bolin took my phone from my grip.

At first, I thought it was because he objected to me fiddling with it while I was driving, but he didn't comment on that. He held the screen up so that it was side-by-side to his phone which was still tucked in the dashboard holder.

"If the GPS tracker is still on him," Bolin said, "Duncan is right in that area."

"As a bipedfuris," Jasmine whispered.

Fresh fear swept into me. What if Radomir knew all about my son and his current location? What if he'd commanded Duncan to *attack* Austin?

I drove faster, hardly caring when the tires slipped on the snowy pavement and we skidded onto the shoulder. Bolin scrambled to find a secure spot in the back, and Jasmine gripped the oh-shit handle.

"We're fine," I said. "It'll be fine."

But would it?

24

"IF IT HELPS," JASMINE SAID AS WE REACHED THE MAPLE FALLS GAS
station and store, a building with a modest clock tower on the
roof, "the address he sent *is* on the internet, listed as an Airbnb."

She waved her phone, but with night encroaching and the
snow coming down hard, I didn't glance over.

"Can you find anything about a contest that mentions it?" I
asked. "One that would have closed and declared a winner a week
or so ago?"

It hadn't occurred to me to look that up before. Of course, I
hadn't imagined Austin would be in *danger* before. If those
bastards did something to my son and his friends because I'd had
the audacity to take back artifacts they'd stolen from *me*, I would
kill them. I'd turn wolf, go completely savage, and kill them
without a single regret.

I turned left onto the road heading toward Silver Lake.

"Nothing on Google or Facebook that I can find." Jasmine
shrugged. "But something like that might not list the address of
the prize. Even if you book a vacation rental yourself, you don't
usually get that information until you've paid."

"Yeah," I said though a niggling feeling in my gut made me wonder if this had been set up as a trap from the beginning.

Radomir knew where I lived and where my mother lived. Given his fondness for spying on my family, it wasn't hard to imagine he'd learned Austin was home for the holidays. I might have found it suspicious if my son had won a contest out of nowhere, especially if he hadn't entered anything, but his friend, Oakley? From what I remembered of the kid, he wasn't a genius. I was fairly certain he'd gone to college on a sports scholarship. The thought that Radomir had researched my family so thoroughly that he'd learned about Austin's friends and arranged all this disturbed me greatly.

"Stalker creep," I muttered.

"What?" Jasmine lowered her phone.

"Just a hunch."

I glanced at my phone still mounted to the dash next to Bolin's. Duncan's dot had stopped moving near the southern bank of Silver Lake. I imagined him hoisting Austin over his shoulder and taking him to Radomir.

Frustrated, I grabbed my phone again. We hit a slick spot, and the van swerved before I could get it back under control. Something rolled out from under the passenger seat, and Jasmine looked down.

"Do you want me to try calling him again?" Bolin crept up to our seats and reached for my phone, looking like he would snatch it from my grip whether I agreed or not.

For the safety of my passengers, I put my hand back on the wheel. "Reply to his text, will you? Tell him... we slid off the road and blew a tire in the snow, but we'll be there in an hour."

"I hope that's a ploy in case his captors are monitoring his phone," Bolin said, "and not a prediction."

"Let's hope." I waved at the map.

We were five minutes from the address, but, as I'd noted,

Duncan had stopped to the south of it. That looked like a park, all forested with no houses nearby. If he'd dragged Austin in that direction, and Radomir was waiting there...

Should I go there first?

Jasmine patted around at her feet and lifted whatever had rolled out and bumped her. "You brought salami for the incursion?"

"I brought a couple in case I needed to bribe family members to let me in to see Mom." I was surprised Emilio hadn't slipped in and snatched the salamis while we'd been inside.

"I guess it's good that we'll have rations if we slide off the road and get stuck in a snowbank." Jasmine lowered the meat log to her lap. "Better than having to eat each other to keep from starving."

Bolin laughed. Nervously?

Jasmine looked back at him.

"I'd think that more of a joke if I didn't know..." He glanced at me. "Things."

"Are you missing the days when you didn't believe in were-wolves?" I asked.

"A little bit, yes."

A plow passed us coming from the other direction, but it hadn't scraped our side of the road yet. I bit my lip as we approached the turn for the park, tempted to drive in and search for Duncan, but my phone rang.

I reached back and snatched it from Bolin's grip. Austin's name was on it.

"What's going on?" I demanded.

Austin hesitated. I imagined someone with a gun pressed to his head.

"I'm being asked to request that you make sure to bring a magical case and medallion." His words came out calmly, but he spoke quickly. He was worried and in trouble.

"Your kidnappers should have made that request *before* we started driving to that address," I said.

"You don't have either?" a male voice asked.

That wasn't Radomir, whom I'd originally dubbed Mr. Raspy. Nor was it Abrams, who had an accent not unlike Duncan's. This sounded like a garden-variety thug. I *hoped* that was all we would have to deal with, but I doubted it.

"Who am I talking to?" I eyed the GPS tracker on Bolin's phone again.

Duncan's dot remained in the same spot in the park by the shoreline. Or maybe he'd gone into the water for some reason? It was hard to tell.

"If they don't have any of the artifacts, there's no point in any of this." It sounded like the guy was talking to someone else, not me. How many thugs were there?

"I don't have the medallion." I *did* have the case. Normally, I wouldn't announce that, but if that was what they wanted, and they decided to kill Austin because I hadn't brought it...

"What about the wolf case?" the man asked. "You have it?"

"Austin, are you okay?" I asked. "What's happening?"

"I'm—" He broke off with a grunt of pain.

"If you bastards hurt my son, I'll kill you all," I shouted. No, it was a scream. The frantic protection instincts of a mother had kicked in, and my skin pricked as my emotions threatened to bring forth the wolf.

Jasmine looked over at me with concern. I wouldn't be able to drive as a wolf—or control myself. But imagining them hurting or killing Austin... I almost didn't care.

Something broke in the background—it sounded like a vase or dish hitting the floor.

"I told you to stay put or we'll throw your dead body in the lake," someone said. "All we need is her kid."

Jaw clenched, I glanced at the map again. We were almost to

the cabin. The breaking vase implied that was where they were, not the park. Duncan's dot hadn't moved much in these past minutes. Maybe Radomir was waiting at the park with him, intending to send him in when I arrived.

"Do you have the case or not?" the first speaker said into the phone. "Your kid is fine. *For now.*"

I wanted to threaten him further, to reach through the phone and strangle him, but I needed a few more minutes to get there. Better to keep him talking.

"I have it."

"Okay, good. That's the most important one, they said."

"Radomir and Abrams? What do they want it for?"

"A memento. You bring it, and we'll trade it for the kid and his dumbass friends. You screw around and— Here, tell your mommy what we'll do, kid."

An agonizing moment passed in silence, and I imagined Austin licking dry lips.

We'd reached the first of the houses along the lake. Many were dark, no lights on, no tire marks in the snowy driveways. Probably unoccupied vacation homes. The lots were large and treed, the driveways winding back from the road before reaching their destinations. I forced myself to slow the van so we wouldn't miss the Airbnb cabin.

"I'm okay, Mom, but they clobbered Mark. There are a lot of guys, inside and out. And there's a shaggy wolf that almost killed Oakley when he tried to escape out the back."

Damn it, was the GPS wrong? Was Duncan at the cabin?

Thank the moon I hadn't wasted time pulling into that park.

I envisioned Radomir with his controller, standing in a snowy yard and ordering Duncan to attack my son's friends. It would be against his will, but that wouldn't make it any better. An image of blood drops spattering all over the snow entered my mind.

"We're stuck inside and—"

"That's enough," the speaker said, cutting Austin off. "Bring the case, Valens. Put it on the porch, and we'll let the kids go. If not, the wolf will tear out your son's throat."

The call ended before I could snap a furious rebuttal.

"Duncan won't do that," Jasmine tried to assure me.

"Three more houses, and we're there." Bolin pointed through the windshield. "That should be the driveway down there."

There were car tracks on the snowy road ahead. We weren't the only ones driving around out here tonight.

I turned off the headlights and pulled over before we reached the driveway, then cut off the engine. The odds of us sneaking up on those guys, especially with a werewolf helping them, were low. But if we drove right up to the cabin, they might open fire immediately. There was no way they would give me my son after I dropped off the case. It wouldn't be that easy.

"Bolin and I will go around to the back and come in from the lake." Jasmine reached for the door handle. "We'll try to surprise them and give you an advantage. Or at least a distraction."

Potions clinked in Bolin's pocket as he climbed out of the van with her.

"Be careful," I warned. "They may have guns with silver bullets."

"Those... shouldn't be extra harmful to me." Bolin frowned and looked at Jasmine.

"They wouldn't be any *less* harmful than normal ones," she pointed out.

"True. We will attempt to avoid them."

Wishing I had bulletproof vests to distribute, I hopped out of the driver's seat, the chill night air startling after the warmth of the van. I debated whether or not to grab the case. Leaving it in here wouldn't be safe, but neither would taking it up there. If they didn't see it in my hands, they might shoot Austin.

Grimacing, I grabbed it and headed for the driveway. Already, adrenaline flowed through my veins—adrenaline and magic. Taking a deep breath, I willed the latter to subside.

If I turned into a wolf in front of my son... I didn't know what would happen. Would he be shocked? Disgusted? Feel betrayed that I'd kept the secret from him his entire life?

The snowy driveway curved between trees as it led to a timber-sided A-frame cabin with a covered porch. A light was on by the door, and more lights glowed inside, but the curtains were drawn, keeping me from seeing in. A shadow stirred at one of the windows. Someone looking out? Another window was dark, but I could make out the muzzle of a gun in a gap in the curtains. The thugs must not have believed my text that I was an hour away.

I walked slowly to give Jasmine and Bolin time to get around to the back of the cabin. But not too much time. These guys would be watching the backyard too.

I passed a lit mailbox shaped like a snow-capped mountain and walked up the driveway, the snow crunching softly under my shoes. It covered ferns and salmonberry bushes dotting the front yard between the trees.

With my eyes focused on the windows and doors, I almost missed a furry wolf padding out to stand in the driveway. Duncan? A warning growl emanated from his throat.

Anger rather than fear suffused me. How could he be working for those assholes? And why couldn't he fight the magic?

As the wolf turned to face me fully, my thoughts of betrayal halted. It was too small to be Duncan. Besides, I knew him well and would have sensed him this close. Maybe the GPS tracking app had been correct and he was back down at the park. This was another powerful werewolf, one as strong as—and oddly similar to—Duncan, but...

"Oh."

It was his clone. The kid I'd traded a chocolate bar with in exchange for my mom's medallion.

Maybe those growls meant he didn't believe it had been a fair trade.

He padded toward me, jaws parted, and I tensed, the urge to change coming over me. The urge to defend myself, to *fight*.

Could I take him? Maybe. When the kid was full-grown, he would be as strong as Duncan, but I doubted he was now.

But I didn't want to fight Duncan's clone. What if I lost control and killed the kid?

"Are you under their magical coercion too?" I held my arms out to appear unthreatening. "I know you're young and probably haven't been out in the world much, but you don't want to work for those guys."

The wolf padded closer, growling. I backed up the driveway, debating how to get him out of the picture without changing to fight him.

Still gripping the case, I wondered if the lid would open if the kid drew close enough. Probably not unless he changed into a bipedfuris. Even if it opened, the artifact inside would only heal me from a bite or poison, not help in a fight.

At the cabin, one of the curtains stirred. A familiar face peered out. Austin.

I could make out someone big looming close behind him. It wasn't one of his friends.

"They're jerks, and they don't want the best for our kind," I told the wolf. "Have you met other werewolves, or have they kept you isolated?"

The wolf paused and cocked his head, one ear flickering.

"You're probably lonely without any friends to play with. If you come with us instead of working for them, I can introduce you to some of the young wolves in my pack." I hadn't seen any of the kids since returning, but I had little doubt that some of my younger half-siblings or maybe nieces and nephews had children. "What are you? Eight years old? You should be playing instead of working for bad guys."

That elicited another growl. Maybe he didn't believe Abrams and Radomir were *bad guys*?

"You should have a chat with Duncan about them. Have you met him yet? Spoken to him? He can tell you *all* about Abrams. He's your brother, you know."

The statement drew another pause and head cock.

"The age difference is probably confusing, but you could ask him all about it. He'll talk to you. I'm sure of it."

The wolf looked to the south. In the direction of the park. Did he know Duncan was down there?

From here, I couldn't detect him, but if the kid had the same kind of power as Duncan, he might have a longer range when it came to sensing magic.

"Have they been feeding you well? I have some salami and summer sausage. Would you like one? You might enjoy a meat snack better than dark chocolate. That's an acquired taste."

The wolf looked back to me, nostrils twitching. Sniffing?

"It's in the van. I can get it." I imagined tossing a sausage log into the woods to distract the kid while I ran for the front door. That might work with a Rottweiler. And Emilio. But I didn't know Duncan's clone well. "I'll be right back."

Hand raised, as if that would prompt him to stay, I backed into the street and strode toward the van. My senses told me that he remained in the driveway. I set the case down and grabbed a sausage log, but, as I turned to walk back, a whisper of magic crossed my skin, raising the hair on the back of my neck. It felt similar to what I'd sensed before when someone had been using the device to summon Duncan—to *control* Duncan. They were using it on the kid.

When I reached the start of the driveway, I waved the sausage.

But the magic plucked at my senses again, and it seemed to wrap around the wolf. The fur on his back rose, and he snarled and charged at me.

25

I TOSSED THE SAUSAGE LOG INTO THE DRIVEWAY BETWEEN THE WOLF and me, then ran back to the van, shoes slipping in the snow. Snarling and driven by coercion magic, the kid ran past my offering and came right after me.

Heat flushed my body, and magic made my skin tingle with the promise of a change. At least Austin wouldn't see if I did it in the street.

I jumped into the van to block the wolf from reaching me but also so I could buy myself a moment. I yanked my jacket off, leaving my phone on the seat, and reached for my shoes.

A thump on the hood startled me—the wolf.

Claws scraped on metal, gouging the paint. Jaws snapped as he tried to bite the glass windshield. That wouldn't work, but he was smart enough to figure out another way in.

I tore off the rest of my clothing as another wave of magic swept through my veins. Before I morphed completely and lost the ability to grab things, I flung the van's side door open. When I leaped out, I landed on four legs—four paws.

The wolf jumped down from the hood but faltered when he saw me in my lupine form.

The change stole my human thoughts and my memories, and all awareness that this was Duncan's clone fell from my mind. His aura and scent were somewhat familiar, but I saw only an enemy and snarled at him, crouching and ready to spring.

He'd come after me when I'd been in human form, but he hesitated to face me as a wolf. He backed a few steps and glanced toward a log of meat lying in the snow. He half turned away, but more magic whispered through the air, seeming to come from around a bend in the road behind me. The power brushed me, making my hackles rise, but it flowed into the wolf.

Snarling, he spun back toward me and crouched to spring.

I charged before he could, rushing at him. With my powerful legs, I reached him in an instant, jaws snapping through his fur and flesh. I tasted blood.

When our bodies crashed together, my greater size let me bowl him over. He rolled into the snow and down a slope at the side of the road. I leaped after him, biting and taking a chunk out of his flank. He yelped, a pitiful cry that floated through the trees and out over the lake.

In this form, it wasn't in my nature to show mercy, but I paused anyway. This was a young wolf, one who wasn't truly a great threat. If he didn't attack again, I could let him go.

Leaving blood in the snow, he rose, but only halfway. He kept his head low and backed away from me in a sign of submission.

The creak of a door opening reached my ears. It came from the human den, a place that was of interest to me because enemies lurked within. No, I remembered. More than that gave it significance. The humans within had taken one of my offspring prisoner.

Growling, I stalked through the trees toward the structure, barely registering that the young wolf had slunk away. He paused only to pick up the meat log in the street, taking it in his jaws and padding into the trees on the other side of the road.

Light spilled from the doorway of the human den. A man with a rifle stood framed by it, the weapon pointed toward the tree-filled yard. He peered into the woods. Looking for me?

A *crash-thump* came from inside the den behind him. My offspring trying to escape? Or being beaten?

I stalked toward the structure, intending to spring upon the man, to slay him for presuming to harm my offspring. His rifle emanated slight magic, and I knew the projectiles loaded within it could badly hurt me. It didn't matter. I had to eliminate the threat to my family.

A deep howl came from the south, from behind more human dens and more trees. It was familiar. The howl of the one I'd wished to make my mate.

A higher pitched howl came from across the road. The youth.

Alarm made my paws freeze as a realization struck me. Those howls had different pitches, but their owners were of the same blood. In my core, I knew this to be true. That was the offspring or... a younger sibling of my ally's. And I'd attacked him, left his blood in the snow. Would my ally be angered?

The man on the porch fired his rifle toward the sky, the crack deafening to my keen ears. Snow fell from branches to plop onto the ground. The man pointed his firearm into the woods again, not toward the front yard but to the side, in the direction from which my ally's howl had come.

Did he think that had been me howling? Perhaps, for he squinted in that direction.

Making my paws as silent as I could, I circled the front yard to come at the man from the other side. Believing the threat came from the south, he didn't look toward the north, and I approached from that direction.

His finger tightened on the trigger. Did he see something? Was my mate coming?

Taking advantage of the man's distraction, I ran the last few steps and sprang. As I soared over the railing of the porch, he must have heard or sensed me. He whirled, pointing the rifle at my chest.

Midair, I couldn't do anything to dodge. Someone—my human offspring—lunged out of the doorway and hit my enemy using a pole with a pointy end. It struck the man's padded jacket enough to shift the aim of the rifle.

The firearm boomed, the bullet blazing silver through the sky as it passed my ear. An instant later, I slammed into the man's chest.

My offspring jumped back into the den but not before I glimpsed blood dried on his chin and a blackened eye. Fury blasted through me, and I snapped savagely at the rifleman. Emotion surged through my veins, the magic making me wild. This time, I didn't try to restrain those savage instincts. The man fell to his knees underneath me, and I bit and tore, ripping into clothing and flesh and muscle. He screamed, trying to get his arms up, but I knocked the rifle aside, and he lacked the strength to push me away.

Crashes and cries came from within the cabin. Fear for my offspring drove me to finish off my enemy quickly. After I ripped his arm away from his neck and ended his life, I leaped into the warmth and light of the human den.

Another wolf was inside. Duncan?

No, it was my female relative. She fought a bearded man, her jaws wrapped around his rifle as she tried to tear it away. My offspring and three other young men were in the space, ducking or attacking more big thugs with handguns and rifles. One weapon went off, and a lamp shattered and fell to the floor, dimming the room.

Beside a fireplace, a back door stood open, and a familiar redheaded man crouched there. His pockets clinked, magic emanating from items inside, and he threw a sphere to the floor, at the feet of a man aiming a handgun at my niece. It kept our enemy from firing as he glanced down. His foot stuck, and he shouted in anger and aimed the handgun at my ally in the door.

My niece released the rifle of the man she'd been wrestling with and whirled, biting the other gunman in the leg. I rushed toward the thug she'd turned away from. He bled from several bite wounds, but that didn't keep him from aiming his rifle at my niece. I sprang and crashed into his back at the same moment as my offspring stepped in with the pole again, cracking our foe in the head. The man went down, the rifle skidding across the floor, as I tore chunks out of his hip and legs.

"Where did all these *dogs* come from?" one of the young men yelled.

"They're wolves." That was my offspring. "Don't you know anything?"

"Imagine my embarrassment at not being able to tell what exactly is going on. This is chaos!"

"I told you it was suspicious that you won a contest you never entered," someone else said. "This was a set-up from the beginning."

"As long as the wolves don't bite us," someone said weakly from a corner, another young man who grimaced as he gripped a broken arm. His face was as bruised as that of my offspring. A victim.

I bit my enemy again, hard. He cried out, trying to escape, but couldn't with my weight on him.

"I... don't think they will," my offspring said, confusion in his voice. He jogged past, glancing at me, then sprang upon the fallen rifle and picked it up.

One of the thugs who'd been down rose up and struck the boy who'd called us dogs. The conversation halted.

I started to rush over to help, but an engine roared in the front yard. Outside, a gun fired, and I spun in that direction. Headlights flared through the windows, and shouts sounded as car doors slammed. Reinforcements had arrived.

26

THE ROAR OF AN ENGINE AND FIRING OF GUNSHOTS MADE ME hesitate to run onto the porch. A snarl sounded from the trees beside the driveway. My ally?

Numerous men had jumped out of an armored vehicle, rifles pointed toward the den—toward the door where I crouched. I slid most of my body behind the wall for cover. Instead of firing at me, the men paused and looked toward the snarls.

Yes, I sensed that Duncan had arrived. Further, I easily spotted the bipedfuris because something glowed golden around his neck. A powerful magical item hung there, along with another item of lesser magic that did not glow.

"Radomir's controlling him," one of the gunmen barked. "He's on our side. Get the girl, and find the case."

The riflemen strode away from their vehicle and toward me.

"Are those our guys?" someone asked from the den behind me.

A thump sounded—one of my offspring's friends striking the speaker with a pointy iron stick that smelled of ash. My niece continued to fight with a big, muscular man who remained upright, kicking at her with powerful legs. Some magic enhanced him. I wished I could turn back to help her, but the first rifleman had reached the porch. He didn't know that I crouched right beside the door, and he strode forward without hesitation.

Hoping his body and the railing would block the others if they fired at me, I rushed out to meet him, jaws snapping for the gun. Finger on the trigger, he lifted it to shoot, but, with my speed, I reached it first. I clamped down on the cold, bitter-tasting metal and ripped the weapon from his grip. It clattered against the wood side of the den.

"Shit." He leaped back, making room for his allies. "Shoot it— *her*!"

Before anyone could, the bipedfuris charged out of the woods and grabbed one of the gunmen. Sinking his claws into our foe, he elicited a scream of pain as he hefted the man from his feet and hurled him against a tree.

"Radomir!" one of the riflemen shouted in alarm, jerking his weapon toward the bipedfuris. "Your beast is out of control!"

Knowing the weapon contained magical bullets that would harm our kind, I rushed off the porch and at the man. I had to protect my ally.

Duncan roared and sprang at someone aiming a rifle in my direction. He had to protect *me*.

We tackled our foes, taking down even those with enhanced strength. We had the magic of the werewolf, and our power was greater than theirs.

A great wrenching of metal sounded as the bipedfuris not only tore a rifle from a man's grip but bent the metal, destroying it before tossing it aside.

I bit the hand of my closest foe, fangs crunching through bone and tendons to ensure he wouldn't wield a weapon again. Though we were outnumbered, we had speed and strength that the humans lacked. The magical medallion hanging from the bipedfuris's neck bounced about on his furred torso as he leaped to battle a new foe, and its golden glow beamed all about, high-lighting blood in the snow.

My wounded foe rolled away from me, leaving more blood behind. I started after him, but a back door in the armored vehicle opened. An older man stepped out, a magical device clenched in his hand.

"You *will* obey me," he shouted, pointing it at the bipedfuris.

Magic sizzled in the air, and an orange beam shot toward my ally, connecting with a glowing scar above his eyes. I hesitated, remembering this device and when I'd seen it used before. It had forced my ally to turn upon me, to *attack* me.

The bipedfuris roared and spun toward the older man. His arms spread wide, his fangs appearing long in the golden light from the medallion.

The orange beam glowed brighter.

"I command you to leave my people alone," the human ordered, but was that a hint of a quaver in his voice? Of uncertainty? "Kill the female, and bring me the case."

After making sure no rifles were pointed at the bipedfuris, I crept toward the older man. If I could get that device away from him...

The golden light from the medallion flared, bathing the bipedfuris's face and more. It ran along the orange beam, encasing it and then somehow making it disappear, its power overriding that coming from the device.

With another great roar, the bipedfuris ran across the snow toward the vehicle, toward the older man. Duncan raised his muscled arms, claws gleaming in the golden light.

Someone inside the vehicle grabbed the older man and pulled him back inside. The door slammed shut an instant before the bipedfuris reached it. The driver hit the accelerator and sped straight toward me. Though startled, I leaped aside before the armored fender reached me. The vehicle skidded in the snow, clipped a tree, and spun around.

The bipedfuris leaped onto the roof, claws raking the metal with screeches that hurt my ears. Even armored, the vehicle wasn't a match for his power, and he tore into it.

I snarled in approval, wanting him to rip the old man out, to forever end the threat to my family and my allies. As the driver regained control of the vehicle, I sensed something in the snow where the old man had been. The control device.

The armored vehicle sped up the driveway toward the street with the bipedfuris atop it. Duncan smashed his claws into one of the side windows. Not as heavily armored as the metal frame, it broke under his assault.

One of the downed men in the yard rose to his knees, a rifle in his hands. He aimed it at the bipedfuris.

I charged, surprising him, and his shot went wide. But the crack of the weapon startled the bipedfuris, and he glanced back. The armored vehicle drove under a thick tree branch before reaching the street, and it struck Duncan hard enough to knock him from the roof.

I bowled into the man who'd fired, snapping at the rifle and tearing it from his grasp. He rolled away, trying to crawl toward the device in the snow. I halted him with a powerful bite to his shoulder. As he screamed in pain, I sprang upon the device and crunched down. Tiny pieces flew into the snow as magic sparked painfully in my mouth.

Not caring, I endured the pain and destroyed the device completely. Never again would it be used to control my mate.

After being knocked off the armored vehicle, he'd landed on his feet, but the vehicle had reached the street. It raced off at a reckless speed, one even a werewolf would struggle to match.

For a moment, the bipedfuris gazed after our fleeing enemies, as if he might try to catch them, but then he turned toward the driveway and strode toward me. The orange glow on his forehead had disappeared. He eyed the pieces of the control device in the snow, then tilted his head back and howled.

I almost joined in, but movement and muttering on the porch drew my attention.

My offspring, his friends, and my niece and druid ally had come outside, witnessing the end of the battle.

The man I'd bitten stirred and crawled toward the woods. I considered ending the threat he represented, but a vestige of my human self crept into my thoughts and suggested that killing a man in front of my offspring could be a bad idea. The savageness that had earlier made me care nothing of ramifications faded, and I did not chase down my enemy.

He and the other thugs capable of doing so slunk off into the woods. The bipedfuris gazed after them. Also thinking of chasing them down?

He did not. Instead, he looked toward the street, in the direction the vehicle had gone. *Those* were the enemies he regretted letting escape, I knew. The old man. The one who'd presumed to control him.

I padded over to stand beside him, to support him. If the old man continued to be a problem, we would deal with him. Together.

He patted my back, claws raised so they did no damage. There was something familiar about the medallion that hung around his neck. Its glow had lessened, allowing me to see a wolf head engraved into the front, the jaws parted to show fangs. When I returned to my human form, I would ask him about it.

"Definitely not dogs," one of the young men muttered from the porch, eyeing us.

"No," my offspring murmured, looking stunned.

EPILOGUE

BACK IN HIS HUMAN FORM, DUNCAN DROVE WHEN WE LEFT THE cabin. With snow still falling, I was happy to let him have the wheel. Bolin rode in the back with Jasmine, who'd also returned to her human form. Soon after the battle, I'd changed back and spoken to my son. He hadn't said much, mostly that he planned to return to Shoreline with his friends in the morning. I'd been tempted to grab his ear, throw him in the van, and say he would ride back with his mother. *Now*.

But his eyes had been haunted, and I had the feeling he wanted some time before dealing with what he'd seen—with deciding if his brain would accept what his eyes had witnessed. And maybe I needed a night's sleep too before having to face questions I didn't know if I was ready to answer. For now, he was safe. Tomorrow would be soon enough to deal with the rest.

Tonight, I would ask Duncan how the hell he'd found the male version of the Medallion of Memory and Power, the match to my mother's artifact.

But before I could bring it up, and only scant minutes into our journey, Duncan turned left. The van headed into a snow-blanketed park, evergreens rising up on either side of the road and hiding the sky.

"This is where you were before, isn't it?" I asked.

"Yes. I need to pick something up." He winked, tapped the medallion, then removed it from around his neck and placed it in the cupholder. Not explaining further, he parked and hopped out.

Soon, he returned with a large black case over his shoulder, snow dusting the lid. It was the same one I'd watched the biped-furis take out of his van at Mom's cabin. After storing it in the back, Bolin and Jasmine raising eyebrows but not asking anything, Duncan returned to the driver's seat.

"My SCUBA gear," he explained.

"I did wonder what was in there—and how you, in your biped-furis form, thought to grab that. Did Radomir compel you to do so?"

"No. You did."

"Me?"

"Technically, it was your mother's medallion, I think. Though the message seemed to be conveyed through the talisman. It was hard to tell."

"The, uhm, message?" I remembered all the weird glowing magic and magnetism between the talisman, medallion, and artifact, but how could a *message* have been conveyed? By inanimate jewelry? Or had the mushroom artifact somehow been responsible? I remembered the brief notion I'd had of it being pleased.

"Kind of a vision."

Okay, I'd had a couple of visions of my own, so that made more sense.

"It conveyed to me that I would find the matching medallion at the bottom of a lake. *This* lake." Duncan waved toward the shoreline, though the water wasn't visible through the woods from our position. "But it also seemed to suggest I'd need to hold my breath for a long time to reach it. It was deep in the water, in the mud under a rocky shelf that I barely squeezed past. All these years, the rock and mud have been muffling its magic so nobody sensed it. I didn't detect it until I was almost on top of it."

He smiled, looking pleased by the adventure he'd had. It had been, I supposed, a much more lucrative treasure hunt than many he went on.

"You were able to grasp that you needed SCUBA gear as the bipedfuris?"

"Yes, the bipedfuris is bright." His smile turned a touch smug. Proud of his furry form, was he?

"Did you *use* that gear as the bipedfuris?" I gaped at the thought of a big werewolf swimming around with goggles, a mouthpiece, and a tank on its back.

"Alas, no. I had to change into my usual self. The water was *freezing* without fur to keep me warm."

"It is winter."

"Quite."

"And you found the medallion out there? All this time, it's been at the bottom of a recreational lake surrounded by vacation homes?"

"Well, if your archivist was right about the timeline, this was probably all wilderness back then." He shrugged.

"It's amazing that you were able to resist the control device and detour here."

"It wasn't much of a detour, and finding this is what Radomir wanted me to do." Duncan ticked the medallion. "Also, he was staying in that cabin at one point, so I've been in the area before."

"That cabin?" I pointed my thumb back toward the road. "The one Oakley won a stay in?"

"If I'd known the address, I could have told you that was a ruse from the beginning. Radomir rented it for the winter. I don't know how he—or more likely Abrams—got the information, but he *knew* the medallion was somewhere up in this area. I'm sure he didn't know it was that close."

"You said before you didn't know where he was staying." I texted Austin right then and told him to make sure to pack up and leave extra early. I doubted Radomir would return that night and risk running into Duncan again, but if I'd known *he* had been staying there at one point...

"Oh, I didn't when you asked. He's been bouncing around from place to place. He'd cleared out of that cabin and was in a hotel the last time he'd summoned me." Duncan shrugged. "Like I said, he was worried you and your pack would retaliate if you found him."

"Oh, I would have." I remembered chomping down on the control device in my wolf form. Even though it had been satisfying, I wish I'd also gotten to chomp down on Radomir. At least the device was gone. So far, Duncan didn't seem to be suffering any ill effects, but, when I'd turned back into my human self, I'd worried I'd made a mistake. All along, I'd only wanted to *steal* it.

Duncan put the van in gear and took us back out to the main road. "I'm afraid I didn't sense your sword when I was near Radomir's armored SUV."

"Did you expect to? It wasn't his thugs who robbed me."

"No, but I'd wondered if there might be a connection between Radomir and the vandals who've been terrorizing you and your apartment complex. It may be, however, that these covens of evil are harassing you independently of each other."

"It would be a shame if only *one* such organization was making my life difficult."

Duncan nodded, his expression pensive as he gazed through the windshield. He might have won a victory by finding the medallion, but he must still lament that the sword had been stolen.

Even though he hadn't spoken a word of blame, I couldn't help but feel chagrined that I had allowed that to happen. As valuable as the magical blade was, I should have hidden it when I wasn't practicing with it. It wouldn't have fit in the heat duct under the bed alongside the case, but I could have stashed it *somewhere*.

"All this means," Duncan said, "is that we'll have to deal with them independently."

"You'll stick around to help?"

"*Certainly,* my lady. Especially now." He ticked the medallion again. "I acknowledge that this rightfully belongs to your pack and isn't mine to wear, but since it helped me fight off the magic of the control device, I hope your family will allow me to borrow it until we can deal with your problems. Radomir has many more magical artifacts at his disposal, and it would be useful to have."

"My family doesn't even know you have it. You can borrow it for..." I almost said *as long as you want*, but my mother hoped to see it returned to the pack before she died. "For a while, I'm sure. You found it, after all. My pack wouldn't have any clue it was still around if not for you."

"I *did* find it, and I quite enjoyed the challenge of doing so, but your family is known to keep tabs on you—and me, being rather enjoyably in your proximity so often. I shouldn't wish for them to spot me with it around my neck and assume I intend to keep it. Even if the most belligerent werewolves are gone, the others might join forces to forcibly remove it from my person."

"We could pelt them with salamis if they try."

"I don't know if they'll be as food motivated as an eight-year-old boy," he said.

"You saw him take it, huh?"

"Certainly."

"Were *you* that food motivated as a pup?"

"I'm that food motivated now. Why do you think I keep coming to your aid?"

"Because of the chocolate I give you?"

"Embedded with such delightful items as bacon bits, cacao nibs, and coffee beans, yes."

"And here I thought my natural allure was what drew you."

"Your allure is quite lovely."

"But not as lovely as dark-chocolate-smothered bacon bits?"

"Well, on par with that, certainly."

"I'm touched."

Duncan bowed his head toward me. "I should like to take the medallion to your mother—your pack—and assure her that I have no intention of keeping it. Then I can politely ask if I might borrow it until we've eliminated the various threats to your livelihood. I would also like to put an end to whatever megalomaniacal plans Radomir and Abrams have for the artifacts. I trust you wouldn't be opposed to driving them out of your state."

"I'd like to drive them off a cliff."

"That's an option. Cliffs are abundantly present in your mountain forests."

"You're stirring up my fantasies."

"By speaking of forests and cliffs? I'd prefer it if it was my masculine appeal that aroused fantasies in you."

"We don't always get what we want." Though it had been a long day and night, and I worried about the future, I managed a smile for him and relaxed, even dozed for a while, until we turned into the parking lot for Sylvan Serenity.

For this late an hour, there were a lot of cars with headlights on. It was almost midnight and, with the snow, one wouldn't have expected people to be out.

Not surprisingly, more than one police vehicle was parked next to my truck. Officer Dubois stood on the sidewalk near them, Rue a few steps away. I couldn't tell if she was handcuffed, but my stomach sank as the officer looked toward us.

Abruptly, I was glad Austin had stayed behind. I didn't want him to watch me be arrested. When he stepped onto his plane to return to Air Force training, I wanted him to remember me as a hero.

"The bobbies in this city enjoy spending a great deal of time here, don't they?" Duncan asked.

"It's my allure. They're drawn to it."

"Even the female officer?"

"Oh, she's *especially* drawn to it." I grimaced.

Seeing Rue reminded me of the potions she'd given me, including the one I didn't want to take, the one that could allow me to locate the hideout of the motorcycle thugs. Maybe... to get the sword back, I would suck it up and consume it. Suck it *down*, rather.

I bared my teeth, my esophagus rippling with distaste at the thought, but I owed it to Duncan to find the weapon. Not only because it had been a generous gift but because he wanted me to have it. Even with the medallion around his neck, our enemies remained out there, and it was possible I would need the sword again. Just in case.

Duncan pulled into a parking spot, and Dubois headed our way. If she arrested me, I wouldn't have a chance to suck anything down. Hopefully, I wouldn't need a sword in jail.

"Do you think salamis would work to bribe her into pretending she didn't see us change?" Duncan asked.

"Sadly not. She's not a werewolf."

"Alas for her to go through life so handicapped."

I snorted and climbed out to face her. Rue waved. Did she look... cheerful under the glow of the nearest parking lot lamp? If nothing else, she wasn't handcuffed.

"Good evening, Ms. Valens," Dubois said.

"Hi."

"Your apartment complex has been deemed a locale of special interest."

"Fantastic. Why don't you let the owners know? I'm sure they'll want to add that to their marketing materials."

"It's for sale? I suppose that doesn't surprise me."

"Yeah, strangely the owners aren't delighted by the increased crime in the area." In *this* area specifically.

Dubois frowned. "We are attempting to address that, but we only have so many officers, and, as you've observed, our presence here isn't always enough to deter criminals."

"Yeah." I braced myself, waiting for her to bring up my werewolfness. There was no way she *hadn't* figured that out.

"I lost my partner last night," she said grimly. "We weren't expecting such an organized attack. That was a mistake."

"They were more than I expected too." I didn't mention the glowing purple weapon that had been like daggers to the brain.

Dubois met my gaze. Here it came...

"I believe you saved my life," she said.

I didn't answer, expecting her to say that it didn't matter. She knew I'd been responsible for the deaths weeks before. She knew what I was and would arrest me.

After a few silent moments, Dubois raised her eyebrows. "That *was* you, wasn't it? There were two, ah, wolves, but the black one... had your eyes."

"Huh." I didn't see a recording device, but that didn't mean she couldn't have one active in her pocket. My gut told me not to admit anything.

"From what I saw, I no longer believe your tenant is training attack wolves." Dubois waved toward Rue.

"I told you *that* from the beginning," Rue muttered. "As if my famil— my *cat* would have allowed that. She gets huffy even when one of those two has been in the apartment." She pointed at me and at Duncan.

So much for my attempt not to admit anything.

"I can imagine," Dubois murmured. "Anyway, I came to let you know that we'll increase the number of officers on patrol around this area, and that I'm not... arresting your tenant."

"Or anyone else here?" I asked warily.

She looked toward Duncan and then me. "Not at this time."

"Oh."

Dubois smirked and said, "You're welcome," before heading to her patrol car.

"Thanks," I called after her.

Duncan had waited for our conversation to finish, but now he joined me. "Perhaps you were correct about her being drawn to your allure."

I shook my head, having a feeling Dubois merely believed that she owed me one. "*You're* the one she saw naked."

"And yet she comes back to visit *you*. Strange."

"Indeed." I looked at my phone to see if Austin had called or texted, but he hadn't. There was, however, a message from Lorenzo.

A word of warning. The pack wise wolf, who is quite attuned to magic and the artifacts of our kind, believes the medallion you seek may be about in the world again.

Amused, I looked toward the cupholder in Duncan's van. He'd been right. There was no way the family wouldn't have learned that he had it.

Yes, I replied. *We'll come see you about it tomorrow.*

"Should I be nervous?" Duncan asked as he drove us through Monroe and out toward my mother's cabin.

We'd waited until midmorning to head out, since I'd wanted to be there when Austin returned, but he'd gone straight to his room without saying much. I worried he would need months rather than a few hours to process that his mother was a werewolf.

"The whole pack has seen you as the bipedfuris now." I opened my purse, fished out my GAS envelope, and tucked a twenty-dollar bill under the bobblehead doll on the dash. Since we'd driven Duncan's van all the way to Maple Falls and back the night before, I owed him extra for gas money. "I don't think anyone is going to mess with you over borrowing the medallion."

"If you really thought that, you wouldn't have stopped to buy all those salamis, including the gourmet summer sausage made from wagyu beef."

"They got some new offerings in at the farm store. I wanted to support them. Though I'm not sure about the beef-and-cranberry one the clerk assured me is fabulous. Wolves aren't that known for hoovering fruit out of cranberry bogs. Maybe Emilio will eat it."

Duncan's knowing gaze promised he believed I had changed the subject on purpose.

"Okay, I don't know if they'll be delighted by the idea of you wearing it. I figured some meat bribes couldn't hurt."

"I thought so. That's why I got these early this morning." Duncan reached behind his seat and pulled out a Trader Joe's bag stuffed with sausage and salami logs as well as bars of dark chocolate.

I drew out some of the bars. They had cacao nibs *and* espresso beans in them and promised 70mg of caffeine in each serving.

"You want my family to be perky while they try to rip the medallion off your neck?"

Duncan eyed the label as I pointed to the caffeine amount. "It's possible I didn't think out that choice well."

"You should have visited the cannabis store instead. Weed is known to mellow out werewolves, and it goes well with chocolate. I even have a recipe for pot brownies."

"An interesting thing for a mother of two and a generally upright citizen to admit."

"Marijuana is legal in Washington." *Now*, it was. I'd possibly acquired that recipe *before* that change had been made. "And mothers of two often unruly boys *need* mellow time now and then. Trust me."

"I do." Duncan gazed thoughtfully out the windshield.

I wondered if he was thinking of his young clone brother. Had he gotten to speak with the boy yet? Did he want to? Having a clone wasn't the same as having a child. And a sibling more than forty years younger than oneself had to be a weird thing.

When we arrived, we found numerous family members around the property, most in wolf form. They sure liked to hang out here, didn't they?

Jasmine stepped out the front door. Maybe she was the reason the pack had shown up. Either she or Lorenzo could have told them I would come visit this morning.

"There are no secrets in a family, I suppose," I murmured.

"Did your pack *grow*? There are wolves here I haven't seen before."

"Extended family."

"Maybe I should have brought more salami."

"I think so."

Numerous sets of lupine eyes turned toward us—toward *Duncan*—and I suspected Jasmine had mentioned the medallion. This close, the werewolves might also sense it.

As we parked next to a couple of trucks, Lorenzo stepped into the doorway, fully clothed today, and said something to Jasmine. Duncan, perhaps feeling presumptuous about wearing the medallion, removed it from his neck and handed it to me.

I wanted to assure him, once again, that he'd found it, after it had been lost for generations, so nobody would object to him modeling it or even borrowing it for a while, but I couldn't speak for the rest of the pack. In a logical world, they would feel the same way I did, but when did family ever act logically?

"Not a lot of Mr. Spock werewolves," I said.

Duncan looked over at me, making me wonder if I should explain my thoughts, but he waved at the wolves and said, "Most of them *do* have pointed ears."

He hopped out of the van before I could reply.

With Lorenzo waving for us to come into the cabin, I didn't delay further, merely grabbing some snacks—bribes—and heading for the porch steps. I spotted Emilio in wolf form. He glanced at the medallion but focused on what *really* mattered to him and wagged his tail. I put a salami in his mouth, trusting his sharp teeth would be capable of removing the plastic wrap if he wanted to eat it in that form. A couple other wolves came up, blocking the steps until I also gave them meat gifts. When I ran out, they turned to Duncan, and he delved into his grocery bag.

"I'll reserve the chocolate bars for those in human form," he said, finding a way between the furry obstacles to set stacks of them on the porch railing. "I've not tried eating desserts in my lupine state, but I understand dogs can't consume chocolate, and our GI tracts aren't that different from theirs."

"Theirs are far inferior," came Mom's voice from the cabin. She stepped up beside Lorenzo and leaned on him. Right away, her gaze latched onto the medallion in my hand. "They're like vultures and crows, scavengers that will eat anything."

"I think you can deliver the chocolate bars to her and her discerning palate," I told Duncan.

"Yes. Come in." Mom pointed at the medallion rather than the bars. *That* was what she wanted delivered.

Duncan and I joined her and Lorenzo inside. Jasmine slipped out to give us privacy.

"You found it," Mom said quietly as I set the medallion on the table.

"Duncan found it. I just drove up to pick him up afterward."

I thought about mentioning the dramatic night rescuing Austin and his friends, but she'd made it clear that she didn't care about my sons. They weren't werewolves, and thus, in her eyes, they were as inferior as dogs. We'd argued over that before, and I didn't want to again. Besides, she looked rough this morning and leaned on Lorenzo again when he came over. There'd been a time —most of her life—when she wouldn't have leaned on anyone for anything.

"It was a most delightful and perfect pick-up," Duncan said. "Luna brought my own van to me. Quite thoughtful."

I expected Mom to ignore him and examine the medallion more closely, but she only ignored his silliness and nodded politely at him.

"Where was it?" she asked. "It's been gone my whole life."

"In the chilly depths of Silver Lake near Maple Falls," Duncan said. "I've magnet-fished in another body of water called Silver Lake that lies not too many miles north of Luna's home. They don't have the most creative or imaginative names for places here, do they?"

"Maybe you'd prefer the likes of Mukilteo, Puyallup, and Quileute?" I asked. "We have those names too."

"I don't know," Duncan said. "Do they mean Silver Lake in another language?"

I snorted. "They might."

"That you've found our pack's missing medallion means a great deal to us," Mom told Duncan.

"It was an honor to quest for something of value to Luna's family," he replied. "I was wondering... Well, we discovered that it has the power to nullify controlling magic." He waved to his forehead but didn't continue on. Maybe he didn't want to admit to being susceptible to that in front of my mother?

I didn't point out that she'd been there when he'd been clutching his forehead the day before and fighting not to give in.

"I wondered if I might borrow it for a while," he said. "Luna did destroy the device that was being used specifically on me, but those who held it have many other magical artifacts. Until we've dealt with those men, it would be ideal to have extra protection against such items."

Mom picked up the medallion, turning it over in her hands several times as she examined it from all angles. I expected her to object, to say that the pack couldn't risk losing it.

"I believe," she said slowly, lifting it toward Duncan, "that you may be meant to wear it."

He blinked. "*Meant* to?"

"You went on a quest to find it and succeeded when nobody else has, and you are of the Old World with the ability to turn into the bipedfuris. I believed before that you would be a good mate for my daughter, to give her powerful werewolf offspring, but now I think it is more than that."

"Oh?" Was that wariness in Duncan's tone?

Worried I knew where Mom was going with this, I didn't blame him for it.

"You were meant to impregnate my daughter," she said.

I slumped and groaned. Why did she have to bring that up every time Duncan was here?

"That's really romantic, Mom," I muttered.

"I was hoping for recreational hunting and frolicking before talk of impregnation came up." Duncan's tone was light, but his eyes had grown haunted.

Mom handed the medallion to him. "You may use it while you are in the area and working with my daughter. Or until... Well, you have a place in the pack now. If you want it."

"I'll think about it. Thanks." Eyes still haunted, Duncan only met my gaze briefly before walking out.

I shook my head, afraid my mother would drive him away. Offspring weren't what *I* wanted from him. We hadn't even had sex yet. I just liked him and enjoyed his company and wished the world would leave us alone long enough that we *could,* as he'd said, hunt and frolic recreationally.

"He would be an acceptable mate for you," Mom told me, "and a capable alpha for the pack."

"I have no doubt of that," I said.

What I didn't know was if Duncan wanted either of those things.

THE END

Made in the USA
Columbia, SC
17 June 2025

59521104R00155